"*Hatteras Moon* has more twists and turns than a giant blue marlin on a 70-pound line. Pitch-perfect dialogue and flesh-and-blood characters who linger long after the story's stunning climax."

—Paul Ruffin, Director of *Texas Review Press* and author of the novels *Castle in the Gloom* and *Pompeii Man*.

"*Hatteras Moon* ... combines elements of Ernest Hemingway, Joseph Conrad and Tom Clancy. If you need to add a book to your summer reading list, this one is definitely it."

—Chantelle MacPhee, *Journal of Multidisciplinary Studies*

HATTERAS MOON
by Stephen March

ISBN 9781938467288

A BEACH MURDER MYSTERY BOOK
www.beachmurdermysteries.com

Published by

köehlerbooks ™
an imprint of Morgan James Publishing

5 Penn Plaza, 23rd floor
c/o Morgan James Publishing
New York, NY 10001
212-574-7939
www.koehlerbooks.com

Publisher
John Köehler

Executive Editor
Joe Coccaro

In an effort to support local communities, raise awareness and funds, Morgan James Publishing donates a percentage of all book sales for the life of each book to Habitat for Humanity Peninsula and Greater Williamsburg.
Get involved today, visit www.MorganJamesBuilds.com

Hatteras Moon

A BEACH MURDER MYSTERY

Stephen March

NEW YORK

VIRGINIA

For Danny Couch
And in memory of Gary Hardison—
Hatterasmen good and true

...death will come to you out of the sea.

—Homer, *The Odyssey*

Prologue

On a hot summer night in 1972, Virgil Gibson was returning to Hatteras Island with four members of his football team—Leon McRae, Sam and Billy Coultrane, and Jack Delaney. Jack was driving his father's '49 Nash. They had gone to a dance at the old Casino in Nags Head. Jack stopped the car on the middle of the bridge over Oregon Inlet and said he was going to jump off. They all got out, laughing, half-drunk, none of them believing he was really going to do it. Jack took off his shoes and shirt and climbed up on the railing, facing the sea. The water was phosphorescent in the moonlight, the mouth of the inlet full of whitecaps.

Raising his arms, Jack stood there a moment, as if he were calling down some mysterious power from the sky.

"Get down from there, you dumb-ass!" Virgil yelled. The wind threw his voice back in his face.

"He ain't going to jump," Leon said.

Jack turned to smile at them, and then he stepped off the railing, disappearing over the side. Virgil leaned over the railing, looking for him. The wind sounded like a waterfall.

It was seventy-six feet down to the water.

"Jesus Christ," Billy Coultrane cried. "Jack's done killed himself!"

Virgil thought this might be true, but then he saw his friend floating on his back. "Jack!"

"He can't hear you," Sam said.

"Crazy damn fool!" Taking off his shirt and shoes, Virgil climbed up on the railing.

"I'm going in after him."

He stood there a few seconds, looking down. He was thinking about the twenty dollars he had borrowed last Friday from his father and that he and his mother hadn't been on speaking terms since the past Wednesday, when he had stayed out until three a.m. playing poker with Jack, Sam, and Billy. It occurred to him if he drowned, he would leave the world estranged from his mother and owing his father money.

"Get down from there, Virgil," Sam called.

Virgil shut his eyes and stepped off the railing.

The wind roared in his ears, and when he hit the water he kept sinking until his feet touched the sandy bottom. His chest and left arm felt like they had been hit with a baseball bat. Using his legs and his right arm, he swam straight up. When he reached the surface, he was surprised by the power of the current. There was no way he could swim against it. He floated on his back, looking up at the arc of the bridge. In the sky, the full, burning moon was encircled by a milk-white haze.

One by one he watched the others jump in, too.

Jack, Sam, and Leon swam to shore. The Coast Guard fished Virgil and Billy out of the mouth of the inlet just before dawn. The wind had flipped Billy's feet out from under him so he hit the water on his side, breaking his back and bruising his pancreas. Like Virgil, he had survived by floating.

Virgil had three cracked ribs and a broken left forearm.

When the Coast Guardsmen got him out of the water, the first thing Virgil asked was, "Is Jack Delaney all right?"

I

Jack Delaney was in his black Corvette on the bypass, getting ready to turn into the visitor's center, when he noticed a wasp on his dashboard, moving its antennae up and down in a slow, pendulous rhythm. Until he had seen the wasp, his mind had been on Herrara, whom he was to meet at one p.m. on the airstrip behind the Wright Brothers Memorial. He was uneasy about the meeting, and the wasp's sudden appearance was unnerving: He was allergic to its venom. He downshifted, and then turned onto the driveway. The noon sun made everything stand out with eerie clarity: the granite obelisk on the hill, the concrete visitor's center, the metallic cars in the parking lot, the glass booth at the entrance. Driving slowly and keeping an eye on the wasp, he pulled into the parking lot at the end of the driveway. He decided to hit the thing with his wallet, but before he could get it out of his pocket, the wasp performed a nervous dance with its back legs, aiming its antennae at him. He got out of the car fast, the wasp shooting by his ear. Under the circumstances, he considered it to be a possible sign of bad luck.

He looked at his watch. It was twelve forty-two. He got back into the Corvette and transferred his snub-nosed .38 special from the glove compartment to his pocket. Picking up the backpack from the floor, he locked the car, slipped on the backpack and started across the grassy field between the visitor's center and the monument. The runway was west of the monument, behind a row of trees at the end of the field.

He was sweating, and he had a throbbing pain behind his eyes.

At the end of the field he started up the walkway that wound around the ninety-foot hill. He could feel the breeze off the sea. When he reached the top, he sat on the steps leading up to the monument. To the east the sea was a slice of hard bright blue, sandwiched between the line of cottages and motels and the lighter blue of the sky. The wind was out of the southeast, so he knew Herrara's pilot would fly in over the Kitty Hawk Bay in order to land into the wind. He watched a Piper Cub rise above the trees and head into the clouds. Most of the planes that used the airstrip were for tourists taking air tours of the Outer Banks.

A woman and a boy were walking around the monument, the woman reading aloud the words inscribed on its base: "*In commemoration of the conquest of the air—*" Jack knew the words by heart—*"by the brothers Wilbur and Orville Wright, conceived by genius, achieved by dauntless resolution and unconquerable faith.*"

He heard Herrara's plane before he saw it. He stood up and went down the hill toward the airstrip, remembering how he used to come up there to skateboard with Sam and Billy Coultrane back in high school.

The plane came in low over the bay and dipped below the trees. As Jack approached the end of the runway he saw Herrara's twin-engine King Air taxi to the end and pull off into a parking area. Jack opened the gate and walked over to the plane. Two men got out, both wearing sunglasses. One was Rafael, Herrara's chief body guard. Jack didn't know the other man.

"Hey, Rafael," Jack said. "How you been?"

"Reflux is giving me hell."

"They got medicines for that."

"Yeah, shit don't work that good if you ask me. Raise your arms, I got to search you."

"What the hell for?"

"New policy, man."

Rafael patted him down, taking his .38. While Herrara's other bodyguard examined the backpack, another man stepped out of the plane and stretched. Jack guessed he was the pilot.

"He's waiting for you," Rafael said.

Jack went up the steps and into the plane, wondering why they had searched him and taken his gun. He could feel a pulse beating in his temple.

Herrara was on a couch in the rear compartment, along with a Latina girl in a miniskirt. A solidly built man with wavy black hair, he had on a white shirt, open at the collar. Jack could see the top section of the gold cross he wore on a chain around his neck.

"Jack, you look at this island from the air, it's just a little ribbon of sand out in the ocean. Big storm would blow everything into the sound."

"It's worth the risk just to live here," Jack said. He sat in a chair across from the couch, holding the backpack on his lap.

"Tell me about risk. You can drown in your bathtub, choke on a piece of steak." Herrara looked out the window. "So this is where aviation got started, huh?"

"That's right."

"The monument marks the spot where the Wright boys took off?"

"They launched their plane in the field below."

"How long were they in the air?"

"Not long. Less than a minute."

"Most desirable things don't last long." Herrara smiled at the girl, who looked to be about sixteen. She was working on a wad of gum. "This is Marta. She wants to be an American citizen." He said something to the girl in Spanish. She nodded, smiling. "*Sí, sí.*" She had bad teeth.

"All the poor people on the planet want to come to America. In Miami, we got thirty-nine different flavors of ice cream, twenty-four-hour TV, drive-through funerals, replacement parts for your body, plastic surgery to make you beautiful. This is the land of unlimited possibilities, the place where dreams come true."

"I got your money."

"Dump it on the floor."

Jack dumped the money out on the floor of the plane, twenty bundles of hundred dollar bills—three hundred and fifty thousand dollars. The girl's eyed widened. She had stopped working on the gum.

"Give the backpack to Rafael."

Rafael took the backpack and handed it to the other man, who took it off the plane.

"What's got you spooked, Lupe?" Jack asked. "They already checked that out."

"This business requires a man to be careful."

"You never been this careful before."

"Business is getting competitive, amigo. Used to be plenty of room for everyone. Now people are fighting over the same territory."

"I'm just a fisherman."

"I'm your fairy godmother, too." Herrara nodded at the money. "How much is there?"

"Half of what I owe you, like I said on the phone."

"When will you have the rest?"

"To be honest, I'm not sure."

"You're way up in the air, Jack. Dancing on a wire."

"You know how much I lost when my trawler went down?"

"Not my problem."

"I always pay my debts. I'll get the rest to you as soon as I can."

"Hey, Rafael, hear what Jack said? He'll pay me as soon as he can. Some joke, huh?"

"You shouldn't worry so much," Jack said. "Haven't I always paid you?"

"You should worry more. Worry about your health. Thirty days. I don't get the money by then, I'm going to be upset. That will bring much misfortune and suffering. You don't want that. Believe me."

Jack smiled at the girl. "Good luck."

"Have a nice day," she said slowly, flashing her decaying teeth.

"I got business to take care of," Herrara said, scowling.

"I'll be in touch."

"Thirty days, Jack. No bullshit."

Rafael followed Jack off the plane. Once they were outside, Rafael returned the backpack and his gun, unloaded. "*Hasta mañana,* fisherman Jack."

Jack slipped the empty revolver into his pocket and walked back across the field toward the visitors center, carrying the empty backpack. Every step he took made his head throb. He watched Herrara's plane rise above the trees and ascend into the sky. He had always gotten along fine with Herrara, but then he had always paid on time, too.

Driving out of the park, he stopped by the booth at the entrance. The Park Service collected the entrance fee as visitors left in order to prevent traffic from backing up on the highway. A young woman in a brown uniform sat in the booth.

"One dollar, please."

He looked through his pockets but he didn't have any change. His wallet was empty, too. "Don't seem to have any money with me," he said, embarrassed.

"Hard to hold on to money these days." She smiled and waved him on through. "Catch you next time."

He drove south along the beach road, past all the motels and hotels, remembering how ten years earlier he could drive for miles on the beach road in winter and not see a soul, not even a light on in the cottages. Even during the tourist season, a man had some breathing room, and the beaches were clean after the tourists left. Now, new cottages, motels, and restaurants were going up, the county averaged sixty thousand tourists on any day in August, and the beaches were littered with their trash—aluminum cans, cigarette butts, fast food wrappers. Houses were getting too expensive for an ordinary working person to buy.

He drove to Whalebone Junction and on down Highway 12 toward Hatteras, thinking about the snow geese that winter on the Outer Banks. He liked to see white flocks descending in droves from the sky and to hear them honking as they fed and rested in the marshes. They would be leaving for their northern breeding grounds soon, but they would return in the fall. The snow geese always came back.

Jack drove across the bridge spanning Oregon Inlet and into Cape Hatteras National Seashore. Then he began looking out the window for the snow geese. He had made some mistakes and had a run of bad luck, but that was life. You get knocked down, you pick yourself up and go on. First thing he had to do was finish paying Herrara off. That would be hard to do with his trawler gone, but he would find a way. After that, he would need to buy another boat. No use in trying to get a job with a suit and tie. The sea was where he belonged, just like the snow geese belonged to the sky and the marshes.

As he drove south toward Hatteras, he kept looking for the

snow geese. That took his mind off the image of Herrara's King Air disappearing into the clouds with his threats and a third of a million dollars—half of the money Jack still owed him.

II

The night Jack was born, his father, Jubal, was awakened by water. The Pamlico Sound had risen to the bedroom window and Jubal could hear the waves striking the glass. In a flash of lightning he saw his wife, Mae, sleeping beside him—her black hair tangled, her skin bleached by the exploding light, her fingers interlocked over her swollen abdomen. It was after one a.m. when Hurricane Iona had slammed into the Carolina coast just before midnight with one-hundred-and-thirty-mile-an-hour winds and a sixteen-foot storm surge that devastated Atlantic Beach and flooded Beaufort and Morehead City to the north. The ocean had washed over low areas of the Outer Banks and poured into the sounds.

Jubal awakened Mae. When they got out of their bed, the water was already ankle deep on the floor. Years later, Jubal told Jack's friend, Virgil, how he and Mae waded and swam out to his truck after the engine was submerged. Trapped in the rising water, they climbed an oak behind the house, where Jubal made Mae as comfortable as he could in a bed of branches. Mae's labor had already begun.

"Her pains were coming every two minutes," Jubal said. "It was raining fish hooks and nails, and the wind was screaming like a thousand demons out of hell. But the worst thing was the snakes. Every time lightning flashed I could see them, coiled around the limbs above and below us, slithering along the branches. Seemed like half the snakes in the swamp had took shelter in that oak. I delivered Jack right there, cut the cord with my pocket knife, and held him inside my raincoat to keep him warm."

That was how Jack had gotten his nickname, "Hurricane Jack." It wasn't, as some people believed later, due to the way he played football. In high school Jack was a star halfback who racked up more yardage than anyone in the history of Hatteras High or the entire Tobacco Belt Conference. He could run a hundred yards in a hair over ten seconds and cut to the left or right so fast he would leave his bedeviled pursuers grabbing the air.

Virgil and Jack first became friends in the eleventh grade, after the coach let Virgil warm the bench for the Hatteras Hurricanes. Virgil only played once that season—in the last quarter of a game with the Mattamuskeet Lakers from the mainland. The score was twenty-four to six. His teammates praised him for his "heart," but he lacked the size, skill, and speed to be an intimidating player. Although Jack was the star, he remained humble about his superior skill. He always said he was part of a team and each member was equally important. That was just Jack's way—one of the many reasons Virgil liked him so much.

During his senior year, Jack received football scholarship offers from Carolina, Clemson, and the University of Virginia, but the Vietnam War intervened, and he was drafted at the end of his freshmen year at Carolina. He served in a special guerilla unit that launched night attacks on the Viet Cong. Near the end of his tour he was shot through the legs while carrying an injured soldier during a fierce firefight. Jack spent four months recovering in a stateside hospital and returned to Hatteras Island with a Purple Heart and a Bronze Star.

Jack's war injuries ended any chance for a career playing football. He worked for Jubal on his trawler, *Sea Horse*, plying the sea and the sounds for fish. He lived with his parents and his sister, Elena, in Buxton, in a soundside house built of lumber salvaged from shipwrecks. The family had moved to Hatteras Island from Stumpy Point, a small fishing community on the Pamlico Sound, when Jack was four years old. In 1978, when Jack was twenty-four, Jubal died of an aneurism, leaving his trawler to Jack, Mae, and Elena. Jack worked the trawler a couple of years before buying out his mother's and sister's shares. He later sold *Sea Horse* and bought a bigger trawler, *Lucky Strike*. Virgil didn't know when Jack started smuggling marijuana, but by 1987 he had a three-story beach house in Avon, two oceanfront lots in Hatteras, a new Corvette, and a cigarette boat said to be the fastest vessel on the Carolina coast.

They stayed in touch after high school, exchanging a few letters while Jack was in Vietnam. After he returned home, Virgil saw him several times a year, usually on one of his trips home to see his parents in Buxton. The family had moved to the Outer Banks from Raleigh during Virgil's freshman year in high school, the same year his father, Charles, retired from the U.S. Postal Service. The move to Hatteras had been his dad's idea. Margaret, Virgil's mother, disliked the island the entire time she lived there. She could never quite adjust to the wind, sun, sand, flies, and storms. "The problem with this godforsaken place," she'd say, "is that it has absolutely no mercy." After Virgil's father died, she moved back to Raleigh. By then Virgil was married and trying to teach college freshmen, most of whom had grown up in front of TV sets, how to write a coherent paragraph. Laurel College, where he worked, was in Indian Creek, a hundred and twenty miles northeast of Hatteras. He went duck hunting with Jack every winter, and Jack would usually call him in the fall when the bluefish were running. Virgil would cancel classes and slip away to the Outer Banks for a couple days of fishing aboard Jack's trawler.

Although his wife, Allison, referred to Jack as "that gangster friend of yours," Jack Delaney was a welcome splash of color in Virgil's world of committee meetings, petty politics, and one too many bored students whose idea of hell was reading a book. Who would have ever guessed that he, Virgil Gibson, went fishing with a marijuana smuggler born into this world in a tree of snakes?

In early May of 1988, Virgil visited Jack at his home near Buxton on Hatteras Island. That was when Jack told him about losing his trawler. He had sunk *Lucky Strike* in about ninety feet of water off Ocracoke Island by pulling out the drainage plugs in the engine room. He and his crew then swam two miles to shore, eluding the Coast Guard cutter that had been chasing them through the fog.

The trawler had ten tons of Colombian marijuana in the hold.

"She was insured, wasn't she?" Virgil asked.

"Insurance company doesn't want to pay. They want to send down divers to examine the wreck. Coast Guard must have tipped them off."

"What are you going to do now?"

"First thing I'm going to do is throw a party."

"A party?"

"That's right. Next Saturday in Hatteras. Can you and Allison come?"

"We're not living together now."

"Sorry to hear that, Virgil. Whose idea was that?"

"Mine."

"How's Allison?"

"Pissed off."

"There someone else?"

"No. Fire just went out."

"You need a place to stay?"

"No, but thanks for the offer. I'm renting a cottage in Nags Head. Got a good deal on it because it's a year-round rental. Figure I'll use it as a weekend retreat after I go back to teaching in the fall."

"Let's see, you and Allison been married about eight years, haven't you?"

"Eleven." Jack had come to their wedding barefoot, in a rented tux.

"Time sure flies by, don't it?"

"Sometimes." Virgil was sure time did fly by for Jack Delaney, but lately time had been dragging for him. He stared at the sea through the picture window in his den and tried to remember the last time he had done something dangerous. "What time does the party start?"

"Come around noon. Food should be ready by then."

Jack had his party on a sandy, treeless island in Hatteras Inlet, one of several created when the inlet was dredged for the ferry channel. He told Virgil to meet him at a boat ramp about a mile south of the ferry dock.

Virgil got to the ferry dock a little before noon and followed the sandy road off of Highway 12 to the unmarked road that went down to the boat ramp. He could hear the booming bass line coming from the island. The road was lined with four-wheel drive vehicles. He parked his Jeep and walked down the path, through the tall grass and bushes to the ramp. About half a mile from the shore, the island was a wafer of sand against the gray-blue sky and sound. He could see people moving around. He took off his shoes and socks and dangled his feet in the water. Soon he saw a boat pull away from the island and head his way. It was Jack in his cigarette boat. He stored it in a boatshed on a canal at the end of a cul-de-sac across from his house in Avon. He rented the space from a retired postman who used to play checkers with Virgil's dad. Jack had dug the ditch back from the canal and built the shed over four salt-treated pilings. He used an electronic winch and a boat bar to keep the boat out of the water when he wasn't using it.

Tying his shoes together by the laces, Virgil hung them around his neck and waded out to meet him. Jack had on jeans and a tight blue T-shirt, which revealed his muscular chest and biceps. The young woman with him had chestnut-colored hair tied back with a red bandanna. She wore jeans and a T-shirt, too. Her suntanned skin was the color of honey.

"Glad you could make it," Jack said as Virgil climbed into the back seat of the boat. "Bobbie, this is my friend, Virgil."

"Hi, Virgil," Bobbie said. They shook hands over the seat. She handed him a beer from a cooler in the front as Jack's boat shot forward. Virgil leaned back and popped the top on the can, enjoying the feeling of wind and sun on his skin. Fine day for a party, he thought.

Jack cut the engine near the island, letting the boat's momentum carry them to the sand. He jumped out and pulled it farther ashore. As Virgil stepped out, some terns swooped down on them, trying to peck their heads.

"They're not used to company," Jack said, laughing. "They nest over on the west end. I've got that area roped off, but we still make them nervous."

There were at least a hundred people on the island. Some just stood around; others were lying on blankets or sitting in deck chairs and at wooden tables off to the right of Jack's boat. Beyond the tables a five-piece band was playing Van Morrison's old hit, "Tupelo Honey." Two diesel-fueled generators powered the band's electric instruments and sound system.

They walked across the sand toward the tables, stepping around the sunbathers. Some of the women were topless. Virgil didn't see anyone he knew.

Past the tables, a fish stew simmered in an iron kettle on a window grate over a firepit dug in the sand. Nearby, there were several beer kegs and a row of coolers. Beyond the kegs, two men and a woman in a bikini grilled fish.

"Let's go check on the fish," Jack said.

Virgil saw Sam and Billy Coultrane sitting at the first wooden table, along with big Leon McRae and his cousin, Mike Jennette. Leon, whom they had nicknamed "Freezer" back in high school when he was the Hatteras Hurricanes's most formidable lineman, smiled and waved. "Look what the cat drug in, boys."

"How the hell are you, Virgil?" Sam said. Two years older than his brother Billy, Sam was lean and tanned. He had grown a handlebar mustache since Virgil had last seen him.

Virgil shook their callused hands, a little embarrassed by how soft his were by comparison. The brothers didn't ask about Allison, probably because they already knew that she and Virgil no longer lived together. Leon had been married and divorced twice, and he had a couple of kids somewhere. Sam had separated from his wife. Billy, like Jack, had never been married. With his blue eyes and blond hair, Billy didn't even look related to Sam, whose hair and eyes were a rich, dark brown, like walnut.

"Virgil, you're an educated man," Billy said. "I wish you would tell me what happened to all of the virgins? They used to be like shells on the beach. Now you can't find one to save your life."

"Gone, just like the dinosaur. You still fishing for a living?"

"Not right now. I'm on vacation." Billy grinned, showing the gold-capped tooth that replaced the one knocked out in a game between Hatteras High and the Columbia Wildcats. It was the night Jack scored two touchdowns and kicked a field goal to win the Tobacco Belt Conference.

"Billy, you wouldn't know what to do with a virgin," Leon said.

"Billy *is* a virgin," Mike said, and everyone laughed.

Jack and Bobbie came up to the table. Bobbie had a plate of grilled fish; Jack, a bucket of stew.

"You boys ready to eat?" Bobbie asked.

Jack set the bucket on the table, along with a ladle, and began uncovering the bowls of food. "We got potato salad, slaw, cornbread, and collards." Bobbie and Jack sat down, and everyone began eating.

"Trout tastes like it was just caught," Virgil said.

"We caught them this morning," Leon said. "Jack, Al, and me hauled the nets in before sunrise. Had them cleaned and on ice by nine."

"Sea trout are down to thirty cents a pound in Hatteras," Billy said.

"Shrimpers are taking a beating, too," Sam said. "Imports are killing them. A plate of shrimp today is most likely coming from China or Mexico. How the hell can an American fisherman make a living?"

"Just have to depend on luck," Jack said.

"Speaking of luck," Leon said. "Lenny Rollins's sure ran out on him."

"You talking about the Lenny Rollins who owns the tackle shop in Nags Head?" Virgil asked.

"That's right," Leon said.

"What happened?"

"He washed up on Ocracoke beach yesterday. In a plastic bag, with three cinder blocks chained to him."

"Nor'easter brought him in," Sam said.

"Why would someone want to kill Lenny Rollins?" Virgil

had talked to Lenny several times in his tackle shop. A friendly, easy-going man, he was always eager to give his customers advice on fishing.

"Maybe he owed someone money," Sam said.

"Can't collect from a corpse," Billy said.

The ferry to Ocracoke was going by in the channel. The tourists were looking at the island and waving. Some of them had binoculars.

"Lenny Rollins was a decent guy," Jack said, frowning.

The party broke up just before dark when the mosquitoes started swarming. Jack organized clean-up squads to go around the island, picking up trash and putting it into garbage bags. Another group loaded the tables, generators, drums, portable johns, chairs, and set-up for the band onto a trawler.

Jack took Virgil back to the boat ramp. A big gold moon hung low in the east. Virgil was sunburned and his legs were sore from dancing in the sand. He had danced first with Bobbie, and then later with a bikini-clad woman with a tattoo of a cobra on her stomach. He was still a little drunk. On the way back to the cottage he was renting in Nags Head, he was careful to stay under the speed limit and to the right of the yellow line. He kept picturing the cobra's head, swaying just above the woman's navel as she danced.

IV

A couple of weeks after Jack's party, Virgil met him for dinner at a restaurant in Nags Head. Jack said he had a job—as a charter boat captain, taking tourists out to fish the Gulf Stream.

"It's been years since I've been out on a charter boat," Virgil said.

"We'll change that. When can you go?"

"Anytime, really. I'm not doing much this summer except reading. Can you make much as a charter boat captain?"

"Enough to keep food on the table."

"How do you like it?"

"I like being on the water. But some of the clients are a pain in the ass. Like this guy I took out today. He was pissed because he only got one yellowfin. Nobody was catching fish out there, but all this fool could understand was that he's paying six hundred bucks a day to go fishing so he's supposed to catch fish. A lot of these tourists got no understanding of nature, Virgil, no respect for it. Look at the way they leave the beaches and the trash they throw in the sea. Know how many sea turtles die from eating plastic bags every year?"

"No."

"Hundreds. They think the bags are jellyfish and eat them, and then the bags stop up their guts. Kills them nice and slow. Old loggerhead can live a hundred years, spend his life roaming the oceans of the world, eating jellyfish, fighting off sharks, and then he dies because some jerk throws a Ziploc over the side of his boat."

"I'm sorry to hear that."

"Not half as sorry as the sea turtle who eats the bag."

The waiter appeared at their table with fresh drinks: bourbon for Jack, brandy for Virgil.

"These are courtesy of Mr. Meyers," he said.

A burly, gray-haired man sitting at a nearby table waved at Jack and then lifted his drink in a mock toast. The man was accompanied by a blonde in a black dress.

"Who's that?" Virgil asked.

"Raymond Meyers."

The blonde was looking their way. She had the kind of sculpted face you see in cosmetics ads: wide-set eyes, high cheek bones, full lips. Even in the low light, Virgil could see she was gorgeous.

He wondered why Meyers was buying them drinks, but he didn't inquire about it. He figured if Jack wanted him to know he would have told him, and Jack didn't comment.

The telephone ringing in the cottage snapped Virgil out of the spy novel he was reading while lying in the hammock on the back porch of his cottage.

He got up and went into the kitchen to answer the phone.

It was his mother. Calling to find out how he was doing. He told her he was fine, and she wanted to know how close he was to the ocean.

"About thirty feet at high tide. It lulls me to sleep every

night."

"Isn't that a little too close? I've been reading in the paper about cottages down there falling into the sea."

"That was along another section of the beach, where the erosion is worse. It also happened during a storm. I'm really quite safe."

"You're not hanging out with Jack Delaney, are you?"

"I've seen Jack, Mama. Saw him the other day."

"That's certainly reassuring. You know when you were younger, just about every time you got in trouble he wasn't far away. I'll never forget that night you boys jumped off the bridge."

"That was a long time ago."

"I'll try to remember that. By the way, Allison wants you to call her."

"What does she want?"

"She wouldn't say. She asked for your number, and she was quite indignant when I wouldn't give it to her. She said, 'Margaret, are you trying to keep me from reaching my husband?' I told her you were doing research and didn't want to be disturbed."

"She probably wants to talk about a property settlement."

"Don't you dare give her the house."

"I don't care about the house."

"You helped pay for it, didn't you?"

"Yes."

"Then you should keep your share of it. Let her buy you out. Or you can buy her out."

"I'll think about it, Mama." He shut his eyes, picturing the house where his marriage had ended. A two-story brick box on a dead end street. You couldn't tell it from a million others.

Virgil's mama spent awhile telling him about her hay fever and arthritis. He listened patiently. After they hung up, he called Allison.

"I didn't realize you were going to be *incommunicado*," she said.

"Just got the phone put in this week,"

"The number is non-listed."

"What can I do for you?"

"You could let me know what's going on."

"I'm not coming back, Allison."

"I think you should know that every one of our friends thinks you've completely lost your mind."

"Did you call for a specific reason?"

"If you're going to continue down this road, we've got issues that need to be settled, Virgil."

"What do you want to do?"

"I'd like to have the house."

"Fine. Take the house."

Allison was quiet a moment. He could hear her breathing. "What about the money, the stocks, our personal property?" She didn't sound as tense now that the house issue was settled.

"You can have whatever you want in the house. We can split everything else fifty-fifty."

"I put more than you did in the stock account."

"I paid the down payment on the house—but I'm not going to argue about this. You want more of the stock account, fine. We can split it sixty-forty."

"We need to put this in writing."

"Why don't you get a lawyer to draw up an agreement?"

Silence, then:

"Virgil, is there someone else?"

"No."

"I don't understand what the problem is then."

"I don't even know where to begin."

"I think you need professional help," Allison said, and she hung up.

Virgil went back out to the hammock and tried to read, but

he kept thinking about Allison. He had met her their senior year in high school at a party in Manteo on Roanoke Island. She was slim then, and she wore her russet hair long. On their third date they took a beach towel and a jug of wine up to Jockey's Ridge, which, at that time, was the tallest sand dune on the East Coast. They sat at the back of the dunes, looking down on Roanoke Sound. The water looked like obsidian in the moonlight. They passed the wine jug back and forth, laughing and talking, and when the wine was gone they made love. Afterward, in his drunken, grateful state, Virgil told her he loved her.

"Don't be silly," Allison said. "You don't even know me yet."

That was Allison. Practical, hardworking, single-minded, a woman with an instinctive and immediate grasp of the bottom line. When they had first met, he was a dreamy and unfocused kid with a Hatteras accent and limited knowledge of the world. In retrospect, he could see that she must have seen him as a Herculean challenge, a project requiring her Germanic single-mindedness and attention to detail. They were married their senior year at the University of North Carolina at Chapel Hill. They lived in Chapel Hill until Virgil earned his doctorate in English. Allison had already earned a master's degree in business administration. Virgil got his first teaching job at Elon College, west of Chapel Hill. Allison was working for a company in the Research Triangle. Three years later he got a tenure-track job at Laurel College in Indian Creek. The college had a position for Allison, too: an assistant vice chancellor for business and finance. Their lives there fell into a familiar routine. Friday nights they played bridge with Virgil's department chairman, Miles, and his wife, Eunice. Saturday night's dinner out was followed by their weekly lovemaking session.

Three years after they moved to Indian Creek, the vice chancellor for business and finance retired, and Allison moved up a notch into the position. Virgil received tenure the following year, and he decided it was time for Allison to get pregnant, a subject on which she had always been oddly reticent. Although she wasn't enthusiastic about the idea, he talked her into going off the pill. He began reading books on child care and picturing himself changing diapers, reading to the kids at night. But Allison's period kept coming, regular as an electric bill. A fertility specialist in Raleigh diagnosed the problem: Allison's fallopian tubes were blocked. Laser micro-surgery would improve the odds, he said, but the results couldn't be guaranteed. Virgil was surprised and disappointed when Allison declined the surgery.

"It's not worth the trouble or the expense," she said, and she began listing the practical benefits of remaining childless: more free time; no worry and expense regarding child care, doctors visits, and schools; more money to spend on vacations and invest in retirement accounts.

He tried to persuade her to consider the surgery, but she was adamant. "Frankly, Virgil, I don't really want to be a mother."

Virgil was aggrieved about the possibility of never having kids. Conversations on the subject always ended up making them both tense and angry, so he eventually stopped broaching the issue. But after that door was closed and locked, little things he didn't appreciate about Allison began to annoy him—her obsessive need to control their money, for example, and the nasal tone of her voice when she was angry or agitated. Sex became increasingly perfunctory, bereft of much emotional context. When he tried to talk to Allison about this, or any matter of importance, she would usually dismiss his concerns with a platitude: "There are ups and down in any relationship, Virgil. We just have to take the good with the bad."

One afternoon a composition student named Monica Simpson visited him in his office. She was wearing a low-cut black dress.

"I came to see you about my grade," she said. "I want to know what my average is."

Virgil opened his grade book, looking for her name, although he knew she was failing.

"Looks like a low D," he said. Freshman composition required a C to pass.

She eased back in the chair across from his desk, hiking her dress up. "What can I do to bring my grade up?"

"Do you have your graded essays with you?"

"No."

"If you bring all your themes in, I'll go over them with you and see if I can pinpoint the problem."

Her dress inched higher. She wasn't wearing any panties.

"When I try to express my thoughts on paper, they seem to disappear."

He forced himself to look in her eyes.

"How are you doing in your other classes?"

"OK." She shrugged. "Yours is the one I'm really worried about. I can't seem to get a handle on it."

"Do you like to read?"

"Not really."

"Maybe you aren't trying hard enough. Writing is a form of thinking. It takes discipline and work."

She ran her hands along her bare thighs. "I'm willing to do whatever it takes to pass your class, Professor Gibson." Leaning back in the chair, she spread her legs so that he could see what she was offering him.

"I have some work to do," he said.

After the student left his office, Virgil shut the door and put his head down on his desk. His hands were trembling. He was frustrated and angry with himself. Instead of passively overlooking his student's attempt at sexual bribery, he should have told her that her behavior was manipulative and immature, and he should have lectured her on the importance of taking her education seriously.

I should have told her to pull her damn dress down, he thought.

On the way home that afternoon, he bought two bottles of wine. He drank the first one, waiting for Allison to come home. When she arrived, he coaxed her into drinking a glass with him, after which he attempted to seduce her on the couch.

She wasn't in the mood.

"Why can't you wait until later?" she asked. She meant Saturday night. It was about the only time she was in the mood.

Sitting beside her on the couch, Virgil watched her read the afternoon newspaper. He remembered the way he had seen her that night on Jockey's Ridge, her long hair wine-colored in the moonlight, the easy way she had given herself to him. She was stocky now and she had a double chin. Her russet hair was cut in a no-nonsense bob.

"Last night I dreamed I was walking on the beach," he said. "When I looked back, I saw I wasn't leaving any footprints in the sand."

"Virgil, are you drunk?"

"Possibly."

"You've been working too hard. Just let's wait until Saturday. You know that's our regular time for sex."

But Saturday was when he told her he was moving out.

As he lay in the hammock, he remembered his dad telling him his life had been just one big routine until they had moved to Hatteras. They were thigh-deep in the surf at the Point, trolling for fish. "I only lived for you, your mother, and the peak moments which I nearly always experienced here, fishing at the Point," Charles Gibson said. "Most people are zombies the majority of their lives, Virgil. I've spent most of my life being a zombie, too. But now I can see that what really matters is what makes you feel truly alive."

Virgil tried to remember the last time he had felt truly

alive. There had been times when he had felt that way in the classroom, when both he and his students were fired up with the passion of learning, and a number of times making love with Allison, mostly in the beginning, but those days were gone now. He felt cheated somehow. *I've been a zombie, too.* Not only that, he had no idea what it would take to make him feel more fully alive. But whatever it was, he was determined to find it, and leaving his loveless marriage had been his first step.

He was getting ready for bed when Jack called. "Hey, you want to go deep sea fishing with me tomorrow morning?"

"Sure."

"Meet me at the Oregon Inlet Fishing Center at six. I'm taking out a party of four so there's plenty of room. You can go as my guest."

"I can pay my share."

"This one's on me."

"What should I bring?"

"Lunch. Maybe something to drink."

"Who are the others?"

"I only know one of them—guy named Meyers. He bought us drinks the other night."

"Sure I won't be in the way?"

"No way. We're going to use you for bait."

Virgil laughed. "See you at six."

"The name of the boat is *Eva Marie*," Jack said.

V

As Jack piloted the forty-seven foot sport fisher *Eva Marie* through Oregon Inlet, the water outside the cabin window was metallic gray in the early morning light. Virgil could see Dave Swain, Jack's first mate, on the deck, putting hooks into the bait fish. There were four other people in the cabin—Raymond Meyers, the blonde Virgil had seen at the restaurant, and Meyers's two male companions. Meyers and the blonde, whose name was Nicole, sat on the starboard couch, across from Virgil. The younger of the two men, Sid Hinton, sat in a chair to Meyers's right. His narrow, sharp-featured face reminded Virgil of a ferret. The other man, C.C. Thorne, sat on the couch next to Virgil, on the portside of the cabin; he was reading *The Washington Post.*

Meyers, a thick-chested man with a wide, fleshy face, looked to be in his early fifties—considerably older than the woman he was with, who couldn't have been more than thirty. Virgil had difficulty keeping his eyes off her. Nicole had what he would call genetic class: wide-set aquamarine eyes, a finely shaped nose, sculpted cheeks, long legs. The book she was reading was James Joyce's *Ulysses,* a complex, experimental novel set in Dublin in 1904 that few people he knew had ever been able to finish. Even those who claimed to have read it all the way through had needed an accompanying key to understand it. This immediately piqued his interest: He wondered why she was reading it.

"Jack tells me you've never been out to the Gulf Stream before," Meyers said. He had noticed Virgil staring at Nicole.

"That's right," Virgil said. "I hate to admit it, considering I graduated from Hatteras High."

"What are you doing now?"

"I teach English at Laurel College."

Meyers nodded. His supercilious expression made Virgil feel sized up and dismissed as a person of little importance.

"Teach any radicals?" C.C. asked, looking up from his newspaper. Although his tone was neutral, his icy blue eyes had a hint of hostility.

"What do you mean by 'radical'?" Virgil asked.

"People who want to destroy the American way of life."

"I'm not sure what you mean by 'the American way of life,'" Virgil said. "But the most radical thing that's happened at Laurel College since I've been there was a panty raid on one of the women's dorms."

C.C. Thorne returned to his newspaper without comment. The other two men looked bored, but Virgil noticed the woman looked up from her book and smiled at him.

They were passing beneath the bridge that spanned the inlet, connecting Bodie Island with Hatteras Island to the south. Looking up at the bridge, Virgil had a flashback of the night he had followed Jack off the bridge into the water below—the sensation of falling, the sudden immersion in the water, the pain radiating through his arm. It seemed like a dream now.

The woman was looking at the bridge, too.

"There's Hell's Gate," he said.

"Why do you call it that?" she asked.

"That's what the fishermen call it. A lot of trawlers have gone down in this inlet. It keeps filling up with sand because of the offshore currents."

"Nikki, I want you to take off my shoes," Meyers said, "and rub my feet."

Virgil hoped Nicole would tell him no. But she put down the book, knelt before him, took off his shoes and socks, and began rubbing one of his feet.

"That's it," Meyers said, closing his eyes. "That's nice. Just like that."

Later, up on the flying bridge, Virgil asked Jack how he had met Raymond Meyers. Jack was at the steering station, wearing Bermuda shorts, a white T-shirt, and a Cat Diesel Power cap.

"I met him a couple of years ago, through a mutual friend, guy I served with in Vietnam. Raymond was looking for someone with a boat. He hired me to do a job for him."

"A job?"

"I dropped some crates off in Belize. He didn't want to go through regular channels."

"Any idea what was in the crates?"

"I didn't ask."

"What does he do for a living?"

"He sells police and military supplies to foreign governments," Jack said. "Chili, El Salvador, Israel. His company's main headquarters is in Norfolk. He comes down here weekends on his yacht. You ought to see that thing, Virgil. It's got to have cost at least three million bucks."

"Why does he come down here?"

"To see the blonde. She lives in Kitty Hawk."

"She seems too classy for him."

"If all the good women left the sorry men, whole civilization would fall apart."

"No doubt about that."

Jack was studying a display screen mounted on the console by the wheel. Virgil asked about the geometric designs on the screen, which were red, blue, and green.

"It's a sonar color scope. Lets you see everything happening in the water around the boat. It works on sound. The colors are determined by the strength of the returning echo."

Jack pointed to a clump of tiny blue dots. "That's a school of fish, probably trout. This thing can give you a digital reading of the course, speed, and range of the school. You can also get depth, water temperature, your own speed, and position. Pretty cool, huh?"

Virgil pointed to a blue form on the lower right hand corner of the screen. "What's that?"

"Shark. That gentleman is a perfect killing machine. He can smell a drop of blood in the water up to half a mile away."

Someone was calling Jack on the boat's radio. He picked up the receiver. "What have you got, Red Man?"

"We're in a school of yellowfin. Got four in the past thirty minutes."

"I'm on my way. Thanks." Jack turned to starboard in the direction of the other fishing boats. Then he called down to the cabin on the intercom to tell the others to get ready to fish.

When Jack got close to the other boats, Virgil climbed down to the deck. Raymond Meyers, Sid, and C.C. were sitting in three of the boat's fighting chairs, which were bolted to the deck on swivels. The boat's outriggers dropped down, spreading out the fishing lines. The sea was blue as a window in a cathedral.

"Red Man's been hauling them in," Dave said, nodding at one of the boats. Tan and blond, he didn't look much older than one of Virgil's students.

"What's he been getting?"

"Looks like yellowfin."

The line popped out of one of the clips holding it in place, and the rod bent down fast. Virgil could hear the drag clicking.

C.C. Thorne grabbed up the rod and jerked back hard on it. A vein popped out in his temple as he cranked the reel.

It took him about ten minutes to get the fish up to the side of the boat. Dave gaffed it with the sea witch, and, holding the line in one hand, the sea witch in the other, he lifted the fish over the gunwale and dropped it into the fish box—a fine yellowfin tuna, black and silver, streaked with iridescent yellow and blue.

"You got a buffalo," Dave said. "Looks like she'll go sixty pounds."

"Nice fish, C.C.," Raymond said.

Virgil wanted to fish, too, but he had had too much of the boat's rocking. His inner ball bearings were starting to slam into each other, and his stomach felt queasy.

He went into the cabin where Nicole was still reading, and lay down on the couch, his arm over his eyes.

"Feeling seasick?" she asked.

"A little."

"It helps to have a little food in your stomach." She offered him a sandwich out of her canvas bag.

"Thanks." He unwrapped the foil and took a bite of the sandwich, a ham and cheese.

Sid came into the cabin, rummaged around in his duffel bag with his back to them, and then went back outside.

"Don't you like to fish?" Virgil asked, after a while. The sandwich had made him feel a little better.

"Sometimes. I feel more like reading today, though."

"How do you like *Ulysses*?"

"I like Buck Mulligan and Leopold Bloom. I'm not sure yet about Stephen Dedalus."

"Why is that?"

"He seems to take himself a little too seriously."

"How so?"

"Well, he wouldn't grant his mother's deathbed request to kneel and pray."

"He was rebelling against organized religion."

"She was his mother and she was dying. What harm would it have done to say *The Lord's Prayer*? It's just words."

"Stephen redeems himself by his guilt."

"That's too late to help her, though, isn't it?"

Virgil considered her comment about *The Lord's Prayer* being "just words." He was trying to think of a way to pursue the subject when he was distracted by gunshots out on deck. Through the window, he could see Sid firing a pistol over the side. He got up and went out to the cockpit to see what was going on.

C.C. and Sid were looking at the water. Sid held the pistol, a flat, black thing, at his side.

Jack had cut the engine, and the boat was slowing down. Virgil saw Dave look at Sid and shake his head.

"What's he shooting at?"

"A shark," Dave said.

"What in the hell are you doing?" Jack called down from the bridge. Raymond Meyers stood behind him.

"There was a shark following us," Sid said. "I don't know if I got him or not."

"That was a dolphin," Jack said.

"I know what a shark looks like."

"Put that damned thing away!"

Sid didn't move.

"Put it away now, or we're going back in."

Sid still didn't move, not until Meyers jerked his thumb over his shoulder. Then he went into the cabin. Through the window, Virgil saw him put the pistol back in his duffel bag.

After that, they didn't catch any more fish. The other boats caught plenty; Virgil could see them hauling them in, but no one on the *Eva Marie* had any luck. Not even a sand shark,

It was as if the boat was jinxed.

This irritated Virgil, because he hadn't had a chance to fish. On the way back to the fishing center, he stayed up on the bridge with Jack.

"That asshole brought us bad luck," Jack said. "Fool like that has got no business out here."

Virgil put his hand in his pocket and touched the brass casing he had picked up from the deck. "Meyers was up here a long time."

"He invited me to have dinner with him next Saturday night. On his yacht." Jack said this casually, but with a hint of puzzlement. Meyers evidently had some use for him, and Virgil had the feeling Jack wasn't sure what it was.

"Mr. Meyers is a high roller," Dave said, back at the fishing center. "He tipped me a hundred bucks."

"He won't miss it," Jack said.

"He seems like a nice enough guy. But that fool with the gun was a major jerk."

"That's Raymond's nephew."

"He's a weird son of a bitch. And that other one, too— Thorne. Notice his ears?"

"I wasn't paying any attention to his damn ears."

"They're pointed," Dave said. "Like a bat's."

VI

A few days after the Gulf Stream trip with Jack, Virgil got out his rod and reel, packed a lunch, and drove down to Cape Point on Hatteras Island, stopping along the way to pick up cut mullet for bait. Cape Point was the sandy promontory that jutted into the sea south of the lighthouse. The beach was lined with fishermen, their rods sand-spiked in front of the four-wheel drives. A few fishermen were thigh-deep in the surf. Virgil drove through ruts in the sand, out to the edge, parking just above the water line. He hooked a mullet to the bucktail lure, waded into the surf, and began trolling, using a seven-foot rod and an eight-pound test line—a light rig for this water, but he wanted to give the fish a fighting chance. He had been fishing here hundreds of times, mostly with his father, and coming to the Point always made him miss him. About fifty yards to his right he saw a flash of silver, a Spanish mackerel leaping into the air. He moved to the right and cast again. On his third cast he hooked the fish. The mackerel had plenty of fight, and it took him awhile to reel it in.

Awhile later, he hooked something that bent the rod nearly double and set the drag to clicking. By the time he got the fish in to shore, he was sweating and his hands were sore. A big drum, it wasn't six feet away from him when he felt the tension on the rod go slack.

"Son of a bitch!"

The drum had escaped, but that was the risk he had run using the light line.

By late afternoon, Virgil had caught half a dozen more mackerel, two sea bass, and a small toadfish, which he threw back. He packed up the Cherokee and drove on through Buxton, passing their old place on the left near Buxton Woods: a white, two-story frame house surrounded by water oaks. In nor'easters, the old house had creaked and moaned on its foundations, dishes rattled in the cupboards, and the wind howled through the wood slats. A neighbor told him the house had originally been built half a mile away, but that it had floated to its present location in the Hurricane of 1944.

Behind the house was Buxton Woods, a maritime forest where Virgil had ridden a dirt bike along paths on the ridge, smoked cigarettes, caught crawdads, listened to birds calling, climbed trees, and learned to shoot a .22 rifle.

A few miles farther, he turned down a sandy road and followed it back to Jack's mother's house on the sound. There were a few trailers on the road, with children playing in the yards. The closer he got to the sound, the worse the road got, with deep ruts.

Mae Delaney was sitting at a table in the front yard of the one-story house, her white hair blowing in the wind. She smiled and waved. Behind her, the Pamlico Sound was a bold, vibrant blue that bled into the lighter blue of the sky.

"Pull up a chair, Virgil. I'd invite you in, but the power's gone off. It's cooler out here."

"Salt air in the lines again." He sat down at the table, holding the stringer of fish between his knees. "Brought you some fish."

"Thanks. Got a nice mess there. Care for a drink?"

"Sure."

Mae opened a cooler at her feet and took out a Coke. He popped the top and took a long drink.

"How's Margaret?" Mae asked.

"Mom is OK. She's living in one of those retirement communities where everything's planned out. Bingo on Monday night, bowling on Tuesdays, movie on Wednesdays, bingo again on Thursday."

"They might as well put me in a loony bin as to put me in one of them places."

"You and me both."

"Jack was just talking about you the other day. Said you'd moved to Nags Head for the summer."

"That's right. I stopped by his place on the way down here, but he wasn't home."

"Honey, Jack's not staying in Avon now."

"Where is he?"

"I'm not supposed to tell, but I don't reckon he'd mind you knowing. He's staying on a minesweeper in Wanchese Harbor."

"A minesweeper?"

"Lord, yes. Old World War Two minesweeper."

"Why'd he move there?"

"You got me. He just said he needed a change of scenery."

"Maybe he wants to sell his house."

"I'll sure be the last one to hear about it if he does. Know how I found out about him losing his boat?"

"How?"

"Read about it in the paper. That Jack. He's turning my hair white. When's he going to settle down and get married, Virgil?"

"I guess he hasn't found the right woman yet."

"He'd run like hell from her."

"Think so?"

"Honey, does a fat man fart?"

Wanchese Harbor, on the southern end of Roanoke Island, was slate-blue in the evening light. As Virgil drove around the harbor, he could see the fishing boats docked behind the seafood companies. Scattered here and there were the rusted bodies of old trucks and cars. The minesweeper—battleship gray, splotched with rust, listing to one side—was at the south end of the harbor facing the Croatan Sound. He parked his Cherokee and walked over to the harbor. He saw a Jeep in the parking lot next to one of the seafood companies, but no black Corvette. Maybe he's not there, he thought.

"Jack! Jack Delaney," he called.

A dog began barking. Jack appeared at the aft end of the minesweeper. He waved, held up his index finger to indicate Virgil should wait, and then disappeared.

An engine kicked into life. Then Jack came around the side in his Scarab. When he pulled up to the dock, he said, "You've been to see my mama."

"She's worried about you."

"What else is new?" He slapped a mosquito on his arm. "Since you tracked me down, might as well come on in and visit."

Virgil sat on the dock, lowering himself into the boat.

"I couldn't tell if that was your Jeep or not."

"It's all I'm driving now. Sold my Corvette."

Jack steered the boat around to the other side of the minesweeper. He cut the engine, glided in close, and tied the line to a chain hanging over the side. The dog was barking louder now. A rope ladder hung from the gunwale.

"I'll go first," Jack said. He climbed the ladder to the deck. "All right. Come on, Virgil."

Virgil climbed up after him.

Jack was holding a three-legged black dog by the collar. "Let him smell you."

Virgil stepped toward the dog, holding out his hand. The

dog growled. It had a squat, muscular body and a bullet-shaped head. Its right foreleg was just a stump.

"It's all right, Amos," Jack said. "Talk to him, Virgil."

"Don't bite me. I'm a friend of Jack's. That's it. That's a good boy."

The dog smelled his hand and leg while he continued talking to him. Then Jack let him go.

"Where'd you get Amos?"

"Traded a skiff for him."

"Who named him?"

"I don't know. That was his name when I got him."

Virgil followed Jack and his three-legged dog through a doorway, down a flight of stairs to a low-ceilinged cabin lit with two lanterns and furnished with a cot, a footlocker, and a small table. On the table there was a semi-automatic pistol and a journal, bound in leather. Jack had developed the habit of keeping a record of key events in his life back in high school. A pump shotgun leaned against the wall. The cabin smelled of kerosene and mildew.

"Have a seat," Jack said, sitting on the cot. The dog lay at his feet.

Virgil sat down on the footlocker. There was a half-open door in the aft end of the berth. "What's in there?"

"What passes for a galley. It's got a sink, propane camp stove, some cans of food. No water, though. I got to haul that in."

"Who owns this jewel?"

"Buddy of mine. He bought it from the government for the engine. He's letting me stay here awhile."

"What's going on, man?"

Jack picked up a manila envelope from the floor and tossed it to Virgil. "A few days ago, I found this on the front seat of my Jeep."

Virgil opened the envelope and took out some eight-by-ten photographs. The first one was an image of a naked male corpse, minus its head and hands. "Jesus Christ!" The next one showed a man's body sprawled in a car trunk; most of the face looked like it had been shot off. Virgil didn't look at the others.

"I'm a little behind on a debt," Jack said. "Until I catch up I figure I'll sleep better here."

"I've got a few thousand if that will help."

"It won't, but I appreciate the offer."

Virgil slid the photographs back in the envelope and put it on the table. "What are you going to do?"

"I've got the house and a couple of lots. Luckily they're all paid for. I'm trying to sell the lots but that takes time. I hate to lose my house, but I might have to let it go, too."

"How about your insurance claim on the trawler?"

"Company's been dragging its feet. I got a lawyer working on it, but that's about all I can do right now."

Amos sighed, farted, and put his head down on the floor. Jack looked at the dog thoughtfully, rubbing his chin with his hand. "No sense in us sitting around here feeling bad. How'd you like to go look at a whale?"

"A whale?"

"One washed up on the beach near Rodanthe this afternoon. Buddy of mine told me about it. I told Bobbie I'd pick her up after dark and drive down to look at it. Want to come?"

"Sure."

"I want to see it before the tourists find out about it," Jack said.

Jack drove south on Highway 12. Bobbie sat in the front with him, and Virgil sat in the back. Near Rodanthe, Jack pulled off onto the side of the road.

"Lee said it was just past the speed limit sign," he said, pointing to a stake in the sand. "He left a marker for us."

He got a flashlight out of the dash, and they walked up

over the dunes to the sea. The whale was a hundred yards south of them on the beach. It looked big as a boxcar. It had a huge, square head, almost a third of the length of its body, and a single nostril on top through which a labored breath was coming. It smelled like a truckload of dead fish just starting to go bad.

They walked all around the whale, Jack shining the light on its black skin. Its body was marked with hundreds of pale circles of various sizes and an overlapping maze of long white lines. Virgil asked Jack about the markings on its skin.

"Lamprey eels hitchhike rides on them," he said. "And squids mark them up with their tentacles. That's what the old boy eats—those big squids. Those lines are from their beaks."

"Wonder why it beached?" Bobbie asked.

"Might have got hit by a ship."

"Maybe he's just old," Virgil said.

"Poor thing," Bobbie said.

"He doesn't have long," Jack said. "Their organs can't support their weight on land."

Virgil touched the whale's side. It felt like soft rubber. Its breath sounded like a huge bellows. It was a sperm whale, the kind Melville wrote about. Looking at it, he had the feeling he was seeing something that would soon be only a memory, preserved in yellowing photographs, grainy videotapes.

Jack knelt in the sand and pulled back a section of the whale's lower lip, exposing a row of banana-sized teeth. The creature's eye opened, a luminous melon in the rubbery mass of its head.

"Nothing we can do, except keep him company for a while."

They returned to Jack's Jeep and got out a lantern, some beach towels, and a cooler of beer. They set up the lantern and the cooler on the beach towels near the whale's head, then sat down and started on the beer. The sky was eaten up with big, shiny stars.

"I saw some whalers off the coast of Nova Scotia once," Jack said. "It was a Russian ship. They were using harpoons with exploding tips. They picked out a mother with a calf to shoot first. After they hit her, the other whales supported her with their bodies, and the whalers followed them, firing their harpoons. After they shot them, they inflated them with air bags so they wouldn't sink. They must have slaughtered the entire herd."

"What mighty fishermen those guys were," Bobbie said. "Kind of makes you sick, huh?"

They drank beer and watched the heat lightning flashing over the sea, Virgil remembering what he knew about whales. They were mammals, and the bones in their flippers were similar to a human's hand bones. They had a language, musical wails and creaks, that scientists had recorded but couldn't decipher. Some people who studied them considered them to be as smart as humans.

Jack stood up and began taking off his clothes. "I feel like swimming."

Bobbie took off her T-shirt, slid out of her jeans and panties, and followed Jack down into the surf.

Virgil slipped out of his clothes too and went down to the water. It was icy cold. He waded in, shivering, trying to keep his eyes on Bobbie and Jack. They were about fifty feet from the shore, up to their chests. A wave rolled in, and he dove under it, swimming toward them. But when he looked again, he only saw Bobbie.

"Where's Jack?"

She pointed out to sea. "Out there."

Another wave rolled in, and he swam under it. When he surfaced, he saw Bobbie come up out of the water, riding a wave. He dove beneath the next wave, thinking of the whale moving through a dark cool world of its own, guided by powers beyond his ken. He pictured its eye, which seemed to radiate a mysterious intelligence, and he imagined the whale diving down through zones of green and lavender twilight, diving down to the part of the sea that is cold and silent and black, where the pressure is a hundred tons per square foot, then leveling off, swimming past luminescent fish and blob-like creatures, the sonar device in his great domed head sending out echo signals, searching for his prey, the giant squid.

He surfaced again and swam out to the deep water, looking for Jack. He didn't see him. He stopped, treading water. All around him, darkness. The inshore current had already pulled him hundreds of feet south of the whale. The lantern was a tiny flickering light in the distance.

"Jack!" he called. "Jack!" He could feel the immense indifference of the sea to his life.

Something seized his legs, pulling him down. His heart pounding, he kicked free, picturing the blue image of the hammerhead on the *Eva Marie*'s sonar screen.

Jack rose up out of the water, laughing.

"I thought you were a shark," Virgil said.

"Your ass would have been gone if I was."

"Big sharks don't come in this close, do they?"

"Not unless they feel like it."

"Ready to go back in?"

"Sure."

They swam back to the shore and then walked back up the beach to the whale. Bobbie was sitting on a towel. She had put her T-shirt on. Virgil sat down on the adjoining towel and began putting on his clothes. Jack stood above them, drying himself with a towel.

They stretched out on the towels and lay there listening to the surf. After a while, Virgil got up and went for a walk. He could see the lights from an ocean liner, far out to sea. And above that, the stars and a crescent moon. He thought about the photos Jack had received, marveling at his friend's nonchalant attitude toward danger. He admired Jack's ability to live so close to the edge and still take time to appreciate the sad grandeur of a dying sperm whale and a nocturnal swim in the sea.

He walked what seemed like a long way down the beach. Being near the sea again, the nighttime immersion in its cold water, made Virgil feel cleansed somehow. But he knew it was more than just being close to the sea. It was Jack, too—the influence he had always had on him.

When he got back to the whale, he saw Bobbie with her ear against the sand, as if she were trying to listen to the earth's beating heart. Jack was entering her from behind. The whale blocked part of the moonlight, rendering them in chiaroscuro. Virgil backed away quickly, and then he walked north back up the beach, the primal image of their bodies below the whale's milky eye lingering in his mind.

What was it thinking as it watched these alien creatures making love?

VII

July was hot and crowded on the Outer Banks. Some days the traffic was so bad it took Virgil fifteen minutes to drive three miles on the beach road. During his afternoon walks on the beach, he had to be careful to keep from stepping on recumbent tourists, whose physical flaws, normally hidden by clothes, were glaringly evident in sunlight: bloated bellies and varicose veins and cellulite and scars and flabby, spindly limbs. Nothing like a walk on the beach to make you realize how most people, including him, fall far short of the glamorous faces and bodies seen in the media.

He didn't feel he had much to show for the summer. He had left Allison and moved to the Outer Banks in an effort to gain some clarity about his overall purpose in life, but all he had managed to do was catch up on his reading. He dreaded returning to Laurel College for the fall semester. He needed more time than a summer off; he was weary of teaching and of his life there. He decided he needed to immerse himself in a challenging research project, one that would allow him to stay in his cottage through the fall. He would have to pick a topic that his departmental chairman, Miles Fletcher, wouldn't find too threatening. That should be easy, however, since Miles's specialty was British literature.

Virgil had always been interested in the German poet Rainer Maria Rilke, not just for the quality of his work but also because as far as he knew, no one had written a definitive biography about him. Although most of Rilke's work had been translated into at least one language, during the last two years of his life he had written about thirteen poems that had never been translated into English. Virgil had first encountered these poems in the graduate library at the University of North Carolina. He decided they would be a fine source for research and eventual publication of a critical essay.

He gave Miles a call. Following the customary small talk, he got around to asking for the sabbatical.

"This is rather short notice, isn't it, Virgil?" Although Miles had grown up on Virginia's Eastern Shore, he spoke with a slight British accent, an affectation he had acquired at Oxford.

"Yes, it is, but I have an exciting idea for a project I'd like to work on. I'm sure it would reflect well on the department." Virgil told him about Rilke's untranslated poems. "It would be interesting to translate them and then interpret them to see what they suggest about his mind during the last two years of his life."

"I didn't know you knew German."

"My German isn't great. I'll have to work with a collaborator, someone fluent."

Miles was silent.

"This could create quite a stir, Miles. It could make *The Literary Review* or *The Malahat*." Miles loved for members of his department to publish in prestigious literary journals.

"I'll have to take this up with the dean, Virgil."

"I understand. I appreciate anything you can do to help."

A week later, Miles called to tell him he had gotten his sabbatical approved.

"I'll have to rearrange the schedule some, but you'll have your sabbatical. Just make sure you have something impressive to show for it."

"I'll do my best, Miles. And thanks."

Virgil wanted to do something to celebrate his good fortune. He drove down the beach road and stopped in at the restaurant where Bobbie Russell tended bar, according to Jack. The restaurant section to the left was dimly lit, with ceiling fans turning slowly overhead. Virgil went through an archway to the bar, left of the lobby, and saw Bobbie behind the counter. She had on a pink tank top and hip hugger jeans with a wide leather belt lined with brass studs. He hadn't seen her since the night they had gone skinny dipping in the Atlantic.

Her face lit up when she saw him.

"Hi, Virgil. What can I get you?"

"Draft beer. Sure is hot out there."

She set a mug on the counter. "This will cool you off. What's been going on?"

He told her about getting his sabbatical approved. "No classes for a whole semester."

"What do you do on a sabbatical?"

"I'm going to do research on a poet. That's part of the deal."

"Does he write sonnets?"

"I don't think so. You like sonnets?"

"For sweetest things turn sourest by their deeds. Lilies that fester smell far worse than weeds."

"Sounds like Shakespeare."

"That's right."

"You a fan?"

"I never was that strong in English, but I had this one teacher in high school, Mr. Calloway—dude was crazy about Shakespeare, especially the sonnets. At first I thought they were boring, but his enthusiasm was just so strong he taught me to appreciate them—the way they were written and what they were saying. Shakespeare packed a lot of meaning into those sonnets. Must have been hard to have them make so much sense and still follow that strict rhyme scheme—three stanzas of four lines and then the last two lines different."

"The couplet."

"Right. That one about the lilies was a couplet. It's one I still remember."

"Mr. Calloway sounds like a first-rate teacher."

"Had to be if he could teach a bunch of wild-ass teenagers to appreciate Shakespeare."

"You ever think about teaching?"

"Maybe someday. I'd have to go back to college first. Only went two years."

"Why'd you quit?"

"I followed a guy down here. He was a real jerk, but I didn't know that then." Bobbie smiled. "You got to kiss a few frogs before you can find a prince."

Virgil wondered if she was still seeing Jack. He had seen Jack several times since that night they had gone to see the whale, but Jack never mentioned Bobbie.

Virgil was about to ask Bobbie if she had seen Jack lately when two surfers came in and sat down at the end of the bar. Bobbie excused herself to wait on them. Virgil sipped the beer, admiring the graceful way she moved, her easy, animated manner with the surfers.

When she returned, he had his wallet in his hand. "How much for the beer?"

"This one's my treat. To help you celebrate your sabbatical."

"Let me pay you."

"I've never whipped a professor before, but I've always wanted to try."

"Thanks, Bobbie. I appreciate it."

"Good luck on that research. Let me know if you run across any good sonnets."

He stepped outside into the sunlight, still charmed by the way Bobbie had pulled out those lines by Shakespeare. He decided to stop by again and get to know her better. If she was no longer going out with Jack, maybe he could ask her out—as long as Jack didn't mind.

Not that he would. As far as Virgil knew, Jack had never allowed himself to get too serious about one woman.

Virgil never got the opportunity to ask Bobbie out: He learned about her upcoming marriage to Jack by way of a wedding announcement in his mail in early August.

Mr. and Mrs. Robert Russell of Greenville, North Carolina, request the honor of your presence at the marriage of their daughter, Roberta Jane, to Jack Michael Delaney, First United Methodist Church, Greenville, North Carolina. October 14 at two o'clock p.m., 1988.

He was surprised and perplexed by the wedding announcement. It was a little like learning Bigfoot had finally been captured. Jack Delaney had always danced away from serious commitments to women. What had caused such a dramatic change?

Virgil hadn't seen Jack since mid-July. Before Jack moved back into his home, Virgil visited him one other time in the minesweeper. That was when Jack had told him about his meeting with Lupe Herrara at the airstrip behind the Wright Brothers Memorial. Jack had been drinking that night, and he was more revealing than usual. It was one of the few times he had ever discussed his life as a smuggler with Virgil in any detail. Virgil had listened with rapt attention.

The first Saturday after he received the wedding invitation, he drove down to Avon and found Jack at home. He answered the door, holding Amos by the collar.

"Got your wedding announcement. Congratulations."

"Can you come?"

"You know I'll be there, Jack."

"I wanted to do it in Hatteras, but Bobbie's mom insisted on Greenville."

"What made you decide to do it?"

"I've made a lot of bad choices in my life. I'd like to make some sensible ones for a change."

"Sounds like you've given it some serious thought," Virgil said. But Jack hadn't quite answered his question.

"My other big news is I've bought another trawler. I've had her down at the boatyard, getting her painted and rigged for fishing. We're having a party on her tomorrow around noon at Oden's Dock. If you're free, come on down."

"OK." Virgil wondered where Jack had gotten the money for the trawler. "Still can't believe you're finally getting married."

"I'm having trouble believing it myself," Jack said.

The next day, Virgil drove down to Oden's Dock, just north of the Hatteras Harbor Marina, for the party on Jack's trawler, the *Dixie Arrow*. Mae, Bobbie, Leon, and Sam and Billy were there, along with a couple of dozen other people from the island, including Mike Jennette. By Jack's standards, it was a quiet party. There was a keg of beer on deck, but no band, not even a tape player. Fried chicken, potato salad, slaw, and hush puppies were served on the table in the galley in the enclosed part of the trawler on the main deck. Some of the people ate outside on deck, where another table had been set up. Virgil sat between Sam and Billy, who had come with a blonde woman and a boy. The child, who looked to be about six, sat in Billy's lap and ate off his plate.

"He loves Billy," the woman said. She wore a baseball cap, T-shirt, and a necklace of seashells.

"This is Tammy," Billy said, his mouth full of chicken.

"Tammy, Virgil Gibson."

"Hello, Tammy."

"I met you at Jack's party in Hatteras. Remember?"

"Oh, yes," Virgil said, still trying to place her.

"This is Evan," Billy said, jiggling the boy on his knee. "He wants to be a fisherman."

"You might have to wait awhile," Tammy said.

"Billy, you ever had a boat?" the boy asked.

"Sure did. The *Ida Mae*. Beautiful little boat. Had a round stern, a round little bottom. She'd roll like you wouldn't believe. Had a little four-cylinder Perkins diesel in her."

"Where's the *Ida Mae* now?"

"I lost her."

"Let's see if we can find her." The boy jumped off Billy's lap. Everyone laughed.

"I lost her to the IRS," Billy said.

"Who's that?" The boy scowled.

"Hush, Billy," Tammy said.

"The IRS means the Internal Revenue Service," Bobbie Russell said, kneeling beside Evan. "They're in charge of the taxes we pay to Uncle Sam."

"Is that Billy's brother Sam?"

"No, honey. Uncle Sam is just a way of talking about the government."

"He ain't had that course in school yet, Bobbie," Sam said, winking at Tammy.

"Middleman's the only ones making big bucks off fishing nowadays," Sam said.

"That's right," Billy said. "But those buyers will sing the biggest, saddest blues about how hard it is."

"They'll tell you one price while you're out there fishing," Sam said. "Say you get in the trout, and you call in to the dock and ask the price. 'They're seventy-five cents a pound boys, get all you can.' But when you get back to the dock, the price is twenty cents a pound. 'Price dropped, boys. Sorry.' That's the story you hear every time."

"And the dealers always got an excuse," Jack said. "They flooded the market."

"That's a crock," Billy said. "The dealers stick it to the fishermen. That's just the way it is."

After lunch, Jack showed Virgil around his trawler. It was outfitted with a large winch aft of the enclosed housing on the main deck and outriggers that looked to be fifty feet high. The door leading down to the engine room was on the starboard side of the winch. The door to the galley, captain's cabin, and wheelhouse was on its portside.

Jack took off one of the hatch covers in the deck to show him the hole, a damp, fishy-smelling place below deck where the catch was stored. It was about twelve feet deep, twenty feet long, and twenty-three feet wide. The fish were kept in bins on either side of an aisle.

"Any secret compartments down there for grass?" Virgil only asked the question as a joke, but Jack didn't smile.

"I'm out of that business for good, Virgil."

They went back through the door to the housing on the main deck. The door opened onto a hallway. Stairs at the end led up to the wheelhouse. The galley was immediately to Virgil's right. A hatch in the galley led down to the forepeak.

Virgil knelt and looked through the hatch. It was about half the size of the fish hole. He saw four bunk beds, two lockers about six feet high, and a table and chairs in the center of the room.

"That looks cozy."

"Gets a little cramped after a week at sea."

"When are you going out?"

"Next week. The serious fishing doesn't start until October, but we're going to do some shrimping this summer."

"Who's going?"

"Sam, Billy, Leon, and Dave."

Virgil didn't know why he said what he said next: "Do you need another crew member?"

"We could use a cook."

"How long you going to be out?"

"A week or more."

"I'd like to do it."

"You sure?"

"Yes, I'm sure."

"You got the job."

"When do we leave?"

"Tuesday morning on the tide. It's your job to buy groceries."

"Where do I do that?"

"I've got an account set up at Burrus's Grocery in Hatteras. You can go down there Monday evening and buy whatever you think we'll need. I'll give you a note for the store manager. Bring the groceries over to the trawler around nine, and we'll load them into the fish hole."

"The fish hole?"

"Right, that's where we store the groceries. On ice."

"How much should I spend?"

"Five or six hundred."

"What should I buy?"

"Enough food to feed a crew for week. And remember, those boys like to eat."

"I'll be there. And thanks."

"Wait 'til you get back before you thank me."

They went on down the hall, past the captain's cabin and up the steps to the wheelhouse. Jack was showing Virgil the Loran unit and radar system when Bobbie and Evan came in. "I want to steer," the boy said.

Jack picked Evan up and held him to the wheel.

"Look out," he cried, as he steered the wheel, "'cause Hurricane Jack is coming through!"

"Whoa," said Jack. "Whoa, there, boy." But Jack looked as happy as Virgil could ever remember seeing him.

Virgil's mother was upset when he told her he was going to sea for a week.

"You listen to me. It's dangerous on those trawlers."

"I'll be fine, Mama."

"And with *Jack Delaney* of all people. You know he has never been anything but trouble."

"I've told you before Mama, Jack is a good man. And he's straight now."

"Virgil, why are you doing this?"

"For the experience."

"If you want to know what life is like at sea, why don't you rent a movie? Try *Mutiny on the Bounty*."

"It's not the same."

"What kind of work will you do?"

"I'm the cook."

"My God, they'll make you walk the plank."

"Very funny."

"You call me when you get back. I want to hear you're home safe. "

"I will. First thing."

"And you be careful out there. Don't take any unnecessary chances. Remember your father always wanted a son to carry on his family name."

"I'll try to keep that in mind, Mama."

VIII

Virgil was walking to his Cherokee when Dave Swain drove up to the cottage in a pickup truck. It was just getting light.

"Jack told me you signed on as the cook. Thought I'd stop and see if you wanted a ride."

"Sure." Virgil threw his suitcase into the back and got into the truck. Dave didn't look very happy.

"Everything OK, Dave?"

"Wife and me had a big fight this morning."

"What about?"

"She's pissed because I signed up with Jack. She wants all these things—a doublewide, a pony for the kids, trips to the beauty parlor—but when I do something to try and get them for her, all she does is complain. She says, 'Dave, he's a drug smuggler.'"

"She mind you working on the charter boat?"

"Not as much. At least I was home every night. Jack is trying to go straight now. People ought to leave him alone and give him a chance."

As they were crossing the bridge over Oregon Inlet, Virgil realized he had forgotten his wallet, but he didn't ask Dave to go back for it. What use would his driver's license and credit cards be on Jack's trawler?

When they got to the dock, Sam and Billy were up on the main deck, mending a net. Amos was running back and forth, barking at gulls circling overhead. Virgil and Dave took their duffel bags down to the forepeak and set them down by one of the bunks. Then Virgil went up to the wheelhouse. Jack was sitting in the captain's chair talking to an offshore captain on the radio, trying to find out where the shrimp were being caught.

When Jack got off the radio, Virgil said, "I came to see what my duties are."

"Just make sure we don't go hungry. Breakfast is at five-thirty. Lunch is at eleven-thirty and supper is at six."

"There a particular menu you want me to follow?"

"It's up to you. You can talk to the crew if you want."

"Do I have any other responsibilities?"

"Just keep us fed and make sure the captain has coffee."

"That shouldn't be too hard."

"We'll see. By the way, as cook you'll get one share of the catch."

"How much is a share?"

"Ten percent of net profit."

"How about if we go in the hole?" Virgil asked. "Will this job cost me anything?"

"It's liable to cost you some lost sleep."

Virgil went into the galley to study his new work area. There was a refrigerator, stove, sinks, and cabinets full of canned goods. After a while, he went out on deck, opened the hatch, and descended the ladder to the fish hole. It was chilly from the ice packed in the bins. He turned on the light and checked on the provisions he had brought.

The boat was moving. He climbed back up to the deck and watched as the trawler chugged through the inlet. The smokestack on the housing behind the winch belched three black puffs of smoke. Gulls circled overhead, filling the air with their rusty gate cries. The winch, drums, booms, ropes, nets, and chains seemed to radiate masculine energy. He pictured himself in oilskin and boots, working with nets and lines, braving storms at sea, a man among men.

Take it easy, he thought. You're just the cook.

Jack was still up in the wheelhouse when Virgil called the others to eat. He was hoping for a compliment on his meal, but although the crew all seemed to eat with gusto, no one commented on his meatloaf, yams, greens, and hot biscuits.

"Jack eat?" Sam asked, after a while.

"Not yet," Virgil said. "Should I take him a plate up?"

"You mean you served us before the captain?" Billy asked, raising his eyebrows.

"That a no-no?"

"Cooks have been flogged for less than that."

"This is just my first day." Embarrassed, Virgil went up to the wheelhouse to see Jack. "I understand I screwed up by serving the others lunch before the captain. Want me to bring you a plate up?"

Jack grinned and shook his head. "When Billy gets through, ask him to come up and stand watch so I can eat."

Virgil returned to the galley and gave Billy the message. He ate quietly, listening to the others talk about the Coast Guard's tough new policy aimed at casual drug users on boats.

Billy said, "Down off the coast of Florida, Coast Guard seized a two-and-a-half-million-dollar yacht after they found one-tenth of an ounce of pot on her. A butt in a trash can. I'll bet the captain didn't even know about it."

"They confiscated a shrimper down in Southport last week," Dave said. "Found less than an ounce under a crewman's mattress. And they impounded a scalloper from Pamlico County. Charged the captain with having 'a measurable amount of marijuana,' is the way the paper put it."

"Good thing we ain't on the *Lucky Strike*," Billy said. "There was enough weed down in the cracks of that boat to keep Hatteras Island high for a year."

"Ain't no way I'd bring any drugs on Jack's trawler," Dave said.

"Coast Guard would love to catch him with a joint," said Billy. "Wouldn't they sock it to him?"

"They been after his ass for years," Leon said. "I wouldn't put it past them to plant one on board."

"That zero-tolerance policy just shows what a piss-poor job the government's doing of catching smugglers," Sam said. "Colombians got pipelines full of coke running into this country, and the government can't stop it. So they bust a hardworking trawler boat captain for having a butt in his trashcan. That's Uncle Sam for you."

"The Colombians fly tons of coke into jungle air strips down in Central America," Leon said. "And some of those air strips were built with U.S. dollars."

"Now how's that for stupidity?" Leon said. "Government is spending millions to fight the drug trade, but they're paying for the airports to bring the shit."

There was a lull in the conversation, and then Leon said, "Hamburger tastes like a boiled boot."

"Tastes more like rubber to me," Billy said.

Virgil looked at them in alarm. "Is it really that bad?"

They were laughing now.

"Ain't nothing wrong with this food, Virgil," Sam said. "It's a fine meal."

"Take my word for it, professor," Billy said. "It's A-OK."

After he cleaned the galley, Virgil went out on the deck. The sun was high, the sea shimmering with pinpoints of light. In the water he saw two loggerheads, one riding the other's back. A guitar floated near them—where had it come from?

The loggerheads, oblivious to the guitar, bobbed on the waves, locked in their primal embrace.

He descended the ladder to the forepeak where Sam and Leon were sitting at the table playing cards. Billy was in his bunk, reading a paperback. Dave Swain looked to be asleep. They wouldn't start shrimping until dark, when the big shrimp run.

"I just saw two turtles in sexual union," Virgil said.

Billy looked up from his book. "I'd like to be able to do it like a turtle. They do it all day long."

"Billy's a thirty-second man," Leon said.

Billy laughed. "Hell, I'm just getting started good at thirty minutes."

"He's snoring by then," Leon said.

Virgil sat on his bunk and began looking through the cookbook he had packed, flagging recipes that sounded good. The image of the turtles and guitar lingered.

For supper that night, he prepared grilled steaks, baked potatoes, butter beans, sliced tomatoes, and sweet potato pie. When he got everything ready, he went up to the wheelhouse to get Jack.

"Tell Leon to come up and take the wheel watch."

After Leon relieved him at the wheel, Jack came down to the galley, Amos at his heels. The others were coming in, too. Virgil gave Jack a plate and Amos a bowl of Purina mixed with hamburger grease.

"Sam, you and Billy can work the winch tonight," Jack said.

"Aye, cap'n," Sam said.

"How long does it take to learn how to do that?" Virgil asked.

"You got to take your time learning to be a winch man," Sam said.

"There's little barbs in that cable," Billy added. "If you ain't careful, they can catch in your gloves and pull you right onto the winch. That happened to a guy right off the coast of Hatteras. Coast Guard took him off the boat in plastic bags. He was mush. Captain didn't even know it until the dredges come up and started banging on the stern."

"You got to be careful out here, Virgil," Jack said.

Sam said, "The sea can fool you into thinking everything's fine and then turn your ass upside down before you know what hit you. I remember one time we was up off the Grand Banks, towing for flukes off the northeast. We'd had swells running twenty feet plus, big southeast swells coming in. But the ocean was kind of calm. I was in the galley reading, and the seas was behind us. They was off our starboard stern, kind of catty cornered. When they're like that you can't really feel them, because you're towing with the seas. All of a sudden, I heard the captain hollering, 'Quick, get the nets in!' I thought, What the hell is he talking about? I jumped up and looked out the back door, and there was nothing there but a wall of water.

"When that water hit the stern, the bow went down into the sea, and the stern come up. She started rolling over on her side. I grabbed the pipes running through the deck over my head, and about that time my feet went out from under me. The outriggers flew up. One went into the water, the one other slammed into the rigging. I was sure we was going all the way over. But she come back down. I ran to the stern and turned the winch on to pull the nets in. About the time I got the doors coming up I looked up and man, that wave was like a ten-story building! Washed me all the way up to where the net reels was. Whole waist of the boat was flooded. Thought I'd seen the last of this world."

"These shipping lanes can be dangerous, too," Dave said. "An oil tanker can be right on top of you in the dark. Some of these big-ass ships got computers running them. Ain't a soul in the wheelhouse."

"I'll never forget the night we got hit," Billy said. "I was on the *Robert E. Lee*, and we got hit by a Greek freighter about fifteen miles off Hatteras. Beautiful night, clear and starry. I woke up when she smashed into us. Sounded like a freight train running right through the middle of the boat. She was listing to starboard and taking on water fast. There was six of us on board. We just had time to radio for help and get on the life raft before she went down.

"She was under water in ten minutes. That sea was forty-eight degrees. Thank God we had that raft."

"Didn't the freighter try to pick you up?" Virgil asked.

"Hell no! There was a hearing held about it afterwards. And the captain claimed he didn't even know they hit us." Billy was shaking his head. "There's an unwritten rule at sea: You help anyone who needs it. You don't ever know when it will be you needing help."

"Remember when we caught the mine?" Jack asked.

"Lord, yes," Billy said. "Won't ever forget it, either. We was towing for sea bass off the Georgia coast. I remember when we pulled the net up the back. It was all swelled up, and I thought, man we got a load of bass. I flipped the tripper and a few fish come out on deck. So I started shaking it, thinking they was packed tight, and all of a sudden—pow!—bunch of fish hit the deck, and right behind them was a great big spiny monster of a mine. I freaked out. I was ready to dive overboard. The boat rolled, and this thing rolled with it. Everybody was shitting their pants."

"What did you do?" Virgil asked.

"We finally got it to the portside and tied it there so it wouldn't roll." Jack said. "Damn thing was full of nails, shrapnel, hunks of metal. We put it on the beach and the Coast Guard blew it up with one of their cannons."

"When you tow around old wrecks, you can pick up mines or torpedoes easy in your nets," Dave said, looking at Virgil.

"Think how many torpedoes the Germans and Americans

fired that never hit their target. They're on the bottom. They're live, too. That gunpowder was sectioned, and a lot of it is still dry. They're real easy to set off."

"We was lucky," Sam said. "I heard about one boat that dredged up a torpedo. Killed everybody on the deck except one guy who was in the head. Blew him into the sea, still holding onto the commode."

"There's another thing that can be as dangerous as a storm or a torpedo," Jack said. "And that's a captain who doesn't know what the hell he's doing."

"Ain't that the truth," Sam said.

"I know a captain that had a boat get in bad seas," Jack said. "Half the crew was dredging and half was sleeping. He down wheeled to get off a wreck and pull the dredges up, and he flipped her over. They were still trying to pull the dredges up when the damn fool pivoted. She just flipped upside down. Asshole didn't even try to save the boat. The first mate said they were all out there in a Gibbons Buoy, and he could hear the ones who'd been sleeping beating on the hull, screaming for help. They were probably all disoriented down there and didn't know which way to go. Instead of looking for air pockets, they beat for somebody to save them. Pounded on the hull. The mate said he dove down and tried to get in, but an icebox had blocked the way. He couldn't move it. Current pulled her under."

"I think some of these mutinies you hear about, if the truth be known, the captain was inexperienced," Sam said.

"Some of them Mexicans on the Desco boats out of the Gulf don't need no excuse," said Billy. "They hung a captain a few years ago. Went into New Bedford with the captain swinging from the outrigger."

"Another thing you've got to watch out for is pirates," said Sam. "There's a lot of them between here and South America, especially down in the Caribbean. And you've got to be careful, else they'll take your boat and throw your ass overboard for the sharks to eat."

"I keep my pistol handy whenever we get close to another vessel," Billy said. "I ain't taking any chances."

"Cook looks like his drawers are too tight," Sam said.

"You all right, Virgil?" Billy asked.

"I'm OK. Haven't gotten used to the motion yet."

It was true. Virgil had only been feeling a little seasick. He was riveted by their sea stories of danger.

"Virgil's going to do all right," Jack said.

Later, Virgil took a mug of coffee up to Jack. The wheelhouse was filled with rust-colored light. The sun was a red-gold disc on the horizon.

"I've spent my whole life in a box," Virgil said, looking out the window at the lavender and magenta sky.

"Don't be so hard on yourself."

"It's true. I've never done anything exciting. I've always lived through books, with other people setting the rules."

"Every dog has his day."

Virgil noticed Jack's left forearm was red and swollen,

"What's wrong with your arm?"

"Wasp stung me."

"I didn't know there were wasps on ships."

"Must have had a stowaway."

"That's a nasty lump."

"Didn't used to be allergic. Bobbie gave me some pills to carry, but I left them at the house."

"What made you decide to settle down with her?"

Jack was silent so long, Virgil thought he wasn't going to answer. Then he said, "When I was about ten years old, Jubal and me were coming back to Hatteras, and we saw two snow geese by the side of the road. Jubal stopped the truck and when I got out, one of the snow geese flew off. The other one couldn't get away; its wing was hurt. Someone shot it. I picked it up and sat with it in the back of the truck all the way home. Its mate followed us, flying overhead. I wanted to fix the hurt goose back up so it could fly. Jubal told me it wouldn't work, but I was stubborn. I got the vet to patch it up, and I made a pen for it outside the house. The other goose kept hanging around. It would be outside the house in the morning when I'd wake up. I've always admired that snow goose. Figured it knew something I didn't."

"What happened to the injured one?"

The wheelhouse was darker now, Jack's face outlined against the flaming sea.

"It died," he said.

At dusk, Jack began trolling in a channel. Virgil went outside to watch.

The outriggers were down. He looked at the steel cables running from the winch to drums on either side, on up through the outriggers, back down through hooks on the aft deck near the stern, and then out to the metal doors that kept the net spread open.

Sam and Billy were standing ready by the winch. Leon was at the stern. Virgil didn't see Dave.

Jack came down from the wheelhouse and said something to Sam, who immediately let out more of the steel cable.

Virgil asked Sam what he was doing.

"Letting out the cable ten more fathoms," he said, easing up on the foot pedal that operated the winch. "Them doors ain't shining enough."

"Shining?"

"Doors get a shine on them from rubbing against the bottom."

A while later, Virgil noticed the trawler had slowed down considerably. He asked Sam why.

"Nets filling up," he said.

"With shrimp?"

"That's what we're hoping." Sam grinned. "If it ain't shrimp, let's hope it's a school of horny mermaids."

The winch creaked and squealed as it pulled the nets up. Sam hooked a whip line around the winch and pulled the tail bag up out of the water with the block and tackle hooked to the mast boom. As the net heaved up out of the water, it looked like it was full of glowing reflectors.

Leon swung the boom around, bringing the net over the side of the boat to the long wooden table at the stern where Dave and Billy were waiting. Leon joined them. When the bag spilled its mass of shrimp onto the table, the crew set to work, culling. The shrimp were jumping like popcorn in hot oil. Mixed in with the shrimp were crabs, jellyfish, eels, a stingray, fish, sea grass, and rocks. Wearing rubber gloves, the crew sorted the shrimp out into different baskets, according to their size. Eels, flounder, and crabs went into a bin. They raked out the jellyfish, grass, and fish they didn't want onto the deck, then kicked or threw them through the scupper plates in the gunwale, back into the sea.

Leon kicked a stingray out of the way and the spine impaled him through his boot. He began hopping up and down and cursing.

"Hold still, Leon," Billy said, "so I can get it out."

Billy cut off the spine with a knife, and then pulled out the imbedded segment with pliers. Leon went back to work without even taking off his boot to look at the damage.

Quick as the net was empty, Sam let it out again, and the towing started all over again.

Feeling nauseous, Virgil went down to his bunk to rest.

The crew worked all night harvesting the shrimp. In between tows they came down to the forepeak to rest, still wearing their boots and oilskins. Their naps were brutally short. Several times, Virgil was jarred awake by the sound of Jack's voice, *"Haul back, boys, haul back!"*

He slept fitfully. When his watch alarm woke him at four-thirty, the others were lying in their bunks in their oilskins and boots. The forepeak reeked of shrimp. He got dressed and went up to the galley to fix breakfast—pancakes, sausage, and scrambled eggs.

The crew was taciturn and red-eyed at breakfast. They hadn't even finished eating yet when Jack's call came down from the wheelhouse. "Haul back, boys!"

"When will you all get to take a break?" Virgil asked

"When we finish catching all the damn shrimp," Sam said, pushing back his chair.

But that was the last haul. Around nine, they brought the nets up, cleaned off the deck, and the crew went down to the forepeak to sleep.

Virgil took Jack a cup of coffee. The swelling in his arm had gotten worse. The wheelhouse smelled of nervous sweat.

"Don't you ever sleep?"

"I'll take a nap in a while."

Leon's foot was infected from the stingray's spine. He had been limping all afternoon. When he took his shoe off after supper, the foot was swollen and discolored.

Jack told Virgil to fix a pan of hot salt water. Then he went up to his cabin for his first aid kit.

When he came back, Jack knelt at Leon's feet, lancing the wound with a sterile needle. Jack pressed gently on the swollen area, pushing pus and blood out. Leon's face reddened, but he didn't make a sound.

"Now let it soak awhile," Jack said, wiping off the foot with a sponge.

"Hell of a thing to see just after supper," Billy said.

"Billy, you just got a weak stomach," said Jack. He was preparing a syringe to give Leon a shot.

Leon sat there, his pants leg rolled up, his foot in the water, cursing the manta ray.

"Goddamned things are bad luck."

All during the night, Virgil was awakened by Jack's voice booming down through the hold, *"Haul back, boys, haul back!"*

The next afternoon, the horizon was the color of an eggplant. The sea was dark and slimy looking, as if it were mixed with motor oil.

Virgil took Jack up his coffee. He was talking to someone on the radio.

"She's pretty rough right now," the voice said, amid much static. "We hit her around nine o'clock. We've got sixteen-foot seas, and they're getting worse. You ought to be feeling it by ten or so. Storm is moving your way."

After Jack got off the radio, Virgil asked whom he had been talking to.

"Trawler boat captain west of here. We're in for some rough weather."

The muddy light dimmed by the hour. By six o'clock it was nearly dark as night.

The storm struck about ten.

Virgil lay in the bunk as rain pounded the deck and hull and the ship creaked and shuddered on the swells. Lightning flashed at the portholes, creating eerie, strobe-like pulses of light in the forepeak. He slept for a while but woke up with a strange sensation in the pit of his stomach, like he was coming down too fast in an elevator. The trawler was rising and falling. It seemed to rise forty or fifty feet before it crashed down.

"She's a bad one," he heard Billy say.

"How do you sleep in this?"

Billy threw him a rope. "Tie yourself to the bunk."

Using the rope, Virgil secured himself to the bunk, counting the seconds between waves. Eight seconds between top and bottom. He felt helpless, out of control. He was afraid the ship would break into pieces, hurling them into the cold, wild sea. He thought of the inflatable life raft attached to the roof of the housing behind the smokestack. What good would it be in this violent sea if the ship went down?

The forepeak was full of the sour stench of vomit. Dave Swain was leaning over the side of his bunk, heaving onto the floor.

Someone else was throwing up, too.

Virgil untied the rope and sat up. He barely had time to hold his head over the side before the churning contents of his stomach spewed onto the floor.

"Heave it out, boys," Billy said. "More room outside than there is in."

The storm ended by dawn. They went up on deck to inspect the damage. The galley was a mess. Pots, pans, and dishes everywhere, some of them broken, and food strewn over the floor. The refrigerator had come loose from its moorings, and the door hung open.

After Virgil cleaned up the galley, he went up to see Jack in the wheelhouse.

Jack's eyes were bloodshot. The dog lay, panting, in the corner.

"It was rough down there," Virgil said.

"I know. I was going head into the seas. I was afraid she was going to smash the windows in the wheelhouse."

"Didn't you throw up?"

"Knew it was coming, so I ate light."

"I didn't eat that much, either, but what I did have is down there on the floor." Virgil bent down and scratched Amos's head. The dog wagged his stump of a tail, licked his hand. "What do you do up here in a storm?"

"Hold onto the wheel and ride it out. The wind throws

that water up and you can't see anything. You've got so much disturbance down in the troughs, you can't use radar. You get ghost ships, all kinds of false images on the screen."

"Sounds scary. Can you eat?"

"Yeah."

"I'll fix breakfast as soon as I take a shower. Then we've got to clean the forepeak."

Virgil made oatmeal, toast and scrambled eggs, but the crew wasn't very hungry.

"I remember the night the *Amazing Grace* went down," Billy said. "We was on the radio talking to her captain, and we lost contact with her. Man, those seas was like mountains. Busted out all the windows in the wheelhouse. I didn't think we was going to make it. The next morning we heard the *Amazing Grace* was gone. I think Jack was the last person to talk to the captain."

No one said anything.

Virgil was getting sick of the smell of diesel fuel. He could smell it everywhere—on deck, in the galley, down in the fish hole. He could even smell it when he was taking a crap.

The enforced intimacy was grating on his nerves, too. He had begun noticing every fart and cough in the forepeak.

He envied Jack the privacy of his cabin behind the wheelhouse.

Jack began towing again just before dark. About an hour later, the crew pulled in the first haul of shrimp.

Around ten, when Virgil took Jack coffee, he was talking to someone on the radio.

"We need help," a voice said.

"What's the problem?"

"Generator's down. We got no lights, no radar. Nothing."

"Want me to call the Coast Guard for you?"

"We just need some fuel filters for the generator. Got any spare ones?"

"I think so."

"You got a man who can work on her? My engineer's hands are all swelled up from fish poison."

"We'll take care of it. Be there in about ten minutes."

"Roger," the voice said.

Jack put the microphone back on the hook. Virgil asked him what the trouble was.

"Trawler's down," he said, pointing to a dot on the radar screen. "They need some help."

Virgil looked out the window, but everything was dark.

"Can you fix the generator?"

"Sure. Sam can, too. We should have them back up in less than an hour." Jack turned the wheel to starboard. "Holler down and tell the others, will you?"

Virgil went down the stairs and called down through the hatch to tell the others that Jack was going to help some fishermen on a nearby trawler with generator trouble. Then he went into the galley to make a fresh pot of coffee.

Billy came in and sat down at the table.

"What's the trawler's name?"

"He didn't say."

"Say she's got something wrong with the generator?"

"Yes. And a sick engineer."

"It's a lonesome feeling to be dead in the water like that."

Virgil thought the men on the other boat might want coffee, too. But the can he kept the coffee in was almost empty. He had four more cans in the fish hole. He went outside and headed toward the fish hole to get the coffee. Sam and Dave were standing by the starboard gunwale, waiting to board the trawler. Virgil could barely make it out in the darkness. Billy came out and joined them. He was wearing his pistol in a holster on his belt.

"Who's going to work on the generator?" Virgil asked.

"I am," Sam said.

Virgil lifted the hatch cover and went down the ladder to look for the coffee. He couldn't help from marveling at Sam and Jack's diverse skills. They could not only captain a trawler boat, they could also man winches, work trippers, cull fish, and fix generators. Maybe on his next trip out he could learn to operate a winch or work the tripper. In the fish bin, digging around in the ice, looking for the coffee, he spun a little fantasy, imagining a new Virgil Gibson—hard-muscled, tanned, capable, a professor turned fisherman. He would settle down with a Hatteras or Wanchese woman and live in a saltbox house by the sea, fathering towheaded children with cheeks plump from eating clam chowder and fish stew.

He was on his way up the ladder, the can of coffee under his arm, when he remembered the frozen strawberries in another bin. His strawberry shortcake had been a hit with the crew at supper. He decided to make some more in case any of the other shrimpers came aboard the trawler. He was full of good will toward these men who needed their help. Although he had only been shrimping a few days, he already felt a bond with them. They were all united in their human vulnerability out here on the cruel and beautiful sea.

He found the strawberries and went back up the ladder. Halfway up, he heard the staccato burst of automatic weapons fire. It was immediately followed by a muffled explosion. He lifted up the hatch cover and peeped out. On the deck he saw a man's leg. He opened the hatch a few inches more to see who it was.

It was Billy. Lying on his back. His eyes open, his lips moving like he was trying to speak.

"Billy!"

Virgil couldn't quite make out what he was saying, but it sounded like he was telling him to hide.

He closed the hatch and climbed down the ladder, his shock and incredulity giving away to terror. He picked up the things he had dropped and put them into the bin. And he stood in the aisle, listening to the crack and roar of the weapons. It was like another storm breaking over the ship.

The only possibility Virgil could think of was pirates. But what would pirates be doing off the coast of Hatteras? And what would they want with Jack's trawler? Did they think he had drugs aboard?

He wanted to help the others, but what could he do without a weapon? And, anyway, hadn't Billy told him to hide?

He climbed up into one of the bins and began digging out a hole in the ice. He dug down to the shrimp, and then lay down in it, covering himself up with shrimp. The smell was overpowering. He could feel their antenna, their legs on his face and head and hands.

The gunfire continued.

Maybe they're filming a movie, he thought, and no one told me. They're all up there laughing now at me, shivering in the fish hole.

But recalling the shock and pain in Billy's eyes, he knew that the horrific violence on the deck above was as real as the ice against his skin. He wanted to burrow deeper in the shrimp, but he was already having trouble breathing.

He didn't know how long the gunfire lasted. The relativity of time becomes painfully acute when you are buried in ice, hiding from killers who have appeared out of the darkness of the sea.

After the shooting stopped, there was a period of silence. Then he heard, ever so faintly, the sound of footsteps on the deck. Whoever is up there will come down here sooner or later, he thought. He prayed it would be Jack Delaney.

He heard someone coming down the ladder. Then, footsteps in the aisle.

"I tell you, I saw five of them out on deck yesterday," a voice said.

"We got five."

"But that doesn't account for the one in the wheelhouse. There were five out on deck and one in the wheelhouse. That makes six."

"Boat might have been on automatic pilot."

"I think there's someone else here."

"Where the hell is he, then? We've looked everywhere."

"Everywhere but in here."

Virgil heard someone digging around in the ice with a shovel.

"Didn't you have someone watching when they boarded?"

"He had car trouble and didn't get there until after they left."

More digging.

"How many IDs did you find?"

"Five, including the captain's."

"Five IDs add up to five men. How many beds were made up in the crew's quarters?"

"They only had two made up. But there were three more sets of sheets out. I think it's possible there were five crew members, not four."

"Other set of sheets could have been for the captain."

There was the sound of more digging, but Virgil couldn't tell where it was coming from. He could hear shrimp and ice striking the floor.

Then he realized someone was digging in the bin he was in.

His heart was pounding so hard he imagined that the man above him could hear it through the ice and shrimp.

"I'll be damned if I'm going to dig through all this ice and shrimp," the man in the aisle said. "We'll be here all night. Even if there was another man here, he must've jumped overboard. I'm going up and get her ready to torch."

The other man kept on digging.

I'll be face up when he finds me, Virgil thought, so I'll get shot in the front.

But a few seconds later the man stopped digging and climbed out of the bin. Virgil could hear him walking back and forth in the aisle.

Then, finally, steps going up the ladder.

He could still hear them moving around on the deck.

He heard the other trawler's engine start.

He's hiding somewhere, waiting, he thought. It's a trick to get me to come out of his hiding place, just like they tricked Jack and the others with the story about the shot generator.

On the other hand, he knew he couldn't stay where he was, trapped in a burning ship.

When he couldn't stand it anymore, he raised up out of the shrimp and ice, half-expecting someone to cut him down with a machine gun.

But the fish bin was empty.

He could smell the smoke. They had left the hatch cover off.

He climbed the ladder and looked out. Smoke was pouring out of the windows of the wheelhouse. Flames ate into the deck of the boat from the enclosed section to the stern. Billy lay face down under the culling table. Dave lay nearby, curled up in a pool of blood.

Someone was lying over the winch.

Virgil crawled toward the winch, through an aisle in the middle of the flames, burning his palms on shell casings, cutting his hands on glass from the lights on the booms. There were bullet holes everywhere—in the galley, the gunwales; even the box containing the inflatable life raft.

The person hanging over the winch was Sam.

Virgil found Jack by the outer wall of the galley. His left hand was missing, and there was a line of holes stitched across his chest. The floor was covered with blood.

Virgil fell to his knees when he saw his friend. He sat down beside Jack and put his hands over his face, sobbing without tears. He sat there until he became aware of the heat from the fire against his skin, and he thought, *this is what hell is like.*

He stood up, still in a daze, and opened the door to the housed section of the main deck. The hall was full of smoke. The light in the galley was still on, and he could see Leon on his back on the floor of the hallway. Virgil bent over him, feeling for a pulse, and then went into the galley.

Jack's dog was under the table, a clump of blue entrails protruding from a hole in his side. He had been shot in the head.

Coughing now from the smoke, he went back out to the main deck. He was getting ready to jump over the side into the sea when he remembered the hatch covers; about three feet by five feet, they were on a plywood frame and filled with foam rubber. He went back through the flames to the fish hole. One of the hatch covers had caught fire, but the other one was intact.

Picking it up by the rope handles, he went to the portside of the ship and jumped through the flames into the icy sea. The hatch cover slipped out of his fingers when he went under.

He surfaced in a panic, looking around for the hatch cover. He saw it in the light of the flames, about ten feet away. He swam to it and held onto it while he unlaced his shoes and kicked them off.

Using the hatch cover as a float, he kicked his feet, propelling himself away from Jack's trawler. He put his head down and kicked with all his strength, wanting only to get beyond the light, into the shelter of darkness.

The *Dixie Arrow* exploded in a huge rolling ball of fire.

Virgil kept looking back at the flaming ship until it faded to an orange glow. He looked away for a few moments, and when he looked back again, it was gone. There was just the black, fathomless night and sea.

He looked up at the sky, thinking he could get his bearings by the stars, but the sky was like a huge vat of tar. Which way was land?

He saw a light flashing in the distance. Either the Bodie Light or the Hatteras Light—he wasn't sure which. Holding on to the hatch cover, he kicked his feet, heading in the direction of the light.

He saw the blinking lights of a boat and then a searchlight.

Sometime later, a helicopter flew over the sea. As it neared him, he held his breath and ducked under the hatch cover, staying down until his lungs hurt before he came up for air.

Had Jack been able to call for help on the radio? Or were the killers looking for him?

The clouds drifted away, and he could see the stars. He looked for the North Star between Cassiopeia and the Big Dipper, low on the horizon. He kept seeing Billy lying on deck, his eyes glazed with shock; Jack sitting against the wheelhouse, his half-open eyes mirroring the rising flames; Dave lying in a pool of blood; Sam hanging across the winch.

It must have been smugglers, he thought. Someone Jack owed money. But why did they have to kill everyone else, too? And why did they cut off Jack's hand?

He recalled the muffled voices he had heard in the fish hole. One of the men had spoken with a Hispanic accent. The other one's voice had sounded vaguely familiar. Was it possible that he had heard it somewhere before?

Virgil was distracted from this thought by the chilling sight of a dorsal fin, a dozen feet ahead of him. He tried to pull himself up on the hatch cover, but his feet dangled over the side.

He felt a thump against the side of the hatch cover. He

lashed out with his foot, kicking the shark's body as it slid by. There were more, too. He could see the fins. He remembered the way the crew had harvested the shrimp, putting them on ice. Now he was just like the shrimp, prey for these sharks.

He considered how he must appear to them. Like a sea turtle, perhaps. But he smelled like shrimp and blood, he thought. *That gentleman can smell a drop of blood from half a mile away*, he remembered Jack saying that day on the charter boat, when they had seen the blue image of the shark on the screen.

His shirt was stained with Jack's blood. He took it off and hurled it away from the hatch. It floated on the surface. A shark hit it and it disappeared.

He curled up on the hatch cover in a tight ball, alarmed by how low it rode in the sea with his weight on it. Couldn't a big shark raise its head out of the water and seize him in its jaws?

The sharks' presence prevented him from kicking with his feet. He looked at his watch. It was ten past midnight. More than five hours until dawn.

But you won't live to see dawn, he thought.

He remembered how his father used to take him walking on the beach after a storm. They would look for gold doubloons, pieces of blue sea glass, or whelks' egg cases tangled in brown bunches of seaweed. Inside the cases was a necklace strung with milky white discs, each one containing miniature whelk shells. Or sometimes he would find a skate's egg case or "mermaid's purse," a small black pouch with spindly curved horns at each of the four corners. He would give each item to his father, who would put it carefully into a bag he carried over his shoulder. They would store their treasures in the garage behind the house. He remembered waiting with his father behind the dunes for the sea turtles to come ashore in the starlight and lay their eggs in Rodanthe. The first time they had seen a loggerhead crawling out of the water like a prehistoric beast, his father had said, "There's the hand of God at work right there."

Virgil remembered the time he and Jack went to Old Christmas, the winter celebration at Rodanthe, when the islanders get together to drink, eat, and dance—and settle any grudges built up during the year. After midnight, some men led in "Old Buck," the effigy of a mythical wild bull that lived in Buxton Woods, according to local legend. Not long after Old Buck was brought in, the entire room seemed to erupt into a fight, which soon spilled outside. Jack and Virgil had just gone outside to watch. But someone hit Jack, and when another man began fighting him, too, Virgil jumped into the melee, swinging with both fists.

He arrived home at dawn with a black eye, his face cut and bruised, and whiskey on his breath. His mother had grounded him for two weeks. She told his father, "He's becoming a savage in this godforsaken place." His father had replied, "Marge, he's just becoming a man."

"If being a man means fighting and drinking then I'd just as soon he remain a boy," Marge Gibson had replied indignantly.

They were still out there, circling. Why don't they go away?

He remembered sitting in church, listening to sermons. And God said, *Let me make man in my own image, after my likeness: and let him have dominion over the fish of the sea...* but not having read the passage, how could the sharks know? And the congregation standing to sing "The Old Rugged Cross," his father's tenor in his ear, his mother's voice high and shrill, and then his mother saying, "Remember your father always wanted a son to carry on his family name."

God help me, he thought, and forgive the rage that passes all understanding.

When the alarm on his wristwatch went off right under his ear, reminding him to get up and fix breakfast for the crew, he flinched so much he nearly fell off the hatch cover. He could imagine his arm with the watch on it being torn off and swallowed by one of the sharks, the alarm still going off in its belly.

He could see their fins in the moonlight.

The sky turned gray, then blue. The sun was a smear of red light on the horizon. He could no longer see the flashing light, but he could see something else: land. He had floated past the barrier reefs on the tide, and the sharks were gone. His body ached from his cramped position on the hatch cover. He put his legs down into the sea and floated awhile, letting the blood circulate to his knotted muscles. Then he began kicking, pushing the hatch cover ahead of him.

He came ashore in the surf, frightening off a seagull that had been pecking at a fish. He lay in the sand, exhausted. When he opened his eyes, the first thing he saw was the fish, a sea bass.

Its astonished eye stared at the pale blue sky. Its tail flopped once against the sand.

About a mile north of where he had come ashore, he broke into an unoccupied cottage by knocking out the glass in the back door. The cottage was the first in a row of cottages on the beach, and as he collapsed on the bed in the master bedroom, he could hear children shouting and laughing nearby. Although he found some cans of food in the cabinets, the refrigerator contained only a jar of mayonnaise, which suggested the owners hadn't been to the cottage in a while. That was no guarantee that they wouldn't decide to visit while he was there, however. He couldn't remember whether it was Friday or Saturday— an important detail, since the owners would be more likely to come to their cottage on a weekend. He didn't want to be caught in their home in his underwear and jailed as a thief.

But Virgil had a more vital reason for not wanting to be

caught: He didn't want anyone to know he had been aboard the *Dixie Arrow*. Whoever had killed the others would kill him too if they found out he had witnessed their grisly work. He decided to wait there until dark and then walk home along the beach. He was too numb and exhausted to think beyond that.

He had come ashore north of Rodanthe near where the whale had beached. The flashing light he had seen at sea had come from Bodie Island Lighthouse to the north. It was about fifteen miles to the Oregon Inlet Bridge and ten more to Nags Head. It should take him about twelve hours to get home, including rest stops. He wanted to get there as soon as possible after daylight to minimize the chance of being seen.

Searching the cottage, he found a canteen, a flashlight, a watch, a weather alert channel, a transistor radio, a knife, a can of insect repellent, a T-shirt, a section of rope, a parka, a tote bag, a pair of tennis shoes two sizes too small, and pants three sizes too large. He cut holes in the tennis shoes and made them into sandals. He held the pants up with a section of rope.

He listened to the hourly news broadcasts on the radio, but there was no mention of Jack's trawler. He assumed Jack had been unable to radio for help.

He tried to sleep in one of the beds, but he kept having flashbacks of the carnage aboard the *Dixie Arrow*. The killers must have knocked out the radio in the wheelhouse with a bomb. That would explain the explosion he had heard and the gaping wound in Amos's side. Whoever planned the attack had everything carefully planned, even down to the bogus story about the shot generator and the ailing engineer. Not only had they assigned a man to watch Jack's boat when the crew boarded, the killers had also been watching them at sea. He had seen dozens of boats while at sea. Which one had it been?

They must have planned to kill Sam and Billy quietly, and then sneak aboard the *Dixie Arrow* to kill the others, but evidently something had gone wrong, and they'd had to shoot the three crew members in view. Alerted to their murderous presence, Jack and Leon had been able to fight back.

Virgil kept seeing Jack sitting against the galley wall, his mouth open, his eyes staring up at the burning mast, the missing hand.

The hours dragged by.

He fell asleep and dreamed someone was pursuing him through a bomb-ravaged city. A car door slamming woke him up. He jumped up and ran to the window, ready to escape.

But it was a car at the next cottage down.

He left the cottage at dark, carrying the canteen and a canvas shoulder bag full of supplies. He walked south to where he had come ashore, looking for the hatch cover from the *Dixie Arrow*. He found it and buried it behind the dunes. Then he began his trek north, passing lighted cottages and a few evening strollers. He was glad they couldn't see him in the dark. He looked like a derelict in the mutilated tennis shoes and oversized pants with the rope belt.

He passed the old Chicamacomico Life Saving Station. Now being restored, it was one of the twelve original stations on the Outer Banks. Surfmen at the stations had rescued hundreds of mariners from the sea, but hundreds more had died, many of them on Diamond Shoals, the sandbars extending out from Cape Hatteras. The ships, brigantines, sloops, tankers, and schooners had gone down in wars and storms. There were ghosts out there, and now the crew of the *Dixie Arrow* was among them. The tide was out, and the beach was wide and glowing, the sea rocking and shimmering beneath the Hatteras moon. He felt a mystical connection to the sea for having delivered him from death. Yet in his deliverance he felt as if he had been reborn into a strange new world, booming with terror and mystery.

His passage was disturbing the ghost crabs. They darted this way and that on their lightning legs. Caught by the beam from flashlight, they froze, staring at the light with their elevated eyes on shiny black stalks.

Virgil allowed himself a ten-minute rest period every ninety minutes. At one a.m., he sat on the dunes and ate canned beans and crackers, washing them down with water from the canteen. Later, fog and mist rolled in from the sea, and he could no longer see the stars. He began to worry that he had somehow gotten turned around and was walking south instead of north. Once he thought he heard Jack's voice floating down over the dunes.

He reached Oregon Inlet a little after three a.m. and walked across the bridge, the hood of the parka concealing his face from the few cars that were out. Past the bridge he crossed back over to the beach.

At four-thirty, the alarm on his wristwatch went off again. He took it off and flung it into the surf. At dawn, the sea was the color of lead.

He arrived home at mid-morning, his body aching, the soles of his feet blistered and bleeding from his twenty-five mile walk over sand. He let himself into the cottage with the spare key hidden in the ashtray of his Cherokee. He drank a glass of milk, ate a cheese sandwich, and then limped back to his bedroom, where he fell into a deep, exhausted sleep.

He woke up suddenly, his heart pounding, thinking he heard someone in the cottage.

But it was only the wind, rattling the shutters.

Limping into the kitchen, he got a glass of water and drank it down in a few swallows. The kitchen was drenched with red-orange light streaming over the dunes. His feet were swollen and raw, his muscles and joints aching. But he was calm enough now to begin to think. His urge to go to the police was held in check by his fear of reprisal from the killers. Whoever had killed Jack and his crew had the means to execute an elaborate scheme, including a trawler and men with automatic weapons to carry out the murders. What would stop them from murdering him, too? It was clear that his survival depended on concealing his presence aboard the *Dixie Arrow*. When he and Dave had arrived at Oden's Dock, he had seen other fishermen in the harbor, but he had gotten on the trawler quickly, and he hoped that no one would remember having seen him. It was possible Jack had told someone he was going along as the ship's cook. If anyone asked, he would say he had gotten sick and decided not to go.

So far luck seemed to be with him. *I pray no one saw me getting on the trawler.*

After he took a warm bath, he stepped to the sink to shave. His face was chafed and raw from the wind and sand and covered with a black stubble of beard. Shaving, he nicked himself with the razor. The blood brought back images of the carnage aboard the *Dixie Arrow*. His hands trembled so violently he had to stop shaving until he could get himself under control.

When the phone rang it sounded loud as a siren.

He answered on the fourth ring. The caller hung up, and he immediately panicked.

They're watching my house, he thought. They know I'm back, and now they're going to kill me.

He lay down in his bed, trembling with fear; he hoped it had been a wrong number.

To get to sleep that night, he drank all the alcohol he could find in the cottage: two beers, some brandy, and the sherry he used for cooking.

Early the next morning, he drove to a supermarket for groceries. As he pushed the cart through the aisles, he was acutely conscious of the other people around him: a blonde woman with a child in her grocery cart, a fat man poking his finger into the side of a chicken, two teenage girls with sunburned faces. Although they looked normal enough, the shoppers had a surreal quality, like figures made of wax. He began to worry about his mental state. The murders he had witnessed aboard the *Dixie Arrow* seemed like a massive attack against the natural order of things, and now it was as if the whole physical world had been knocked askew. Virgil felt overwhelmed by a need to set things right.

On the counter in the check-out line were copies of *The Coastland Times*. A headline on the front page caught his eye:

Coast Guard Investigates Mystery Fire Near Rodanthe

He read the story in his Cherokee.

A Coast Guard helicopter and boat searched the coast off of Rodanthe early Friday morning after several residents reported seeing what appeared to be a fire at sea.

The first report came in at 11:30 a.m., according to Thomas Gray, commander of the Oregon Inlet Station.

"We sent a boat to investigate," Gray said, "and a helicopter went out from the Elizabeth City Station."

Gray said there were no radio calls for help and there were no ships in the immediate area.

"As far as we're concerned, the fire is a mystery," he added.

The killers had done their grisly job well.

The next time the phone rang, Virgil was immensely relieved to hear his mother's voice on the line. She wanted to hear about his trip to sea. He explained the story he had been rehearsing, that he had gotten sick and had to cancel at the last minute.

"Are you cooking your fish all the way done?"

"I guess so."

"That could be your problem. I just read an article about how dangerous it is to eat certain kinds of seafood without cooking it all the way. A man in Georgia nearly died from eating some poorly cooked tuna. You need to cook it until it's all the way done, with no pink showing."

"OK. No problem."

"Now, I hope you'll put this idea to rest of going out on a fishing trawler, Virgil Gibson. Especially not with Jack Delaney."

"Not anytime soon, Mama."

He was drifting off to sleep when he remembered the leather-bound journal Jack had had with him in the minesweeper. He sat straight up in bed, his heart pounding. *If you can find that journal, maybe you'll know who killed him.* He wanted to get into Jack's house and look for his journal, but the door would be locked. Maybe I can get in through a window, he thought.

He got up at first light and drove to Avon.

When he turned onto the street Jack lived on, he was alarmed to see a black Lincoln Continental parked in front of a cottage two houses down, the engine running. There was a man inside.

He drove on, turning the corner. What was he doing? Was he watching Jack's cottage or just waiting for someone to come out?

He drove around the block and stopped at the stop sign, looking down Jack's street to the right. The car was still there, so he turned left and drove back to Highway 12, heading north to Nags Head. Did the killers know about the journal? Were they watching Jack's house, waiting for someone to come for it?

He stopped to buy a paper, and saw this headline on the front page:

Police Suspect Robbery In Killing Of Avon Man

Someone had shot Leon's cousin, Mike Jennette. The story, with an accompanying photo of Mike, told how Mike's wife had gone to the restaurant looking for him after he didn't come home. She found him near an empty cash register, which led the police to assume Mike had been killed during a robbery. But Mike was a friend of Jack's. Had he been a victim of the killers, too?

Virgil had a sudden sense of panic: He was so desperate to talk to someone, he considered driving to the nearest Catholic church to talk to a priest in a confessional booth. Couldn't he hide behind a screen to conceal his face and identity?

Late that evening, he got a call from Bobbie Russell.

"Virgil, did you go out with Jack?"

"No. I got sick and couldn't go. Isn't he back yet?"

"Not yet, but I thought you were with him."

"I had a bad stomach virus, so I called him the night before and told him I couldn't make it this trip."

"I heard someone say they saw you in Food Lion. I couldn't believe you all were back without Jack calling me."

"I don't know what to say, Bobbie. Weren't they just going a few miles offshore?"

"I think so. Did you know there was a strange fire offshore Thursday night?"

"I read something about that." Virgil thought his voice sounded high and false. Could she tell he was lying?

"And Virgil ... someone shot Mike Jennette."

"I read about that, too. The police think it happened during a robbery."

"Did you know him and Jack were friends?"

"Jack has a lot of friends."

"Things like that don't happen around here."

"That can happen anywhere these days, Bobbie. Try not to worry."

"I can't help it. So many things can go wrong out there."

He tried to say something positive, but, once again, he found he was unable to think of the right words.

"Virgil, you still there?"

"Yes," he said. "I'm still here. Listen, do you have a key to Jack's house?"

"Yes."

"Could I borrow it? I loaned him a couple of books that belonged to my dad, and I want to get them back. My mom has been bugging me about them."

"Sure."

"Are you working tomorrow?"

"Yes."

"I'll stop in for a beer and pick it up."

"OK, I'll be looking for you," Bobbie said.

Virgil returned to Jack's house the next day; the black car was gone. He walked up to the door, trying to appear casual and confident. If someone asked him what he was doing there, he planned to say he had just stopped by to get a book he had loaned Jack. Using the key Bobbie had loaned him, he unlocked the door and went through the living room, into the den. On the table there was a checkbook and a ledger containing a record of Jack's expenses on the boat—how much he still owed on her, the various costs of fixing her up, expenses for groceries, dry ice, gas and other supplies. Everything was written in Jack's uncharacteristically neat handwriting.

He walked down the hall into Jack's bedroom. The bed was unmade, and there were clothes strewn around. On the floor beside the bed there was an empty beer can, dirty socks, and an open copy of *National Fisherman*. He picked it up to see what Jack had been reading, an article about the federal management plan for Atlantic billfish.

On the pillow, there was a long brown hair, the same shade as Bobbie's.

There were pictures of Mae and Jubal in frames on the stand beside the bed and a photo of Jack and his sister when they were children. On the wall over his bed hung an oil painting of snow geese in flight. In a shelf by his bed were some books, a couple of classics —*The Old Man and the Sea* and *The Call of the Wild*—and titles by Mickey Spillane and Elmore Leonard, along with more magazines, a dictionary, a Bible, and Jack's high school yearbook.

He sat on the bed and opened the yearbook, looking at the signatures and notations written in the front: *Good luck, Jack,* Billy had written. *You'll make the pros, yet.*

Dear Jack, you'll always be number one in my heart. Love, Sandi.

Looking at the photos of Jack, Leon, Sam, and Billy in the senior annual, his eyes filled with tears. He put the book back on the shelf.

In a footlocker beneath the window, he found several journals, all bound in leather. He picked up one, opened it, and began reading:

Western Dinh Tuong/Saigon, 1983

Deke Johnson and me were flat on our bellies in a rice paddy in the Delta, eighty yards from a canal we were staking out. Deke said he smelled something funny. "Like what?" I asked. But I could smell it, too.

"It's like the Goddamned circus," Deke said.

I wiped sweat from my face and sniffed the night air, which smelled of rotting vegetation. But there was another smell there, too.

"Elephants!" Deke said. "Fucking pachyderms."

I called my platoon commander, Lt. Holt, on the radio and told him we smelled elephants.

"Bingo!" he said. "Keep your heads down."

We were on the mission because someone in headquarters had learned the VC were moving supplies, including their lethal heat-seeking missiles, through this territory, but we hadn't found any signs of a road or tire tracks. All we found were some elephant tracks and some tread marks left by Ho Chi Minh sandals. That was when we got the idea the VC were moving the missiles by elephants. This was the second night we spent waiting by the canal, about ten miles into enemy-controlled territory. Chopper dropped us off after dusk.

"I can close my eyes and picture the lady on the trapeze," Deke said.

I told him to keep his damn eyes open.

We heard them before we saw them, lumbering along single file. The Cong walking alongside, wearing black pajamas and carrying AK-47s.

"Would you look at that? Deke whispered. "Where the hell did they get elephants? Man, this ain't Africa."

A few seconds later the lieutenant detonated the claymore mines we had set out by the canal. After the mines went off I could hear the elephants bellowing and grunting. Two of them plunged into the canal.

I didn't see any VC, so I aimed at one of the elephants thrashing by the canal. I could see it clearly through the night vision scope. Put three rounds into its head. It stopped moving and lay still.

I heard the shrill, whistling sound of a flare. Saw the arc rising up. Covered my eyes as the flare burst overhead.

Something's wrong, I thought. We should have taken them all out with the mines.

Deke's hollering that he's blind. "Can't see a Goddamned thing."

There was a lot of automatic fire coming from somewhere, but I kept my head down until the flare faded to a green glow in the sky. Then I pulled Deke up and we took off running low through the gelatinous mud, bullets whizzing by my ears. I heard Deke screaming behind me.

"Jack, I'm hit! I can't see!"

I went back for him, picked him up, slung him over my shoulders and staggered on through the mud toward the tree line, about thirty yards away.

Just before we reached cover, something knocked my legs out from under me. I went down on my face. Felt like I'd been hit with a couple of sledgehammers.

Lt. Holt and some other guys dragged us into the trees.

The rest of my platoon was dead or dying back in the field.

I learned later that the elephant patrol was at the head of a larger force of VC that was moving some mortars and machine guns into position along the canal to ambush the 6th Battalion to the north. The VC threw everything they had at us.

The lieutenant called in air support, and a little while later the Cobras rolled in—firing their 2.75 millimeter rockets, and their mini-guns, unloading their mike-mikes.

When the F-14s arrived, the earth shook from the bombs.

I was lying under a tree, next to Deke, who was moaning and laughing at the same time.

"Fucking elephants, who would have thought it? Did you see those beasts jumping in the water? I put a whole magazine into them. How the hell do you kill something that big?"

I told this asshole to shut the hell up. Low point in my whole life. Most of my platoon dead, my legs shattered, and I'd just saved the life of a man who didn't have enough sense to understand elephants can feel pain.

I was medivaced to an evac hospital and then flown to another hospital in Saigon, where the surgeons started trying to save my legs. VC with a 12.7 millimeter machine gun hit me with four two-hundred grain bullets. These bad boys ripped through the back of my legs, splintering bone, shredding muscle. End of my football career, right there.

I woke up after the surgery with my legs elevated and

fluids running through tubes into my veins. White wall to my right. To my left, a man whose face and head were wrapped in bandages. Both legs and an arm missing. Nothing but stumps left.

I tried to talk to the mummified figure but he was too far gone. Drifted off to sleep. Woke up to see a chaplain sitting by my bed, reading from a Bible: "The Lord is on my side; I will not fear. What can man do unto me?"

"Listen, can you read to the guy next to me?"

"He died a little while ago," the chaplain said, wiping tears from his eyes. "I've never seen anyone die before."

"You'll get used to it," I told him.

I drifted off to sleep. Dreamed I was squirrel hunting in Buxton Woods. A group of soldiers were in the woods, dragging some dead elephants behind them with ropes. They dragged the elephants onto the beach then set them on fire. Smoke so thick from the burning elephants it blocked out the sun, made the island dark as night.

As Virgil leafed through the journals, he saw they were from a much earlier time in Jack's life—dating back to high school. There wasn't a single entry within the past two years. The journal he had seen in the minesweeper wasn't among them.

Where could it be?

In a dresser, he found Jack's Purple Star and Bronze Star, his dog tags from Vietnam, and an undated photo of Mae as a young woman. She was holding a baby in her arms. He couldn't tell if it was Jack or Elena.

In the bottom drawer of the dresser he found a snub-nosed revolver. A Smith & Wesson. Unloaded. He held the weapon in his hand, feeling its weight. He pointed it at the wall and clicked the trigger a few times, watching how the cylinder turned to present a new shell to the firing pin on the hammer. The gun looked small and deadly. He found a box of shells at the back of the drawer. He opened the cylinder and slipped five shiny rounds into the chambers. Holding the loaded gun eased his mind a little. He walked down the hallway and looked out the front door. No black car. Slowly and carefully, he searched the entire house, looking in the cupboards, the sink, closets, desks, under mattresses, every place he could think of, but there were no more journals.

He went back down the hall, pulled down the attic stairs by the cord and climbed up to the hot, musty attic. He looked through several cardboard boxes and a battered duffel bag but found nothing of significance. On the east side of the house, he ran his hand along the beam and found the leather-bound journal resting there.

Virgil opened the journal and began reading. It was like hearing Jack speaking to him, outside of time. He had not read very far before he recalled that day on the flying bridge of the *Eva Marie*—when Jack had seemed puzzled about Ray Meyers's invitation to have dinner with him on his yacht. Jack began his story with that visit.

IX

When Jack got to Ocracoke, the sun was setting, and Raymond's yacht, the *Victory*, was anchored in the middle of the whiskey-colored harbor. Jack had left his boat at his mother's house in Buxton and driven to the ferry crossing in his Jeep. He wanted to keep a low profile around the Coast Guard Station at the mouth of the harbor.

He drove around the harbor and parked by the docks. Raymond's man was waiting for him at the end of one of the piers. He was slim, balding, wearing a white uniform. He asked Jack if he was "Mr. Delaney." Jack told him yes.

"I'm Gary Thompson, first mate on the *Victory*. Mr. Meyers is expecting you."

A Carolina skiff was tied up at the dock. Jack followed him down the ladder and sat in a fiberglass seat at the bow while he fired up the outboard motor. The *Victory* looked to be at least a hundred feet long.

Thompson steered the skiff around to starboard, near the stern. A man in a navy blazer stood on top of the boat deck. A boom with two chains hanging from it swung out over the stern. Thompson connected the chains to metal rings attached to the stern and bow. An electronic winch hummed as the skiff levitated up and set down in the cockpit.

The man in the blazer called down from the boat deck to welcome him aboard and introduce himself. He was Raymond's captain, Clay Douglas.

Jack followed Thompson up the steps to the aft deck and through sliding glass doors into the stateroom. Surrounded by windows, the salon was furnished with black chairs and sofas, the carpet fire-engine red. There was a bar and entertainment center at the forward end.

Raymond, C.C., and another man were on a sofa near the center of the room. They stood up when he entered.

"Jack, good to see you," Raymond said, shaking his hand. "You remember C.C."

C.C. had one of those gorilla handshakes—like he was trying to crush your fingers. Remembering what Dave Swain said about his ears, Jack noticed they were pointed.

Raymond introduced the other man, Ed Ryan. Sunburned, wearing a golf shirt, Bermudas. Looks like another goofy tourist, Jack thought. He wondered what he was doing there. He figured he would find out soon enough.

Jack declined Raymond's offer of a drink. He wanted to keep his mind clear.

"Jack, I was just telling Ed about Ocracoke, how it exists outside of time. This is his first visit here."

"It's like walking around in a postcard," Ryan said. "I understand it was once the home of Blackbeard."

"That's right," Raymond said. "He died not far from here, in Ocracoke Inlet."

"Blackbeard was hard to kill," C.C. said. "Had a couple of dozen wounds on his body when he finally went down."

"He'd have made a good Marine," Raymond said.

"Marine, hell," said Ryan. "He'd have made a good Green Beret." He winked at Jack. "Better be careful, these two are retired leathernecks. Looks like I'm outnumbered. You a leatherneck, too?"

"I was in the Army."

"What outfit?"

"Thirty-ninth Infantry."

"Put her there, pal. I was Eighty-second Airborne."

"Jack is just being modest," Raymond said. "He served with the Thirty-ninth's Fourth Battalion"

"The Hardcore Battalion? That was an elite guerilla unit." Ryan, a piss-poor actor, raised his eyebrows in an exaggerated look of surprise. "A snake eater, huh?"

"You here on vacation?" Jack asked.

"That's right."

"First trip to the Outer Banks?"

"Been down here duck hunting a time or two with C.C. You a hunter?"

"Not much."

"I like to hunt duck," C.C. said, "but the best hunting is goose."

"I don't kill geese," Jack said.

"I'll kill one in a heartbeat," C.C. said. "I've got a ten-gauge shotgun with a thirty-six inch barrel, full choke. It will reach out for a goose like the hand of God."

A plump, sunburned woman entered the stateroom through the door near the entertainment center. "Excuse me, gentleman. Thompson has advised me dinner is ready."

Ryan introduced Jack to the woman—his wife, Greta. They all went through the door she had come through, into the galley where a table had been set for dinner. Nicole Andrisson was helping Thompson set the table. She had on a white sundress. Her arms were lean and tanned.

"Hello again, Mr. Delaney," she said, smiling.

She seated him to the left of Raymond, who sat at the head of the table. Nicole sat to his right, across from Jack, the Ryans next to her, and C.C. to Ed Ryan's right. Thompson served dinner—grilled filet mignon, broiled shrimp, mashed potatoes, green beans, a tossed salad, and rolls.

Greta Ryan was talking about how refreshing it was to get out of D.C.

"It's so muggy there now and the drug problem is just horrendous. We live in Fairfax, but you can't escape it. I used to go to an antique shop just off Constitution Avenue, run by this nice little Chinaman. Last week, when I went there looking for a table for our den, there was a wreath on the door. I read in the paper he'd been shot during a robbery, by some drug addict no doubt. You could get some great pieces at his shop, and I don't even know if it will ever be open again. The crime situation in D.C. is a disgrace. Murder capital of the nation."

"Greta, we're on vacation," her husband said.

Mrs. Ryan looked at Jack. "And what do you do, Mr. Delooney?"

"I'm a fisherman."

"Mr. *Delaney* is the captain of a charter boat," Nicole said.

"Oh. How long have you been doing that?"

"About two weeks."

"What did you do before that?"

"Had my own trawler."

"What happened to it?"

"It sunk. Went straight down to the bottom of the sea where the little fishes hide from the big ones."

"Really!"

Nicole put her hand over her mouth, hiding a smile.

After dinner, Raymond showed Jack around the *Victory*. A flight of steps forward of the galley led up to the wheelhouse. He had satellite communications, a radio telephone, and a teleprinter telex. Jack followed him up a spiral staircase to the flying bridge, down to the galley, then down the starboard stairs to a hallway on the lower deck. The crew's quarters and

galley were forward of the hallway. Aft, there were two guest
staterooms, a master stateroom, and Raymond's office. The
engine room was aft of the office. It was a fine setup all right.
A seaworthy home for a millionaire, with backup generators
and pumps, gold-plated fixtures, and a hot tub. And that sweet
young thing Nicole to share the good life with. Jack couldn't
help but feel a twinge of jealousy of Ray Meyers.

Following the tour of his yacht, Raymond invited Jack into
his office for brandy. C.C. came, too. Jack and C.C. sat on the
couch against the wall. Raymond sat at his desk.

"I'll get right to the point, Jack. I've got a proposition for
you," he said. "It will involve some risk, and you'll be operating
completely outside the law. But you'll be very well paid.
Interested?"

"I'm listening."

"Later this summer, a large shipment of cocaine will be air-
dropped off the Carolina coast. The cocaine will be wrapped
in waterproof containers and attached to underwater beacons,
which can only be seen with special goggles. It will be at least
ten or twelve hundred kilos, with a wholesale value of eighteen-
to twenty-million. A boat will pick up the cocaine and transport
it to a remote inlet on the Pamlico, Gull Rock Bay. Know where
that is?"

"Yes."

"From the inlet, the cocaine will be loaded onto a four-
wheel drive, and then driven up through the woods to a field
near US 264, where a truck is to pick it up and take it to New
York. But the cocaine is not to reach its destination. We want
you to intercept the shipment."

"You want me to *steal* the cocaine?"

"That's right. You'll need some additional men. We'll supply
you with all the necessary equipment—weapons, VHF radios,
night vision goggles. And we'll pay you two hundred fifty
thousand, cash. Seventy-five down, the balance when the job

is complete. I'll also pay each man you hire fifty thousand. It's vital that you pick men with no drug or alcohol problems, and we'd like to know who they are. Also, I want it understood that you will never reveal our roles in this. Not to anyone. I want your word on that."

"Hold on, Raymond. Why would you want to steal cocaine?"

"This is a national security issue, Jack. The money from the sale of this coke will be used to support a group of freedom fighters."

"Congress lacks the guts to support them," C.C. said. "These soldiers need supplies, weapons, ammunition, and food. Meanwhile, the Communists are busy exporting their revolution to Central America."

"You're missing an important point here. You steal that cocaine, you're going to have some very dangerous people looking for you."

"You don't have to worry about that, Jack. The coke will only be in your possession a few hours. After you get it you'll take it by boat to an island near the inlet and load it on an airplane. Then you're out of the picture."

"It's too dangerous. You got to raise money some other way. I know a few of these guys, and they don't play around. They'll kill you and your whole family too if you cross them."

"That's a legitimate concern, but we've already anticipated that risk. Members of our network will cover for us by implicating a rival cartel."

"These spics do this to each other all the time," C.C. said.

Jack was quiet, thinking how bat-shit crazy this scheme was. He wondered who the hell had come up with it, who else was involved.

"How do you know the time and location of the shipment? Seems like that would be impossible to nail down, unless you're in the organization."

"We have a very good source. The key information will

come from one of their business rivals."

"They'll give it to you?"

"To associates of ours."

"How are you going to sell that much coke? There are territories for cocaine. Serious turf issues, too. You can't put that much shit out on the street without the major players knowing about it. And then they're going to be knocking on your door. Only they won't come in the daylight."

"You don't need to worry about that part of the operation," C.C. said. "It's all been taken care of."

"I do worry about it."

"It will be sold in very small parcels, to people in the film and entertainment industry," Raymond said. "It will go in so many different directions it will be impossible to trace."

"Why me?"

"Your familiarity with the area, your military record, your reputation. But there's another reason, too. Call it gut instinct. I feel you're the right man for this job."

"Why are you so hellbent on helping these soldiers?"

"They're fighting for us, Jack," C.C. said. "Look at the big picture here. Through Cuba and now, Nicaragua, the Communists have established a strategic base in Central America. If Communism spreads to Mexico, do you see a problem? A hostile nation with a hundred and eighty million people sharing a common border with us."

"If I did agree to do something this crazy, it would only be for the money."

"That's your choice, then. But we're patriots. We believe in our way of life, and we want to maintain it."

"I'll have to think about this."

"I understand." Raymond gave Jack a card with a telephone number on it. "You can reach me at this number. How can we get in touch with you?"

"Leave a message at the Oregon Inlet Fishing Center."

"Don't you have a home phone?" C.C. asked.

"I don't spend much time at home these days," Jack said.

As the skiff descended to the water, Nicole came out onto the aft deck.

"Good night, Mr. Delaney."

He sat in the skiff, looking up at her, her white dress catching the moonlight, her hair swirling around her face.

"Good night," he said.

Raymond's proposition was a dirty deal any way you sliced it, but he needed the money too badly not to give it some serious thought.

He would need at least four or five men. Sam, Billy, Leon—who else? Leon's first cousin, Mike Jennette? A former Navy Seal who served a tour in Nam, he was quiet and steady, a man to trust. Jack wasn't sure he would be interested, though. He just opened a restaurant down in Avon. He might have some financial worries with his new business venture. I could try Mike, though, he thought, that is if my crew wants in. Would they want to take a risk like this? Even with the best planning someone could get hurt or killed, not to mention what would happen if the Colombians ever found out who ripped them off.

Who else knows about this? Jack wondered. Ryan, sure as fire. Who else?

Only plus he could see: a way to pay off Herrara.

If I don't do that soon, he thought, remembering the photographs he had received, I'm liable to end up like Lenny Rollins.

Tuesday afternoon, when he got back to the fishing center, Jack saw Nicole in the crowd that was watching Dave throw the fish onto the dock. They had caught several yellowfin, a yahoo and two dolphins. After the boat was unloaded and the clients left, she came over to the slip. She was wearing sunglasses, a white blouse, and a chambray skirt.

"Looks like you had a good day," she said.

"Not bad. What brings you out here?"

"Stopped by to sell an ad to the fishing center."

"Any luck?"

"Yeah. I usually sell one here."

"I'll bet you're pretty good."

"I get by."

"What's the secret of selling ads?"

"Self-confidence, perseverance. Probably similar to being a good charter boat captain."

"A lot of fishing is just luck—and intuition."

"You seem like the lucky type."

"I get by."

A pretty smile, then: "How'd you like to have a drink with me later?"

"Sure. Where?"

"Sweetwater's, say in an hour?"

"OK."

"See you then."

He watched her hips swaying under her skirt as she walked back up the dock.

"There goes my dream," Dave said. He was hosing down the boat.

What in the hell does she want? Jack wondered.

She was waiting for him in a booth, with a view of the door. A glass of beer and an empty shot glass sat on the table. He slid in across from her, wishing he'd had time to shower. The barmaid took their orders—bourbon on the rocks.

"I'll have to leave her a little extra on account of the way I smell," Jack said.

"Nothing wrong with sweat."

"It's worse when it's mixed with fish and diesel smoke."

"I'm sure you just smell like an honest working man."

"I haven't been called that in a while," Jack said, smiling. "Speaking of work, what does Raymond's friend Ryan do?"

"I think he works for the government."

"Doing what?"

"I'm not sure. Something in the Department of Defense."

"He seems like someone in sales."

"Most everyone is in sales when you get down to it."

"You think everyone has a price?"

"Don't you?"

"No, not everyone."

"What category are you in?"

"The same as you."

"Touché." Nicole laughed and took a drink of beer. "So how'd you meet Raymond?"

"Ask him."

"I did. He gave me a vague answer."

"Why'd you want to know?"

"You two seem very different. Opposites in a way."

"Maybe we just have mutual interests."

"Like what?"

"Fishing."

"Raymond only likes to spearfish."

"Then why he'd charter the *Eva Marie*?"

"You got me."

"Maybe he wanted to spend some time with Sid."

"That jerk? His wires are loose."

"What's his problem?"

"Who knows? Genetics, probably. He's Ray's nephew by marriage. His wife's brother was Sid's father, but he died when Sid was half-grown. Sid's mom was long gone by then so Raymond and his wife finished raising him—until he joined the Marines. If you ask me, he's a pitiful advertisement for Ray's parenting skills. Gun nut. He gives me the creeps. Wouldn't surprise me if he was into some serious S and M."

"What does he do all day?"

"Works for his uncle Ray. Director of security or some shit like that."

"What's C.C.'s connection to Raymond?"

"Old Marine buddies. Now that C.C. has retired, he's supposed to work for Raymond, too, as a consultant or something. But all I ever see them do is drink together and play golf."

Nicole caught the barmaid's eye and ordered them two more shots. She put hers down fast and chased it with a swallow of beer. "You know you're very curious."

"Why is that?"

"You're full of questions, for one thing."

"I've got one more."

"OK."

"Did Raymond send you to see me?"

"Why would he do that?"

"I just like to know where I stand."

"That was my idea." She smiled. "I have another idea. How'd you like to come to my place for dinner Friday night?"

"How about Raymond?"

"No reason he has to know about it."

"Where do you live?"

"Kitty Hawk, one twenty-seven Seaview."

"Got a business meeting at seven, but I could be there later, say by nine."

"I'll leave the porch light on."

Friday night, Jack presented Raymond's proposition to his crew in the minesweeper. Leon had brought Mike along. They all looked serious as safecrackers in the dim light. The first question came from Billy.

"Who's behind this, Jack?"

"I'm not sure who all is involved. Probably some federal guys. The ones who are trying to cut the deal with us don't want their names revealed."

"Fifty thousand ain't bad for a night's work," Mike said.

"Tell you one damn thing," Billy said. "Anybody else but you make me an offer like this, I'd tell him to cram it."

"I'm just laying it out for you all to decide," Jack said. He was thinking money wouldn't be any use to a dead man.

"What if the Colombians find out we did it?" Sam asked.

"They're not supposed to find out. That's part of the deal. The federal guys, or whoever else is in on this, are supposed to pin the hijacking on another cartel."

"How they going to do that?" Billy asked.

"I don't know. I was just told that's part of the plan."

Sam: "You trust these people, Jack?"

"Not really. I've worked for one of them before, and he was a straight shooter. But I can't say I'd trust him. All I know is they do have the money to pay us."

"Why are they so interested in Central America?" Leon asked.

"They hate Communists."

"This is liable to be coming from the White House," Billy said.

"I don't know about that. Only reason I'm even considering it is I need the money. Take some time to think about it. And let me know whether you're in or not. If you're not, then I'm not either. I can't do it alone, and you boys are the only ones I'd trust. I'm going up for some fresh air."

On the upper deck, Jack leaned on the gunwale and looked at the moon's image in the harbor. He had already decided he was willing to do it—that is if the others would go along with it. Nicole, however, was the wild card. After a while, he heard footsteps on the stairs.

Billy.

"Jack, we took a vote. We'll do it, but we'd like sixty grand apiece."

They went down the stairs to the cabin.

"Billy said you boys want in. You decided awful fast. Don't you need more time to think about it?"

"If I think about it too much, I'll get cold feet," Leon said.

"I hocked everything I own to open my restaurant," Mike said. "Sixty grand would give me some breathing room."

"Sam?"

"I don't see any other way for you to get back on your feet, Jack. We need another trawler, and if you don't pay off Miami, you're liable to be food for the fish."

"I'm ready for a cold beer," Billy said.

"I've got a date," Jack said. Just this once, he thought. And that's it.

A muscle was twitching in his left eye.

Nicole lived in a cottage on Kitty Hawk Bay.

She met him at the door, wearing a short black dress that showed off her fine legs. She told him dinner would be ready soon and asked if he would like something to drink. He asked for a beer.

Music was playing on the stereo, a female singer he didn't recognize. Back of the living room was the dining room, with a window view of the bay and the moon.

Nicole served broiled flounder stuffed with crab, wild rice, squash and onions fried with bacon, a tossed salad. Jack liked it better than the meal Raymond had served on the *Victory*. When he told her this, she said, "Let's not talk about Raymond."

"OK."

"I'd rather talk about you, anyway. What do you do for fun?"

"Fish. Mess around with boats. Listen to music."

"What kind of music?"

"Country, mostly. But not that shit you hear on the radio."

"You like Merle Haggard?"

"Lord, yes."

"I have one of his albums. I'll put it on when this is through."

"Who is it?"

"Anita Baker. Like her?"

"I haven't heard much of her music. But I like that."

"Her voice gets under your skin."

"Her singing kind of goes with that view, there," he said, nodding at the bay and the moon shining in the water.

She looked out the window. "My grandmother used to say when you see the moon floating in the water you could make a wish and it would come true."

"Any of yours come true?"

"I'm not very good at wishing."

"What are you good at?"

"Cake decorating."

He laughed, looked at the curve of her throat. He pictured himself kissing her there.

Time to leave, he thought. They had already finished eating.

But her sea-colored eyes held him. When the album went off, she invited him into her living room. He sat on the sofa while she put on Merle. She came over and sat beside him. Merle was singing, "I Always Get Lucky With You."

"You trying to make me happy?" he asked.

"Why not?"

"With that dinner and Merle Haggard, what more could a man want?"

Nicole smiled.

"I'm sure you could think of something," she said.

Next morning, in her bed, she ran her fingers over his legs.

"How'd you get these scars?"

"From bullets," he said.

Saturday afternoon, he used a pay phone in Manteo to call the number C.C. had given him. A woman answered; he asked to speak to Raymond. A moment later,he heard a man's voice on the line. Sounded like Raymond's dumb-ass nephew.

"Give me your number, and he'll call you back."

"I'm in a phone booth."

"He'll call you in five minutes."

Jack gave him the number and hung up.

When Raymond called, he asked to talk to him face to face. "I'll be anchored a couple of miles out from Nags Head tomorrow."

"I can be there about two p.m.," Jack said.

"Looking forward to it," Raymond said.

Jack left the minesweeper at one-thirty in his Scarab. He had tuned her up that morning, and she was running smoothly. He took her through Oregon Inlet at forty-five knots and then opened her up on the sea, turning loose the full power of her Mercruiser Magnum engines. She flew over the wave crests, spending as much time in the air as the water. He traveled the six miles to Raymond's yacht in less than nine minutes.

He circled the *Victory* once before he pulled up to the aft deck, where Gary Thompson was waiting.

He cut the engine and used the electric motor to get in close to the stern. Releasing the automatic anchor, he tied the line around the transom ladder and climbed up to the cockpit.

Thompson escorted him down to Raymond's office. C.C. was there, too.

Jack declined Raymond's offer of a drink.

"I'll do it on two conditions," he said.

Raymond nodded, poker-faced.

"The first one is, I need my share of the money in advance."

"Why's that, Jack?"

"Got a debt I need to pay off. Man I owe does business with the people you want to rip off. I've got to pay him off before something like that goes down around here. That way, no one will suspect I had anything to do with it."

"I told you, all that's being taken care of."

"It's a loose end I don't like. I'll need the money before the job. I don't mean to be hard-nosed about it, but that's the only way I can do it."

Raymond frowned. It was clear he didn't see this as good business practice. Jack had known he wouldn't.

"What's your second condition?"

"I've got four men ready to help. They're good men, and I know I can trust them. They want sixty thousand apiece."

Raymond didn't answer. He was thinking the conditions over, but his face remained expressionless.

"These boys could get hurt or killed," Jack said, although he didn't think the extra money was any real issue. "I don't think that's too much to ask."

Raymond picked up a letter opener. "C.C.?"

"It's your call."

"All right, Jack, we'll help you out this way."

"Double cross us and you're dead," C.C. said.

"I don't like threats," Jack said. "They muddy the drinking water."

Raymond said, "Your word's good enough for us." He looked at C.C. "We're going to trust one another here."

"One more thing," Jack said. "A couple of these boys have been out of work for a while, and it would really help out if I could give them a little money up front."

"I'll give you five thousand dollars for each man in advance, the balance within ten days after the job's done. But I'm going to need to know your men's names."

"Why?"

"Routine background check, that's all."

"I've grown up with these boys. They're like family."

"Of course I trust your judgment, Jack, but the people we're working with are very thorough, and they insist on this."

"I don't like it."

"Look, we've made concessions. You can do this for us. The people I'm working with won't bend on that."

Jack was silent.

"Just write their names down." Raymond handed him a pad and a pen. "After they check out, we'll lose their names. You have my word on that."

Jack wrote their names on the pad and gave it back to Raymond. He put it in his desk drawer without looking at it. "I'll have your money for you next Saturday. Hundreds all right?"

"Fine."

"Meet me right here, same time. C.C., ready to go over the plan with Jack?"

C.C. stood up and spread a map of the Carolina coast out on the desk. Using Raymond's letter opener, he drew an imaginary X off of Hatteras Inlet.

"The cocaine will be air-dropped here. A boat will pick it up, using divers, and take it through the inlet into the sound. We've watched them make these drops twice before, and each time they had a spotter aircraft flying over the sound, looking for other vessels, particularly the Coast Guard. The pilot will be in radio contact with the boat. If everything looks clear, the vessel will go in here"—he pointed the letter opener at Gull Rock Bay—"and the cocaine will be unloaded somewhere near here." He drew another X with the blade.

"That's mostly swamp in there," Jack said.

"The nearest state road is here—three miles east, which runs to highway two-sixty-four. So the first step is to explore the area around the inlet and learn the most likely loading point."

"Only one way through that area by vehicle: old logging road that follows the high ground."

"You'll need to check it out, then select the interception point."

"I'll do that Saturday. What do we do with the cocaine?"

"You'll transport it by boat to this island, near the mouth of the bay"

"That's Hog Island."

"Right. A DC-3 will be waiting for you on the south end. The night before the shipment, you'll need to put reflectors down so the pilot can land safely. He'll need at least half a mile of runway."

"What about the boat?"

"We'll have a cabin cruiser anchored somewhere near the drop-off point."

"I'll need at least three M-16s or AK-47s with electronic sights, night vision goggles, a couple of submachine guns, and handguns for backup. Also ballistic vests."

"No problem."

"I'll need some other things, too. I'll give you a complete list next Saturday."

"We'll get you whatever you need." Raymond picked up another letter opener from the desk and placed the point on Hog Island. "There's a lot riding on this."

"Should be quite a party," C.C. said.

Early Saturday morning, Jack took his boat across the Pamlico to Gull Rock Bay to explore the inlet and the country between the inlet and the state road. Sam, Billy, and Leon went, too.

This part of the mainland was poor and sparsely populated. Watermen who lived in the fishing communities on the sound couldn't catch the quantities of shrimp and oysters available during the 1940s and 1950s. He remembered his daddy saying he could average a thousand pounds of fish a day back then, with just a couple of flat nets and a thirty-two foot trawler. Now, shell fishermen were lucky to get five hundred pounds a day, trawling from dawn until dark. Jubal said the decline in shellfish started with the hundreds of miles of canals and roads the West Virginia Pulp and Paper Company built through the Albemarle-Pamlico Peninsula back in the 1960s. The peninsula lay between the two sounds. In the 1970s, other corporations ditched, cleared, and drained more land for farming. Runoff from all of the canals changed the level of salinity in the marshes and creeks where young shrimp, crabs, and fish matured. "You don't mess with Mother Nature," Jubal said. "But that's just what those damned fool people did."

Jack anchored his boat in the inlet and they walked up the old logging road. It wound around through flat, low country, part swamp, part peat bog, with clumps of shrubs so thick a hound dog would have to back up to bark. They passed cypress and water oak hung with Spanish moss, cat briar, marsh grass, and brackish creeks. Although they had all coated themselves with repellant, mosquitoes and deerflies were all over them. It was hot and muggy in the swamp, with no breeze for relief.

Jack studied the terrain on either side of the road. He was looking for a place with swamp or trees on either side so they couldn't turn around or escape. They wouldn't expect to be hit in the swamp in the middle of the night. He found three possible locations, one close to the inlet, a second one about halfway to the state road. The third possibility was about a quarter of a mile past the second. All three sites had sturdy trees fairly close to the roadbed. He would need them for the chains.

Sam, Leon, and Jack were studying the third site when he heard Billy holler. He was standing in a clump of weeds, shouting and pointing at a red-bellied moccasin crossing the roadbed.

Sam pulled a .22 pistol from his pocket and went down the roadbed, trying to get a shot at the snake.

"Let him go, Sam," Jack called. "You can't kill all the snakes in here."

Billy came huffing and puffing up the road.

"Did you see that son of a bitch? Fucking python."

"He won't bother you unless you spook him," Jack said. "Probably just trying to get out of your way."

"It bothers me just being alive!"

They went on, Billy looking around and grumbling.

About three miles from the inlet, the roadbed ended in a field. Beyond the field was a stand of pines and past that a state road that connected to U.S. 264.

"They'll have a truck or van waiting beside those pines," Sam said.

They squatted in the shade of an oak, passing Jack's canteen around. Leon had fallen behind. Jack told Sam and Billy he liked the third location best. There were good oaks within ten feet of the road. Also, he wanted to keep them on the road with trees rather than the swamp. "They're less likely to make a run for it."

"Ain't that where we seen the snake?" Billy asked.

"That snake will be long gone by then," Jack said.

"Some of his relatives might still be around."

Leon came up the road, red-faced, soaked with sweat. He sat down on the ground, wiping his forehead with his arm. "Damned if it ain't hot."

"Better lay off those Moon Pies, Leon," Sam said.

On the way back to the boat, Billy lagged behind, jabbing weeds and bushes with a stick. Sam told him to hurry up, said he heard they always bite the last man through.

"Sam, let me carry that gun," Billy said.

Back at the minesweeper, Jack went over the plan with Sam,

Billy, Leon, and Mike. He explained that the cocaine would be air-dropped offshore and brought to the inlet by boat. At the inlet, it would be picked up by at least one four-wheel drive vehicle and then taken along the logging road to a truck waiting near the state road.

"If there's only one vehicle, or even two moving close together, we can stop them with chains. But if there are two and they aren't close to each other, we'll have to take the first one out quietly. We'll have to use silencers for this, but I'm hoping we won't have to do much shooting. We'll post a lookout near the inlet and stay in touch by radio."

Billy volunteered to be the lookout.

"Less time I spend in that snaky swamp, the better."

"With Billy down at the water, that will leave four of us to handle the vehicles. After we take the coke, we'll handcuff the drivers and take the vehicle back to the sound where we'll load the cocaine on a boat. From there, we'll take it to Hog Island and load it onto an airplane on the south end of the island."

"Sounds simple enough," Mike said.

Sounds and *is* are two different things, Jack thought.

His damn eye twitch was back.

He was thinking about Nicole again.

Saturday night, he met with C.C. and Raymond on his yacht anchored off Kitty Hawk. He told them about studying the terrain they would be operating and how he planned to stop the vehicles.

"This plan will work best if there's just one vehicle," he said, "but there's always the chance they'll have two. If there's two vehicles close together, we can stop them both at once. The problem comes in if one is way ahead of the other—say because they split the shipment. If we hit it and have to do any shooting—which is likely—the second one will hear us, and we've lost the element of surprise. If there are two vehicles, we'll have to take the first one out quietly."

Raymond said he would include silencers in the supplies.

Jack gave him a list of the other things they would need: four heavy duty one-hundred-foot chains, locks, canned food, flashlights, canteens, handcuffs, insect repellant, masks, knapsacks, hip boots, a pedometer, first aid kits, and five seventy-eight-channel VHF radios with voice-activated headsets.

"I'll have everything by the end of next week. Where do you want it delivered?"

"Old minesweeper in Wanchese Harbor."

"Isn't that a little exposed?" C.C. asked.

"Nobody's going to bother with that old wreck. Besides, I've got a guard dog on twenty-four-hour duty. One more thing, I'm going to use my Scarab to transport the cocaine to the island."

"A Scarab can't transport that much weight," C.C. said. "Not in one trip."

"I plan to pull it on a pontoon."

"Why?" C.C. asked.

"A cabin cruiser would be too easy to spot. A pontoon is low and harder to see. We can pull it right up on land and hide it in the woods, if necessary. And we can make better time."

"Makes sense to me." Raymond looked at C.C. "I knew we had the right man for the job."

"When does this go down?" Jack asked.

"Around the end of July. We'll know the night by the end of the month."

"How much notice you going to give me?"

"At least twenty-four hours. I'm sure you understand how complex this is."

Absurd is more like it, Jack thought.

"By the way, C.C. is going, too," Raymond said.

"I don't like that idea. Nothing personal, C.C., but I know my men real well. We're used to working together."

"You might need the extra firepower," Raymond said.

"Thought you guys wanted to stay out of it."

"C.C. volunteered to help you out. He's got extensive combat experience. And he'll work for free. Sounds like a good deal to me."

Raymond set a black briefcase on the desk. "Quarter of a million. You're welcome to count it."

Jack told him he would take his word for it.

He left Raymond's yacht thinking he couldn't afford to see Nicole again. It was too damned risky. Not only that, he was starting to feel guilty as hell for two-timing a good woman like Bobbie.

Thursday afternoon, he had a message to call Nicole at the fishing center.

He called her on the pay phone outside.

"You want to come see me tomorrow?" she asked.

"How about Raymond?"

"He's not coming down until Saturday afternoon."

Jack was quiet, trying to think of an excuse not to see her.

"Jack, are you free?"

"Yes," he said. "I'm free."

"Why don't you come over a little after seven?"

This has got to be the last time, he thought.

Nicole was fixing dinner when he got there. Shrimp scampi. They ate out on the patio. Jack noticed something seemed to be bothering her. While they were eating, she raised the subject of him visiting Raymond on his yacht. She had seen him come and leave from the top deck. She wanted to know why he was there.

"Business."

"What kind of business?"

"It's confidential."

"I don't like you seeing each other."

"Isn't that supposed to be my line?"

"Very funny. He must want you to do something for him."

"You know this is very good shrimp scampi."

"I'll bet it's something illegal. That would be just like him. He loves to pull strings, make things happen. And he thinks he's above the law."

"Why do you keep seeing him, then?"

"He's got some purpose for you. He's got a purpose for everything and everyone."

"What's his purpose for you?"

"Pleasure."

"You can sure deliver on that."

"You know you're a million laughs."

"I try."

"I think you should know something, Jack. Last year, Raymond hired some men to rob the headquarters of a group in D.C. that was investigating the government's arm sales to anti-Sandinista rebels."

"How do you know that?"

"I overheard him and C.C. planning it with another man. Later, I read in the paper that the place had been burglarized, the records stolen. He wants you to do something like that, doesn't he?"

"Burglary is a little out of my line."

"You'd better be careful."

"I always try to be careful."

"No you don't. You're a born risk taker."

"What makes you think so?"

"It's in your eyes, the way you walk."

"I'm just a fisherman, Nicole."

"And I'm the tooth fairy."

"I'll leave one under my pillow tonight, then."

"Very funny," she said, but she wasn't smiling.

Drifting off to sleep, he pictured Raymond's meaty hands holding the gold letter opener above the blue water on the map, the nails manicured, diamond ring sparkling on his little finger.

This is the last time, he told himself. I've got to leave that alone.

Thursday afternoon when he came back from a Gulf Stream charter, he had two messages in the office of the fishing center: one from Bobbie, the other one from his Realtor.

He called the Realtor first and learned that a retired lawyer had offered one hundred and fifty thousand for both of his ocean front lots. "They're worth more than that," he said.

"I told him that," the Realtor said.

"Tell him I'll take a hundred and ninety."

He hung up and called Herrara in Miami.

"I got your pictures. Old friends of yours?"

"You got something for me?"

"I can pay you half now. The rest in a few weeks."

"You're a funny man, Jack."

"I just want to let you know what's going on, so you won't worry."

"You're the one should be worried."

"I'm sleeping like a baby."

"But not in your house." Herrara hung up.

Jack figured Herrara would give him more time to raise the rest of the money. After all, what use would he be to him dead?

He called Bobbie next. She'd left her work number.

She was concerned that she hadn't heard from him.

"I've been thinking about you," he said. "Does that count for something?"

"Words don't buy much these days."

"You working tomorrow night?"

"Yes, but I'm off Saturday."

"How about dinner? Some place real nice."

"Sounds good."

"I'll pick you up at seven."

The night he took Bobbie out to eat he had the bad luck to pick the same restaurant as Raymond and Nicole.

Nicole was staring at Bobbie, who was wearing a tight-fitting red dress.

Bobbie seemed equally interested in her.

"Did you notice that blonde at the back with the older man?"

"Where?"

"Behind you. But don't look now. That's Nicole Andrisson. Ad rep for *Sea and Sand*. Every time she comes in the bar, the owner drools all over himself."

Jack nodded, studying the menu.

"Do you think she's sexy?"

"She's all right. For a blonde."

The waiter appeared, reciting the specials for the evening. Bobbie ordered lamb. Jack ordered the shrimp scampi.

A little later, Raymond and Nicole walked past them on their way out. They spoke to Jack as they went by.

"How do you know them?" Bobbie asked.

"Took them fishing once."

"Is he rich?"

"I don't know."

"He must be or she wouldn't have her hooks in him."

Jack grinned at her. "Maybe he just has a big, kind heart."

"A big bank account is more like it."

Jack and Sam built the pontoon in the backyard of Sam's house in Buxton. They found the fifty-five-gallon drums at a marina and they took the two-by-fours from an abandoned shack in the woods near Sam's house. Jack towed the pontoon to his mother's house and tied it up at the dock. When Mae asked about it, he told her he was just keeping it there for Sam. "What's Sam going to do with that fool thing?" she asked.

"Guy in Wanchese is hiring him to haul an engine over from Stumpy Point."

Lying to his mama like that made him feel lower than a snake's ass. One more thing to feel guilty about.

Jack woke up out of a deep sleep, hearing a tapping sound on the side of the minesweeper. He grabbed the shotgun, pumped a shell into the chamber, and went up the stairs. Amos was on deck, his ears pricked up, growling. Jack peeped over the gunwale and saw the source of the sound—an empty dingy bobbing in the current. He looked at his watch. It was four-fifteen. His alarm would go off in fifteen minutes.

He went back downstairs to make coffee and make himself breakfast. Hell of a way to start the day, he thought.

Later, going through the inlet on the *Eva Marie*, he remembered what Jubal used to tell him about fishing: "It's a good, honest life, Jack. Clean and decent. Out there on the sea, you don't see man's handiwork. All you see is the spirit of God. There's nobody out there to yarn to you or tell you what to do. You've got to work hard, but it's good work, and there's money in it, enough to live."

He had made a good living at it too—until he had those six bad months. The inlet shoaled over and they'd had to go all the way to Beaufort to get to the sea. There were major, unexpected expenses on the boat, including more fuel, a burned-up power take-off and a shot generator. Debts piling up. And the catch wasn't that good. He could have gotten through it all right, but along came temptation in the form of a man who offered him twenty-five thousand cash for one night's work. All he had to do was meet a ship offshore at night and transport a load of marijuana to an inlet on the mainland. Just this once, he told himself.

But the money was gone in a few months, and he made

another night run and then another. Pretty soon, fishing just got to be a cover for the real business of hauling the grass in from the mother ships at night. He bought his first load from Lupe Herrara's cousin—delivered to his trawler off of Santa Marta by Chibca Indians in motorized canoes. He sold the load to a dealer in Washington, D.C., and made more money than he could have made in six months of trawler fishing. After he ran a few loads up from South America, Herrara began extending him credit on the grass. He would move a load up the coast four or five times a year, paying Herrara off when he got paid. Lupe kept trying to convince him to move cocaine, pointing out how much more profitable it was, but Jack didn't want to fool with cocaine because he knew it killed people. On the other hand, he had never heard of anybody dying from a toke on a joint.

He started investing in real estate, taking vacations in St. Thomas and Cartagena. Herrara set him up with a lawyer who took his drug money and sent it back to him through a dummy corporation in the Cayman Islands. He built Elena a house after she got married and set up a trust fund for his mama.

But except for the trust fund, the trawler, his lots, and the house, most of the money he'd made slipped through his fingers from living like there was no tomorrow. And the load that went down off of Ocracoke really cost him—not just his boat but also seven hundred grand, half of which he still owed Herrara.

He hoped to clear one hundred and fifty thousand from the beach lots. With that, and the money Raymond had paid him, he could settle up with Herrara. Then maybe he could start sleeping easier at night. Back in his house.

He thought of the pictures Lupe had sent, wondering who the unfortunate victims were. And he thought of Lenny Rollins washing up on the beach. Lenny's brother lived in Queens. He was married to a Colombian woman whose family was in the business. During the off-season, Lenny made a lot of trips to New York. Probably moving coke up from Florida. Jack had known Lenny since he was a kid. His family had lived in Hatteras for a few years before they moved to Manteo. Another victim of the turf war.

He was sick of the whole business. His father, Jubal, was right about fishing. The easy money had messed up his perspective. After he paid off Herrara, he could mortgage his house for a down payment on another trawler and go back into fishing. He knew a man over in Englehardt who had a good trawler for sale. He could borrow the down payment and sell his Scarab if he had to. It was not too late to start over.

In the afternoon, when he got back to the fishing center, there was a message at the office to call his Realtor. He called him from the pay phone outside.

"He offered a hundred and seventy-five," the agent said.

"When do you think he can close?"

"Maybe a week, ten days. He's anxious to start building his house."

"Go ahead and draw up the contract."

"It's not a bad price, Jack."

"It's not great, either."

Jack called Herrara and told him he could pay him in two weeks and asked him how he wanted him to deliver the money.

"Wait a minute." Herrara spoke to someone in Spanish, then said, "Jack, I've got to be in New York on the sixteenth. We'll be flying over the Carolinas. I'll meet you at the airport by the memorial around nine at night."

"You can only fly in there during daylight hours. It's illegal after dark."

Herrara, laughing now, said. "We'll be there between six and seven. I wouldn't want to do anything illegal."

Billy came over to the minesweeper to help Jack unload the supplies Raymond had promised to deliver there. They were playing poker in the cabin below when Jack heard Amos growl.

"That's them," he said.

They went up to the upper deck and waited. Bats wheeled and dived in the air above the harbor. Clouds covered up the moon.

They were in a cabin cruiser. Two men on deck, one up in the flying bridge.

Using the electric motor, the captain eased the boat up to the portside of the minesweeper, the side facing away from the road.

One of them called down from the deck, asked if they were ready to unload.

"Ready," Billy said.

Two men carried three crates out from the cabin and set them on deck. The captain climbed down from the bridge and the three of them passed the crates up to Jack and Billy. They lifted them over the gunwale and set them down on deck. The last crate was the heaviest.

The captain climbed the ladder and swung over the minesweeper's gunwale. "Let's get this down below and make sure everything's there." It was Sid, wearing a black toboggan and camouflage paint.

Jack and Billy took the heavy crate down the steps and set it in the cabin. Sid followed them down the steps.

Jack heard Amos growl. He turned to see Sid backing up the steps, kicking at Amos who was going after him. By the time he got up the steps and grabbed the dog's collar, Sid had a knife in his hand.

"Get that fucking mutt out of here before I kill him!"

"Take it easy. He's just doing his job. He's a guard dog."

Jack put the dog into the kitchen compartment and shut the door. Then he and Billy went up for the other two crates.

When they returned, Sid had pried open one of the crates with a screwdriver.

"The portable VHF radios, medical supplies, vests, and handcuffs are in this one," he said. "The heavy crate has the chains and rifles. The subs are in the third one. The ammunition, magazines, and pistols are in that one, too."

They opened the other two boxes and checked everything off against Jack's list. Three AK-47s, two Hechler and Koch machine guns with silencers. Two Colt Delta Unit pistols.

Jack picked up one of the MP-5 machine guns.

"This is a real classic," Sid said. "You ever fired one?"

"No."

"It fires with a closed bolt, using a roller-locking lug system with a fluted chamber to dissipate the heat. This makes for smooth and accurate work. I can put a thirty-round magazine into a five-inch group at thirty yards."

Sid picked up the other machine gun and slipped the laser sight onto the mount.

"This is the silenced version. Silencer slows the bullets down to about nine hundred and thirty-five feet per second. You give up that velocity loss for the advantage of a quiet weapon."

He activated the laser sight, pointing the red dot at the wall.

"It's two inches in diameter at a hundred yards. But you'll be working much closer."

"Looks like something Darth Vadar would carry," Billy said.

"It's a state-of-the-art *weapon*," Sid said.

Jack took one of the night vision goggles out of its box and slipped it on.

"Those Exalibur goggles are made to military specs," Sid said. "They've got automatic brightness control to protect the tubes and maintain the image during muzzle flash."

"Man, I've always wanted to see in the dark," Billy said. "You could do some great girl-watching with those."

"They weren't designed for that," Sid said, with contempt.

He looked at Jack. "I'm to remind you to dump the weapons in the ocean after the job's done."

"I'll consider myself reminded."

Sid gave him a curt nod, and then glided up the stairs, quiet as a shadow.

"Who's the clown with the makeup?" Billy asked. He was trying on a flak jacket.

"You don't want to know."

Billy spun himself around, holding out his arms. "What do you think? Is it me?"

"You look gorgeous, Billy."

Jack tossed and turned in the cabin, thinking about Nicole, remembering her legs wrapped tightly around his back, her scent of limes and sunscreen, her satin skin. Crying his name over and over.

The last time he'd visited her at her cottage, she had immediately brought up the subject of Bobbie.

"Your date was very attractive. What's her name?"

"Bobbie."

"Known her long?"

"Awhile."

"She looks like the earth mother type—those wide, child-bearing hips."

Jack didn't answer.

"What does she do?"

"Tends bar."

"I was a bartender once."

"How'd you like it?"

"I had to listen to a lot of sad stories—and confessions. Like I was some kind of priestess."

"Can't see you as a priest."

"Why not? A lot of cultures have female priests."

"Is that right?"

"The Aztecs for instance. And the Egyptians."

"What are your qualifications?"

"Don't have any. I don't even believe in God."

"Then how could you be a priestess?"

"I could be a priestess for pagans."

"Could you find a flock?"

"Look around you. How many people do you see with genuine faith?"

"I know a few."

"How about you? Moved any mountains lately?"

"Not lately."

"Lots of people claim they believe, but look how they live. Me, I'm honest enough to admit what I am. An infidel."

"You've got to believe in something, Nicole."

She ran her fingers along the inside of his thigh, slipped her tongue into his ear.

"I believe in this, baby."

Chills up and down his spine. *Jesus.*

On Saturday afternoon, they went to Hog Island to practice with the weapons—it was a low, marshy island, six miles from the mainland, fifteen miles south of Gull Rock Bay. They test fired the AK-47s and the Heckler and Koch machine guns with the silencers. All were accurate and easy to control.

Jack and Billy tried out the Colts. Jack thought they had decent accuracy, with a little more recoil than his .45.

"I'd like to have one of these ten-millimeters," Billy said. "I heard the FBI is thinking about going to them."

He emptied an eight-round clip at some coffee cans.

"You only got four of them," Leon said.

"A Colombian is a lot bigger than a can," Billy said.

"But a tin can don't shoot back."

"Think we'll have to shoot any of them, Jack?" Billy asked, putting another magazine into the pistol.

"I hope not," Jack said.

He cruised over to the inlet alone. He wanted to be more familiar with the terrain they would be operating in. It was a clear night, a quarter moon, stars shining through a skein of tattered clouds.

About a mile north of the inlet, he found a small tidal creek where they could hide the boat and pontoon. He cut the engine and tied up in the creek. Walking through the woods to the roadbed, he cut a path through the vines and grass with his machete, marking the trees. Using the pedometer, he measured the distance from the inlet to the site on the roadbed where they planned to stop the vehicles. It was just over two miles. He notched the backs of the trees they were going to use for the chains.

He sat down by the roadbed and listened to the frogs and cicadas. It was important that he get the feel of the place. In Vietnam, he had learned how feeling at home on the land can give you a life-saving edge in a fight. At first he had believed the country's basic mission was right, and it wasn't until near the end of his tour that he really began to question it, especially the way it was being fought. Why fight a war you don't intend to win?

He kept turning the operation over in his mind, looking for problems, trouble areas. Even with the best planning, there was no guarantee there wouldn't be a screwup. What if the Colombians had superior firepower and decided to fight? One or more of his men could get hurt or killed. The vehicles could get so shot up they couldn't use them to haul the cocaine back to the inlet. They would have to carry it, then. And there was always the chance of being spotted by the Coast Guard. Jack felt responsible for his men. Except for Mike, they lacked combat experience. Sam and Leon served tours in the Navy, Billy had been in the Coast Guard. Neither he, Sam, nor Leon had much experience with firearms. They were fishermen, not soldiers.

They're good boys, steady and true, he thought, but could they handle it?

On the way back to the boat, he saw a luna moth fly into the web of a wolf spider. He stopped and watched the moth struggling against the web and the spider's venom.

He smelled something dead in the air.

On the sixteenth, Jack drove to the Wright Memorial and parked his Jeep in the parking lot. He had the three hundred and fifty thousand he owed Herrara in his backpack. He sat on the ledge of the memorial, waiting for Herrara. After a while, he saw the King Air emerge from the clouds.

Herrara's pilot flew a low downward leg over the sound before making a shallow crosswind bank. By the time he turned for his final approach Jack was already halfway down the hill.

Herrara's bodyguards were waiting by the plane. Jack handed Rafael his gun, but they searched him anyway.

Rafael escorted him to the back of the plane. Herrara was on the couch. Red-eyed, puffy faced—looked like he hadn't been sleeping good. At his side he had a MAC-10, an ugly little box of a gun that could empty a thirty-six-round magazine in a few seconds.

"Jack, my old friend," Herrara said.

"How's life?"

"Life sucks, man."

"War still on?"

"Yeah."

"Maybe everyone should call a truce."

"Who knows? Anything's possible. Maybe they'll find the Milky Way is made of cotton candy."

"You know a guy named Lenny Rollins?"

"Worked for the Bunellas family?"

"Used to. He washed up on the beach with concrete blocks

chained to his legs. Left a wife and two kids behind."

"Dangerous world, Jack. What did you bring me?"

"Three hundred and fifty thousand."

"My *associados* will count it. If it's all there, this will make us amigos again, but you should learn to show a little more respect for your business partners. Next time you run into a jam, let me know what's going on. Man owes me money and I don't hear from him, I begin to worry he's forgotten all about his obligations. I saw a show on TV the other night, about how so many marriages suffer from communication issues. Communication is the key, man. You catch that show?"

"No, Lupe. And you know I had a lot on my mind after my boat went down."

"Gets me right here, Jack." Herrara touched his fist to his chest.

Jack looked down at the money. He wondered how long it would take him to make that much fishing.

"Let me know when you want some more *yeyo*, but from now on it's going to have to be cash up front."

"I'm getting out of the business."

"Most people only leave this business one way."

"I'm hoping I can beat the odds."

"*¡Buena suerte!*"

"Thanks a lot."

"I mean that, Jack. From the bottom of my heart."

Jack moved back into his house in Avon. He and Sam hauled the weapons and supplies under a tarpaulin in the back of Sam's truck and stored them in his attic.

He called the number Raymond had given him. Sid answered. Jack gave him the number to his cottage. Sid said he'd pass the message along.

Jack lay on his couch, staring at the phone. It had been nearly three weeks since he had seen Nicole, and he couldn't get her out of his mind. He kept thinking how nice it would be to have her visit him in his own place. After a protracted internal struggle, he finally dialed her number.

He fixed her a Hatteras meal of bluefish broiled with bacon, collards, sweet potatoes, and cornbread. For dessert— a coconut cream pie Mae had made.

Nicole wanted to know why he had been living on a boat. He guessed she had pried that information out of Raymond.

"I sleep better on a boat. Water rocks me to dreamland."

"That way it would be harder for someone to sneak up on you."

"You said I liked to take chances."

"Everything rests on chance, doesn't it?"

"I think a lot of what happens is a result of choices."

"But you never know what's going to happen as a result of those choices. That's where chance comes in."

"But chance isn't everything. You have some influence over what happens to you."

"Strange talk from a man in your line of work."

"A fisherman has got to have confidence."

"I wasn't talking about fishing."

After supper, they went for a walk on the beach. There was a big silver moon over the sea. Amos ran ahead, chasing crabs, barking at the surf, happy to be out of the minesweeper. Jack guessed he had been getting claustrophobic in the cramped quarters.

"How'd he lose his leg?" Nicole asked.

"Got hit by a car. Happened before I got him."

"He seems to do fine on three. He tried to hump my leg while you were fixing supper."

"At least he had the courtesy to wait till I was out of sight."

"You can't trust a dog."

"Sure you can. You can trust him to be a dog."

Nicole laughed. They sat on a piece of driftwood and watched a star fall over the sea, streaming light.

"Is that the secret of trusting someone, Jack? Knowing what they're all about?"

"No. The real secret is in knowing yourself."

"What do you mean?"

"You have to know what you want. You get that right, other things tend to fall into place."

"I try not to want anything too much."

"Why?"

"Because the more you want something, the more likely you are to lose it."

"Must be something you'd like to have."

"Money."

"There you go."

"What else is there?"

"You know I've always liked hard-assed women. The tougher the better."

He was laughing at her now. She grabbed him, pushed him down into the sand. They wrestled a minute before he let her get on top of him.

"Let me hear you beg," she said, tickling his ribs.

"I'm begging."

"Who's the toughest babe you know?"

"You."

"Don't you forget it either, Jack Delaney."

They lay still awhile, his hands on her lower back. He could feel the steady rise and fall of her diaphragm. After a while, they were breathing in time. Jack looked up at the stars and thought how solid and still the earth felt beneath his back, even though it was spinning in black, empty space, and how fast the starlight was traveling toward them, and how those same stars would still be shining long after they were gone.

Amos came back and lay beside them, panting.

The ringing telephone woke him up out of a dream of fishing the Gulf Stream with Jubal.

"It's going down Sunday night," C.C. said. "Reflectors will need to be put up on the island."

"I'll take care of it. What time?"

"Be there just after dark. I'll meet you at the inlet. Use your radio, channel seventy-three. My handle's Black Fox."

"See you there," Jack said.

Sam, Billy, Leon, and Mike met at Jack's house. They waited until dark and then crossed the road to the boatshed, in the subdivision across from his cottage, carrying the weapons in a tarpaulin. They put on the body armor and loaded the rest of the supplies in the V-berth of the Scarab. Jack had towed the pontoon over the night before and tied it up in the tidal creek.

They started across the sound in the dark just after nine, moving through fog so thick Jack couldn't see ten feet. He flipped the silent choice switch, directing the exhaust away from the pipes and down through the hub of the prop, channeling the exhaust underwater. He had mixed feelings about the fog. On the one hand, it would give them cover, but it could also weaken the edge they had with the night vision goggles. And the men making the drop could get lost, miss the inlet, and end up unloading the cocaine in the morning. That would cost them the cover of darkness and possibly the element of surprise, too.

He used Loran coordinates to find the inlet. When they got there he called C.C. on the radio. C.C. said everything was quiet. Jack told him they should be in their positions within forty-five minutes.

He dropped anchor just north of the logging road. They were unloading the supplies when C.C. appeared out of the fog, wearing camouflage fatigues, a flak jacket, and face paint. He was carrying an Uzi with a silencer attached and a pistol in a shoulder holster.

Jack introduced him to the others as "Black Fox." They had agreed on these handles while using the radio: Jack, "Swamp Man"; Billy, "Cowboy"; Sam, "Bluefin"; Mike, "Ranger"; and Leon, "Moon Pie."

Sam and Leon carried the chains. Jack gave Sam the pedometer and reminded him of the spot they had picked out two and one-tenth miles from there. He told him he would meet him there in forty minutes.

He went on around the shore, found the tidal creek, and backed the boat in close to the pontoon. Mosquitoes swarmed all over him, some even biting him through the repellent. His shirt was already drenched in the hot muggy air. He slung the machine gun over his shoulder and climbed out of the boat onto the low ground near the inlet. Wading into the water, he hooked the pontoon to the boat with a chain. He had spare magazines in his pockets, the VHF radio attached to his belt, the headset in place, food and supplies in his rucksack. He slid the goggles down and started through the swamp toward the logging road, stepping in water up to his knees. Except for patches of fog, he could see everything clearly through the night vision goggles: tree limbs, Spanish moss, even bullfrogs croaking by the water.

Thigh deep in swamp, he saw a scaly bump in the water about thirty feet away. It was topped with two red eyes. He eased the Colt out of the holster and kept it aimed at the alligator until he got to higher ground.

He was on the logging road when Billy called him on the radio to tell him he'd heard "a weird-ass noise" behind him.

"What kind of noise?"

"A rustling noise, like something crawling. Think it might be a moccasin?"

"Take it easy, Cowboy. Could be anything."

"Don't those frigging snakes hunt at night?"

"Snakes won't bite you unless you bother them. Just be still."

Might be a possum."

He figured C.C. was thinking that he had hired a bunch of amateurs.

When he got to the interception point, Sam and Leon had the chains locked to the trees. They went over the plan again. For one vehicle, they would follow plan A, with two men on each side of the logging road. Jack told them to stand at forty-five-degree angles from the vehicle, to keep from shooting each other.

He put C.C. and himself in one team, Sam and Mike in the other. He positioned Leon up near the state road so he could let them know who was coming. When Billy radioed that the truck was on its way, he would take the chain across the road and hook it to the tree. Immediately after the truck passed by them, Leon and Sam would hook the second chain up to prevent the truck from backing up. If the driver tried to go to the left or right, he would be stopped by the swamp or trees. Then they would fire a couple of warning shots, tell them to come out with their hands up.

If there were two vehicles traveling close together, they would follow a modified version of plan A, called "A-two." C.C. and Jack would take out the first vehicle. Sam and Mike would take out the second one after they got the chain hooked up.

Plan B would go into effect if the two vehicles were apart. Jack and C.C. would take out the first vehicle since they had the silenced weapons. When the second vehicle arrived, Sam and Leon would quickly hook the chain behind it and then take care of the driver. Jack hoped he would give up without a fight.

Once the first transport was neutralized, he could help Sam and Leon.

"Tell them you're police and that we've got them surrounded," Jack said. "Don't shoot unless you have to."

"What kind of advice is that?" C.C. asked.

"That's the way it's going down."

"What if they run?" Leon asked.

"Shoot them in the legs. Now, let's get in our positions."

Jack squatted down behind a cypress, ten feet from the road and began to wait. He felt reasonably good about their positions. Leon was big and slow, and Billy was too jumpy in the swamp. The way he had it arranged, he and C.C. would take care of the major action.

He was trying to minimize the risk to his men.

After a while, he saw a red dot moving lightly on the leaves above his head—Mike, fooling around with the laser.

He heard a wild cry floating above them.

"What the hell was that?" Sam called.

"Hawk got a rabbit," Jack said.

"How could it see a rabbit in this fog?" Sam asked.

"Hawks got X-ray eyes," Mike said. "Like Superman."

"Swamp Man," Billy said, on the radio. "You read about the coke dealer whose family buried him in a coffin shaped like a Cadillac?"

"No."

"It had a steering wheel and everything. They buried him sitting up at the wheel."

C.C. said. "Amazing number of Einsteins in the world, huh?"

They were silent awhile, waiting, then Jack heard Billy's voice on the radio.

"Swamp Man, I hear an airplane."

"Might be the spotter aircraft," C.C. said.

"Keep us posted," Jack said.

Billy didn't call back, so Jack called him.

"What's happening, Cowboy?"

"Bugs, snakes, and frogs are happening."

"Ants about to eat me alive," Leon said.

"Ants, hell," said Sam. "These skeeters are vampires. Bastards want every drop of blood you got."

"Ain't the ants or the skeeters I'm worried about," Billy said.

"We've got company, boys," Leon said.

Jack heard it, too. An engine. Then he saw the headlights.

A truck. Three-quarter ton Dodge with a long bed. After it passed by, he called Billy and told him the truck was headed his way.

A few minutes later, Billy radioed back to tell him the truck was at the inlet.

Jack asked him how many men he saw.

"Can't tell for sure. Two, maybe three."

Billy said something else but his voice was too low to hear the words.

"What's that again?" Jack asked.

"They're pissing," Billy said.

Jack hoped they wouldn't put up a fight. He wanted to get it over with, without anyone getting hurt. It's just cocaine, he thought. Why should anybody be willing to die for that shit?

But who was he kidding? People were dying every day for a few dollars worth of crack.

They had to be prepared to shoot the couriers if necessary. No other way to do it.

"I hear a boat," Billy said.

"You see anything?"

"Fog, man. It's like being in the middle of a cloud."

Silence, then: "I can't see a damned thing. No, wait—I see a light offshore. They're shining a light on the shore. Dudes in the truck are flashing their headlights."

A few minutes later, Billy reported the boat was at the inlet.

"Looks like plan A," C.C. said. "Time to hook up the chain, Swamp Man."

Just then, Leon called to say another vehicle was headed toward the inlet.

"More the merrier," C.C. said. Jack heard him pull back the bolt on the Uzi.

The second vehicle was a van—not the best choice for this kind of terrain. *More men in the back?*

"You got more company, Cowboy," Jack said. His heart felt like a clock wound too damn tight.

It took them thirty-three minutes to transfer the coke from the boat to the two vehicles. Afterward, Billy radioed to tell him they were on the way.

"The truck is coming first. There's two guys in the cab, one on the back."

"How many in the van?"

"I only saw one."

"Has it left yet?"

"Roger. About thirty seconds behind the truck."

"What about the boat?"

"They're leaving now."

"Get ready," Jack said, into the radio. "We're going with plan A-two."

He slipped on his gloves and pulled the bolt back on the submachine gun.

He heard the truck, saw the headlights piercing the fog.

The truck slammed into the chain, the rear wheels spinning in the earth. Jack started to shout, "Police!" but at that moment he heard the cracking purr of the Uzi, then the sound of the truck's horn.

Gunfire from the truckbed. He could see the shooter through the goggles. Squatting down on the bags of cocaine, shooting wild with a MAC-10. Just wasting his ammo. Jack put the laser dot on his shoulder and squeezed the trigger.

The man spun around and fell off the truck.

All he heard was the sound of the truck's horn. He called Sam on the radio.

"Bluefin. You need any help?"

"Negative, Swamp Man. We got the van. Everybody OK up there?"

"Yeah. How'd it go?"

"Guy in the van gave up. Told him we were cops."

"Where is he?"

"On the ground with his hands behind his head. Ranger's got him covered."

"Did you check the back of the van?

"Roger. Just some big bags in there. How you all doing?"

"We got the truck stopped. Two guys shot in the cab, wounded man underneath. Stay there till I tell you it's OK."

"Ten-four, Swamp Man."

"Can you get a shot at the man under the truck?" C.C. asked.

"I'm going give him a chance to give up."

"What the hell for?"

"Cover me. I'm going in the cab."

Jack crawled forward on his belly until he could see the back of the truck. He saw the MAC-10 on the ground. Then he saw tennis shoes sticking out from under the truck.

No sense in calling out to him—he wouldn't be able to hear for the horn.

Jack crawled back to the front of the truck. The driver was slumped over the wheel, the passenger leaning against the right passenger's door, head shot. The windshield was riddled with bullet holes.

C.C. never gave them a chance.

There was a CB radio in the truck, but they wouldn't have had time to use it.

He opened the door and the passenger fell out onto the ground. Jack slid into the truck and pulled the other man away from the horn. He had a bullet hole in his forehead, another one in his cheek.

Jack moved back into the trees, where he could have a view of the truck.

"Hey, you—under the truck. *¿Hablas Inglés?*"

No answer.

"We can do this one of two ways. You can surrender now and live, or stay under there and we'll finish you off where you are. It's your choice."

"Who are you?"

"DEA," Jack said. "Come on out with your hands up."

After a minute, he heard the man shout that he was coming out. "Don't shoot, I'm giving up. Don't shoot me!"

Jack told him to come out from the back. He was crouched behind a water oak ten yards away.

The man rolled out from under the truck, his left arm in the air. His right arm hung at his side. Jack told him to turn around and face the truck. "Keep your hands where I can see them."

Jack slung the machine gun over his shoulder and drew the pistol. He approached the man carefully, warning him to hold still. He searched him, taking a spare clip for the machine gun from his pocket. The mosquitoes had smelled the blood and they were on him like a plague.

"Now, sit down on the ground."

Moaning, he did the best he could with his wounds.

Jack called Sam on the radio and told him to bring the other man up.

"You guys really DEA?" Jack could smell the sour stench of his fear.

"Don't worry about that. Where you hit?"

"Shoulder and arm. It hurts, man. You got any morphine?"

C.C. stepped around from the side of the truck.

"Move out of the way. I'm going to finish him off."

"No you're not," Jack said.

"Get out of the goddamned way!" C.C. held the Uzi pointed at the ground.

Jack was on him before he could even think, slamming him to the ground, jerking the gun out of his hands. He pinned his arms with his knees and took his pistol, too.

C.C. was spitting and shouting: "What the fuck is wrong

with you?"

"Nothing. Just don't see any need to kill him."

Jack stood up, put the pistol in his rucksack, and slung the other machine gun over his shoulder.

"I want you to stay out of the way. We'll get the job done from here."

"You're making a big mistake," C.C. said.

"You guys ain't DEA," the man on the ground said. "Shit."

Sam and Mike came up with the other man walking in front. His hands were cuffed behind his back. He looked to be just a scared kid.

Jack asked him if he spoke English and he nodded.

"How many men up by the road?"

"One driver."

Sam said, "Unless he's deaf, he's heard the shooting."

"What's your name?" Jack asked.

"Ramone."

"Ramone, you want to live to see the sunrise, don't you?"

"*Sí, señor.*"

"Here's the deal. I want you to call that driver on the radio, tell him you had a little trouble but everything is all right. Tell him you ran into some 'coon hunters and had to shoot them. Tell him they shot out one of the tires, and you'll be up as soon as you get it changed. You do a good job, you live. You do a bad job, you die. *¿Comprendes?*"

"Yes, sir, *comprendo muy bueno.*"

"Let's get up into the truck."

They went back to the cab. Leon took the cuffs off him so he could use the radio.

Jack placed the muzzle of the Colt against Ramone's temple. "Do a good job now and you might live to see your grandchildren."

"Alabama, this is Ramone."

"What the hell is going on down there? I'm just about ready

to haul ass out of here."

"Had a little trouble. Ran into some hunters and had to smoke them."

"Hunters?"

" 'Coon hunters."

"Shame to shoot a 'coon hunter."

"Couldn't be helped, man." Ramone was getting into his part.

"Anybody else hurt?"

"No, we're OK. Be up as soon as we can."

"What's the holdup?"

"Bullet hit a tire."

"Jesus. I got to get out of this business."

"What?"

"Nothing. Ten-four."

Jack told the kid he did a good job and then handcuffed him to the steering wheel so he could drive the van.

Jack had a brief meeting with his men behind the truck. Black rubber bags full of cocaine were piled up about five feet deep in the bed. He told Leon to back up the van until he found a place to pull it off. "Ranger, take the truck down to the inlet and get Cowboy to start helping him unload it. Keep a sharp eye on your prisoner. Grab those two dead guys' guns and round up the kid's weapon, too. Moon Pie, you come with me. You and me and Ramone here are going to take care of Alabama."

Ramone drove the van. Leon sat up front with him. Jack sat in the back with the rubber bags. He pierced one with his knife, tasted the white crystals. The sharp medicinal taste of pure Peruvian.

He told Leon to drop him off on the logging road a hundred yards from the field. "Wait ten minutes, then come on."

"What's your plan, Swamp Man?"

"I'm hoping he'll get out to meet Ramone so I can get the drop on him."

Jack jogged to the field and crouched behind a pine. He saw the tractor and trailer rig parked at the edge of the field, a row of pines concealing it from the highway. He circled the field, staying close to the trees, and came up along the back of the truck. There was lettering on the side: *Baltimore Fish Company.*

He saw the van's lights on the logging road. Leon drove up to the rear of the truck. Jack was waiting on the driver's side.

The door opened and the driver got out. Jack told him to freeze and get his hands up. He had the laser sight on his face so he'd get the picture.

The man raised his hands fast.

"Turn around and put your hands on the truck, your feet out behind you."

Leon came around the front end of the truck.

"Where's Ramone?"

"Handcuffed to the steering wheel."

"What about the radio?"

"I disabled it."

Jack searched the driver for weapons, but he was clean. He cuffed his hands behind his back then climbed into the truck cab and looked around. He found a .357 Magnum with a six-inch barrel on the seat. He yanked the microphone from the radio and then put the Magnum in his rucksack.

As he stepped back outside onto the ground, the truck driver asked if he was a cop.

"No," he said.

"Shit, that means I'm dead, don't it?"

"Not necessarily."

"I hope not. Got a wife and three kids."

"You should have been home with them," Jack said.

Leon drove the van all the way to the inlet. Jack stayed in the back to keep an eye on Ramone and Alabama, although their hands were cuffed behind them.

At the inlet, Billy, Sam, and Al had most of the cocaine unloaded and piled beside the truck. The wounded man was groaning on the ground. Jack gave him a morphine tablet from the medical kit in his rucksack and let him wash it down with water from his canteen. He had been hit twice—in the right shoulder and bicep, both bullets exiting the back. Jack put bandages on him to slow the bleeding. They were non-lethal wounds, but he would need medical attention soon.

The man mumbled something in Spanish. Jack asked Ramone what he said.

Ramone: "Thank you for not killing him."

"I'm going to get the boat," Jack said.

Jack went back up the logging road until he found the path he had marked with the machete. He was shaky now that everything was over. He was sorry about the men C.C. had killed, but glad none of his men had been hurt.

As long as I got the cocaine on the airplane, I've kept my end of the bargain, he thought. Still, the trouble with C.C. worried him. Patriot my ass, he thought. I've seen his type before. Just wants to kill someone to prove how tough he is.

When they got the cocaine loaded onto the pontoon, he asked Sam and Billy to disable the truck and the van. He opened the back of the van and took the cuffs off the couriers.

"Wait until you hear us leave and then go on up the path," he said. "Forget about the van and the truck. We're yanking the cylinder wires out. You can get out of here with that diesel rig. You need to get this wounded man to a hospital. There's hospitals in Edenton and Elizabeth City. Or you can take him to one up in Norfolk."

Two of the men had their heads down. Alabama was looking at Jack like he had just discovered a cure for his terminal disease.

It took them about an hour to tow the cocaine out to the

island.

They came in on the south end near the makeshift runway, but they couldn't see the plane in the fog. Leaving the others in the boat, Jack and Billy walked through the fog until they saw the reflectors. They followed the tracks in the sand to the plane. Jack rapped on the door and the pilot stepped out. He was wearing a Mickey Mouse mask.

"Cute disguise," Jack said. "Borrow it from your kid?"

"No comment."

"How'd you like the runway?"

"I've seen worse, but not by much. You got the shit?"

"Yeah."

"Let's get it loaded, then"

"If you'd pull the plane forward about fifty yards we'll save a lot of time."

"No problem."

"How much is all this coke worth?" Billy asked, on the way back to the pontoon.

"Wholesale, about twenty million," Jack said. "On the street, cut down, maybe eighty million."

Billy whistled.

"That would buy a lot of happiness," he said.

"That shit's all about misery, Billy," Jack said.

He could feel a bad headache coming on.

They returned to the boatshed just before daylight.

Jack told Sam and Billy to take the Scarab out to sea and dump the weapons and supplies.

He drove himself and Leon back to his house. Leon immediately fell asleep on the couch.

Bone-tired, Jack took a shower, grabbed a cup of coffee, changed his clothes, and headed out to work. When he got to the fishing center, Dave and the clients were waiting for him on the dock. The other boats had left.

"Trouble getting up this morning, Captain?" one of the clients asked.

"Fickle alarm clock," Jack said. "Been meaning to get a new one."

All day long he kept seeing the faces of the two men C.C. killed.

A Fish and Wildlife officer found what was left of Alabama and the Colombians. The story made the front page of the Raleigh paper, under the headline, *Five Men Found Shot to Death in Hyde County.*

Jack read about it Friday afternoon at the fishing center.

The state man found the two men C.C. killed in the logging road. Sheriff's deputies found the other three about a half mile farther up the road. They had been shot in the head. The reporter played up the drug smuggling angle, describing the truck with its windshield "sprayed with bullets." The story included a DEA agent's statement that the killings had been carried out by rival drug dealers.

Raymond had apparently been able to deliver on his promise to keep them out of it.

Jack had deep regret about the three men C.C. killed He pictured C.C. coming out of the fog, waylaying them on the logging road just when they thought they had escaped with their lives, ordering them to either kneel or lie down so he could give it to them in the back of the head.

Damn murdering bastard. That's why they sent him along. To make sure there were no witnesses.

He didn't want to see either of them again, but he still had to meet Raymond to pick up the money for his crew. After that, he hoped to God he never laid eyes on Raymond Meyers again.

When Billy and Sam came over that night, he was halfway through a fifth of whiskey.

They had read about the murders in the paper and wanted

to know what happened.

"Black Fox killed them," Jack said.

"Why?" Sam asked.

"Damned if I know, Sam."

"They couldn't identify a single one of us," Sam said.

"There wasn't any need to kill those guys," Billy said.

"No, there wasn't. But there's nothing I can do about it now."

"What about the money they owe us?" Sam asked.

"I'm going to pick it up tomorrow evening. Meet me back here at nine, and I'll have it for you."

"I'm going with you," Billy said.

"I want you boys to stay out of this, Billy. Round up Mike and Leon, and meet me back here at nine."

He got to Raymond's yacht at sunset. The clouds looked like they had been dipped in red paint. Thompson, who was waiting for him near the stern, held the transom gate open for him.

"Evening, Mr. Delaney. Mr. Meyers is expecting you."

Raymond was at his desk in his stateroom.

"Hello, Jack." He didn't stand up or offer his hand. Jack was relieved to see C.C. wasn't there.

Raymond asked him if he wanted a drink. "No drink. I'm just here for the money for my men."

"Have a seat."

"That's all right."

Raymond stared at him thoughtfully, balancing the gold letter opener in his right hand.

"C.C. killed three unarmed men," Jack said. "They weren't combatants. They were prisoners."

Ray Meyers shrugged, turned up a meaty palm. He made no comment.

"Why didn't you tell me that was part of the plan?" Jack asked.

"You were hired to do a job. Let's just leave it at that."

"There wasn't any need to kill them."

Meyers shrugged again, as if this was an issue of minor significance.

Hearing a noise behind him, Jack turned around, half-expecting to see C.C.

But it was Nicole, wearing a yellow bikini.

"Excuse me," she said, wide-eyed. "I didn't know you had company."

"We're busy right now," Raymond said.

"I'm sorry, I didn't mean to—"

"I said we're busy!"

Nicole went out and shut the door.

His face flushed, Raymond reached down beneath his desk and brought up the briefcase. Setting it on the desk, he opened it and turned it around so Jack could see it. "Two hundred and twenty thousand. You're welcome to count it."

"That's all right." Jack walked over to the desk, closed the briefcase, and picked it up. "So long, Raymond."

"Goodbye, Jack," Ray said, smiling now. "And thanks for a job well done."

Jack didn't answer. He just wanted to get out of there.

When he stepped out onto the aft deck, he saw Nicole waiting by the transom, her hair and body bronzed by the dying light.

"What's in the briefcase?"

"Bibles."

"Ever read the story of Icarus?"

"No, who's that?"

"A character in Greek myth. He was able to fly, but he went too far up and the sun melted the wax in his wings. He fell into the sea and drowned."

"Don't know much about myths."

"And you don't know what the hell you're getting into,

either."

"If he's so bad, why do you stay with him?" He stepped close to her, thinking how fine she looked in that light. "Why don't you come with me, Nicole?"

"Jack, don't do this. Not now."

"Come on. Just get in the boat and come with me. Leave that asshole for good."

Thompson came through the glass doors onto the aft deck. Nicole looked at him and then turned back to Jack.

"Goodbye, Mr. Delaney."

"Goodbye." He climbed down the ladder, put the briefcase into the V-berth, hit the switch to raise the automatic anchor, and started the engine.

He opened the throttle up and didn't look back. The boat flew over the swells, leaving the sea like a sailfish then coming down on the aft section of her hull, water blowing all around him like a hard rain.

X

Virgil read Jack's journal with a mixture of fascination and horror. His friend's neatly written account explained how he had gotten the money to pay off his drug debt and buy the new trawler, but it did not answer the main question: Who murdered him and the crew of the *Dixie Arrow*? Considering that Jack had slept with his mistress, Raymond Meyers had the means and a possible motive, but it wasn't clear that Meyers had even known about their relationship.

Virgil pictured Ray Meyers in the cabin of the *Eva Marie* that day he had gone along on the charter trip: his arrogant manner, his imperious tone, his thick torso, and meaty hands. He had had no interest in fishing; he had only wanted to set Jack up for his pitch about stealing the cocaine shipment. And Jack, desperate for money after sinking his trawler, had gone along with it. What other crimes had Meyers and his henchmen committed?

He considered taking Jack's journal to the police but soon discarded this idea. Based on his reading of the journal, the operation Jack and his crew had participated in had very possibly been sanctioned by individuals working for some federal agency. If those same people had also been involved in the murders, once they became aware there was a surviving witness to their plot, Virgil was afraid they would want to eliminate him, too. Also, Jack's detailed recollections clearly implicated Meyers and C.C. Thorne in a variety of crimes, but not the murders aboard the *Dixie Arrow*. If Virgil did go to the police, what could they really do? What other evidence was there besides the journal? Couldn't Meyers and his small army of defense attorneys argue that it was a product of Jack's imagination? It was hard enough to send a drug smuggler to prison these days; Jack himself had smuggled marijuana for years. Convicting a man like Raymond Meyers, with his wealth and political connections, would be just this side of impossible. And if Jack and his crew had been killed by drug dealers—perhaps as revenge for the theft of the cocaine—and they learned that Virgil had been aboard the trawler the night of the murders, it was likely that he, too, would disappear. *No bodies, no witnesses.*

His thoughts kept coming back to Jack's missing hand. He kept trying to think of a reason for it, but no matter what angle he considered it from, it didn't make any sense. What would the killers want with his hand?

Virgil felt overwhelmed by a sense of futility and powerlessness. What to do?

"Can I help you?" The man behind the counter asked.

"I'd like to buy some shells for a thirty-eight special."

"What type of shells do you want?"

"I'm not sure."

"What kind of gun do you have?"

"It's a revolver, with a short barrel."

"Two-inch?"

"I think so."

"Is your weapon for home defense?"

"Yes. But I'd also like to do some target shooting."

"I recommend Plus P hollowpoints for defense, and wadcutters for practice."

"What's the difference?"

"Hollowpoints have more power, and they expand when they hit. Makes a bigger hole."

"I'd like a box of the hollowpoints and three boxes of the others."

"How about some targets?"

"Yes, please."

The man put a pack of targets on the counter beside the boxes of shells.

"You going to be doing a lot of shooting, you might want some earplugs, too."

"OK."

He put a box of earplugs on the counter.

"I don't know much about guns," Virgil said. "I just got this one for home defense."

"Small snub-nosed revolvers are great concealment weapons, but their small size and short sight radius makes them a challenge to shoot with accuracy. You should take it out on a range and get familiar with it. Remember to squeeze the trigger, don't jerk it. And hold the weapon in both hands."

"Any other suggestions?"

"If you ever have to use your gun in self-defense, keep shooting."

"Keep shooting?"

"Right. You know these scenes you see on TV, when a cop shoots a bad guy once and he goes down like he's been hit with a telephone pole? That's pure fantasy. In real life people don't always drop like that when they're shot."

"What do they do?"

"Depends on a lot of different factors, the type and caliber of bullet, where the individual is hit, how much alcohol or drugs he has in his system, his mental state at the time. But you can't count on putting a man down with one, two, or even three shots. He might go down and then again he might not. A man can be shot through the heart and still have enough blood left in his brain to send return fire your way a few seconds. Only sure way to stop someone cold is with a head shot that penetrates to the brain or a direct hit to the upper spine."

Virgil nodded, trying to appear casual and relaxed, but his knees felt weak.

"You seem to know a lot about the subject."

"Used to be a cop." The gun store manager put another box on the counter.

"What's that?"

"Earplugs. For your wife. I'll throw them in for free since you are a first-time shooter."

He drove down to Buxton Woods to practice shooting with Jack's revolver. Deep in the woods he parked on the roadbed and walked along a path until he found a clearing with a small hill at the end. The sun was shining and birds were singing in the trees. He tacked one of the targets to a tree in front of the hill and stepped back fifteen paces. He aimed the revolver at the target and fired five shots, surprised by how much the small revolver jumped in his hands. Then he walked to the tree to see how well he had done.

None of the bullets had even hit the target.

He took more time with the next five shots, squeezing the trigger instead of jerking it. When he went to look, only one of the rounds had pierced the upper right corner of the target.

The birds had stopped singing. He didn't blame them; his ears were ringing from the gunshots.

He put up another target, and returning to his position, he inserted the earplugs, reloaded, and squeezed off five more shots. When he went to look, two had hit the target.

By the time he had opened the second box, he was able to

place all five bullets in the targets, but not every shot was in the concentric rings. Some were on the edge of the target.

Next, he paced off five yards from the targets and began practicing shooting quickly—raising the gun from his side and firing three shots in rapid succession. He concentrated on his grip, stance, breathing, and sight picture. By the end of the third box, he was able to put most of his shots in the black rings of the target.

Although it was clear he needed more practice, he felt he had attained a minimum level of competence with Jack's small revolver. He wanted to know how to use it in case the killers came after him.

I want to take some of them with me before I go, he thought, remembering what they had done to Jack and his crew.

On his way back to Nags Head, he stopped at a station in Rodanthe for gas. When he went inside to pay, he overheard a group of men talking about Jack. "I tell you, Jack Delaney is in South America," one said.

"I don't think so," another speaker said. "You look at who was on that trawler with him—the Coultrane boys, Leon McRae, Dave Swain. I can see Delaney faking a fire like that, but not all of them. Swain has a wife and a couple of kids."

"Hurricane Jack is in Peru right now," the other man said. "Coast Guard and the DEA was on his ass. He set that fire himself and got away on another boat."

"Now how the hell do you know that, Roy?"

"I know Jack Delaney. Knowed him ever since he was a boy. Knowed his daddy, too. Jack always was wild as a damn nor'easter."

"I could believe that about Jack, but not all five of them. I say that boat either went down in a storm or else they're still out there somewhere."

"Jack and his crew are down in Brazil, rared back like Brer Rabbit in the briarpatch, laughing at the DEA and the Coast

Guard, too."

Virgil paid for the gas and left. He thought he should stop by Mae's house, but he wasn't ready to face her yet. He was afraid that she would somehow be able to look at him and sense he was hiding something from her.

Miles called to clear up a "point of confusion" about his sabbatical.

"I had lunch with the dean yesterday, and the subject of your sabbatical came up. He wanted to know if you really knew German. I told him I'd get back to him on that."

"Did you explain I was going to hire a collaborator?"

"We didn't get to that point. He seemed concerned about the issue of your fluency in German."

"I can read it well enough. You can tell him that."

"I'm scheduled to meet with him tomorrow. I'll pass it along."

"Thanks, Miles. I really appreciate your help with this."

"Just make sure you come up with some damn good research on Rilke."

"I'll do my best."

At one time, Virgil would have felt guilty for lying to Miles; he couldn't read German any more than he could play the violin. But now his lie, like the rest of his petty sins, seemed insignificant when measured against the monstrous evil he had encountered aboard the *Dixie Arrow*.

Jack's journal had given him a focal point for his quest to find the killers: Raymond Meyers. Even if Meyers didn't have anything directly to do with Jack's death, Virgil had a feeling he could either lead him to the killers or provide him with some clue that would help him identify them. Remembering that Jack had said his company's headquarters was in Norfolk, he drove up to Norfolk, stopped at a phone booth, and looked in the yellow pages under Import/Export. He went down the list, calling each business and asking for Raymond Meyers. At the fourth number, International Military Supply, Inc., a woman said, "I'll transfer you to his secretary."

Virgil hung up.

International Military Supply was a sprawling complex just off Indian River Road in South Norfolk. A fence topped with barbed wire surrounded the complex. There was a security booth at the front gate. Virgil sat in his car, looking at the complex awhile before he drove back to the Outer Banks.

Even if he found out where Raymond Meyers lived, Virgil guessed he would have an elaborate security system, perhaps including armed guards. How could he get close to him—how could he get time alone with him?

It occurred to him that the quickest and easiest way to get to know Raymond Meyers better was through his mistress, Nicole Andrisson.

He would have to figure out a way to get to know her better.

He called Nicole at the magazine office in Nags Head, where she worked.

"I met you in the deep sea fishing trip," he said. "I was the only one who got seasick, and you rescued me with a sandwich."

"Yes, I remember."

"You were reading *Ulysses*."

"Right."

"Anyway, I called to see about an ad. I'm trying to find a typist and a researcher, someone to help me with an academic project I'm working on. I thought maybe the best way to do it would be to run an ad."

"I don't want to lose a sale, but you might try the classifieds."

"I was thinking a display ad might be more effective."

"It's your money. Do you want to come by the office?"

"Could we just get together for a working lunch?" he asked. "I've spent too much time in offices this year."

"Sure. When would you like to go?"

"How about tomorrow?"

They agreed to meet for lunch the next afternoon at a restaurant on the beach road.

That night, he dreamed he and Jack were on the beach at night, beside the body of the dying sperm whale. They were laughing and talking, and Virgil looked away for a moment, his attention caught by a falling star above the sea. The star left behind a beautiful stream of rainbow-colored light. When Virgil looked back, Jack lay dead beside him, his right hand missing. Virgil woke then and sat on the side of the bed a long time, holding his head in his hands.

When he got to the restaurant, the hostess asked him if he was Virgil Gibson.

"Yes," he said. "How did you know?"

"Just a hunch," she said, smiling. "Nicole is upstairs, on the deck."

He went up the stairs to the bar, wondering how Nicole had described him. Five eleven, average build, in his middle thirties. *A description of an ordinary man,* he thought. *Unlike Hurricane Jack Delaney.*

She was sitting at a table on the deck outside the bar, smoking a cigarette. An umbrella set in the center of the table shielded her from the sun. She wore a sleeveless, turquoise sundress, the same color as the sky behind her, and a pale gold gloss on her lips. She was stunningly beautiful, but even as Virgil smiled and said hello, he was thinking Jack might still be alive if not for her.

"I wanted to wait for you up here while I smoked," she said. There was a file folder and a notepad on the table. "I don't like to pollute other people's air."

"That's very considerate."

"It's a nasty habit. I keep quitting and then starting again. My mom says I should try hypnosis."

"Think it would work?"

"Someone tried to hypnotize me once. He said I was a poor subject."

"It seems like that would depend on whether you trusted the hypnotist or not."

"He wore a toupee. Who could trust a man with fake hair?"

Virgil laughed.

"Are you ready to eat?"

"We can have a drink first."

"Fine with me."

Virgil ordered a Dos Equis. Nicole asked for wine.

She opened the folder and took out a rate sheet. "These are our rates. You get a discount if you run your ad more than once."

"How often does the magazine come out?"

"Every two weeks."

"Guess I could run it six weeks."

"You could get a lot of calls from even one ad. Take my advice and just run it once. If you don't find someone, I'll just give you the reduced rate if you have to run it again."

"I appreciate your help. I don't have a lot of experience with ads."

"It's a racket, like everything else. Anyway, the next thing you'll have to decide is the size of the ad."

He looked over the rate sheet and told her he would like to have a quarter of a page.

"That ought to attract plenty of attention."

After she took down the information for the ad, she asked him how he had been.

"OK. But you know I've been worried about my friend Jack Delaney."

At the mention of Jack's name, Nicole's mouth tightened. She gazed steadily at him, her eyes cool and guarded.

"He went to sea two weeks ago, and he was supposed to be

back in a week," Virgil said. "But no one knows where he is. Down in Hatteras, there's a rumor he set fire to his ship and went to South America to live off his drug money. Coast Guard seems to think his ship went down in a storm."

"What do you think?" The expression in her eyes told him she knew all of this.

"That doesn't make any sense. Jack was getting married, and he had just bought a new trawler."

Nicole ground out her cigarette hard in the ashtray. Her aquamarine eyes seemed to have turned a shade or two darker. "How can anyone know what's going to happen from one minute to the next? You lay down your money and hope for the best, right?"

"Kind of like running an ad?"

"You got it."

He could see he had much work to do. He would have to gain her confidence first and then find things out casually, without acting too interested. That would take time, but he had time. And he would be patient. As long as she was still involved with Ray Meyers, Nicole Andrisson was his best chance to learn more about him—and to find out if he knew who had murdered Jack Delaney and the crew of the *Dixie Arrow*.

I want to catch him by surprise, he thought, smiling at her across the table.

The way the killers caught Jack.

XI

Virgil finally got up the nerve to visit Mae.

When she came to the door, her eyes were red. "Hey, Virgil. Come on in. Bobbie just left thirty minutes ago."

"Bobbie Russell?"

"Yes. I held her right here on this couch. And as I held her, I was reminded of the way Elena cried when John Ballance jilted her for that little redhead from Ocracoke. Honey, she let loose a storm that day. I wanted to tell Bobbie everything would work out, but I knew it wouldn't, at least not the way Bobbie wants it to.

"See, Virgil, I know Jack's dead. Been knowing it ever since I had that dream. I was walking by the sea and I saw him riding a dolphin's back. 'I'm gone, Mama, and they won't ever find me so don't worry about looking,' he said, smiling big as life. I couldn't eat for two days."

Virgil didn't know what to say. He had a compulsion to tell her everything that happened, but he knew he could never do it.

"For years I'd been waiting to hear Jubal was lost at sea, but no, he died right in the living room, coughing up blood. Didn't even want me to call the rescue squad. He knew his lungs were full of cancer, and he wanted to go fast. 'Don't try to keep me hanging on, Mae,' he said, even as I was dialing the number. 'I don't want to go on like this, so sick I can't work, can't enjoy my life.'

"The sea took Jack instead. I had him up in that oak in the swamp with the wind howling like a freight train full of devils and the snakes slithering along the branches and Jubal sitting out there on the limb, hollering 'push, Mae, push!' and me laying there in that bed of branches, pushing with all my might, scared when I finally got him out we'd all be burnt up by lightning. After Jack was born, Jubal kept him warm and dry with his raincoat.

"I was so exhausted that night I felt like someone had drained half my blood out, Virgil. But I had never had any words to describe what I felt when Jubal put Jack to my breast and I felt him all warm and wet against me and heard his little cry."

Mae put her face in her hands. Virgil put his arms around her and held her while she cried.

"I've still got Elena and her two kids, and life goes on," she said, after she'd regained control. "It goes on, Virgil, with all the pain and heartache. It goes on. You know Bobbie came here wanting me to tell her Jack might still be alive. But I couldn't tell her that any more than I could jump over the moon, because I know he's dead. We have to just go on living and remember that everything the good Lord gives us He can take away in the blink of an eye. Bobbie's heart is broken now and she's thinking she'll never love again. But she will, Virgil. She won't ever find another man like Jack. But someone else will come along in time, and she'll start all over again with him. And Jack, he'll fade in her memory. He'll become someone she'll think of every once in a while. Some little thing—a song, a smell, a phrase—will bring him back.

"I was born down here on the water. My daddy was a lighthouse keeper, and I was born right up there in Bodie Island Lighthouse, back when they ran it with oil lamps, and I'll stay here till I die. But I was looking at Bobbie and thinking she won't stay here because this is where her hurt is. She'll go somewhere else just to get away from the memory of Jack. I'll get letters from her at first, and then just a postcard or two, and then a card at Christmas, and then maybe not even that. She'll be settled down somewhere with a husband and maybe a couple of kids.

"All the time I was holding her, I knew I would never ever forgive the sea for taking Jack from me. And the Coultrane brothers, and Leon McRae, and that Swain boy from Wanchese, who left a wife and children behind. I saw Sam and Billy's mama and daddy yesterday. They been to see me nearly every day since they got worried. And Leon's mama has come, too, all of them sick with worry. I haven't told them about my dream, but they know, too. You can see it in their eyes. Laverne Ballance lost her boy, Frank, coming through the inlet, and there've been so many others. That's just the way it is when your menfolk go to sea. The sea takes the ones she wants. And every woman who has a man go out there knows he might never come back, and that's why you try to be patient with them and give them as much as you can when you have them because every time they go you know it could be the last time you'll ever see them."

"Was Bobbie OK when she left? Do you think I should call her?"

"I offered to get her a drink of whiskey, Virgil. Guess what she said?"

"What?"

"'I can't drink, Mae.' We just looked at each other then. When I did, I asked, 'Is it Jack's?' Mae's lips trembled. "She said—'yes.'"

"Do you mean—"

Mae took his hand and squeezed it.

"I just said, 'Praise God.'"

XII

On the second Sunday in September, Virgil drove down to Hatteras to attend a memorial service for Jack and the crew of the *Dixie Arrow*. The service was held at the request of the crew's families, for they had given up on the men returning from sea. According to newspaper reports about the missing trawler, no other trawlers had been in contact with Jack after the fierce storm they had endured, and although the ship was still officially declared as "missing," the Coast Guard believed the *Dixie Arrow* had gone down in the storm. The memorial service took place at two p.m. on the beach near the lighthouse, its black and white spirals vivid against the metallic blue sky. When Virgil arrived, the ushers were setting up rows of chairs in the sand for the family members. He saw Mae, Bobbie, and Elena, along with her husband and their two children. Sam and Billy's parents and grandparents were there, along with Leon McRae's mother, Maude, and his father, Leon Sr. He saw Dave Swain's wife and children, two small boys who looked like Dave. And he saw Tammy, Billy's girlfriend, and her son, Evan, both of whom had been at the party on the *Dixie Arrow* at Oden's Dock.

When the minister began speaking, he had to compete with the surf crashing against the beach. A tall man with iron-gray hair, the minister would have had a commanding presence in a church, but he seemed dwarfed by the backdrop of sky and sea. The minister said that death was the end of all heartache and a welcome release from the suffering of the world. He spoke of the "incredible mystery of God" and of the importance of accepting His will in all matters. The minister concluded the service with a passage from Isaiah

At the end of the service, Virgil went over to Mae and put his hand on her shoulder to let her know he was there. Then he walked down the beach, wiping tears from his eyes. Although he grieved for all of the crew, it was Jack's death that made him feel the most diminished, robbed of some essential part of himself. He pictured Jack's face: his blue eyes radiating humor and intelligence, his brown, windblown hair, his thick chest and muscular arms, and, despite his slight limp from the war injury, his confident, purposeful stride. He remembered Jack standing on the bridge that night so long ago, reaching toward the moon before he jumped into the inlet. He wanted to remember him that way. But the image that kept haunting him was Jack sitting against the galley wall, his hair matted against his forehead, his eyes mirroring the rising flames.

On Sunday, the day of the memorial service, Hurricane Gilbert sideswiped Puerto Rico, the Dominican Republic, and Haiti. On Monday, the hurricane ravaged Jamaica, leaving half a million people homeless and damaging or destroying most of the homes on the island. Virgil watched the satellite pictures on TV. The hurricane seemed to be a living thing, a swirling Cyclops of violence and death. It smashed into the Yucatan Peninsula on Wednesday, and after tearing up Cancun and causing widespread flooding, it finally fizzled out. The hurricane seemed a fitting finale to a year of apocalypse—a

Midwest drought, forest fires in the U.S., rainforests torched in the Amazon, mass starvation and floods in Sudan and Bangladesh. At night he lay in bed, listening to rain pounding the roof and the wind howling off the ocean. The earth seemed such a dangerous place.

He dreamed he was walking by the sea, stepping around tidal pools in the sand. A cloud of light gathered above one of the pools, and it slowly formed into Jack. Then more dead people formed out of the water in the same way, from clouds of misty light. A crowd gathered on the beach, talking about the dead people who had formed above the tidal pools. Jack was trying to tell them something, but he floated away before Virgil could hear what it was.

In his dream, he ran down the beach after him, shouting "Jack, Jack!"

Virgil had lunch with Nicole again. He had gotten no solid responses for his ad for a research assistant—someone fluent in German. He knew it unlikely that a small local newspaper would yield anyone with such credentials. Virgil's primary purpose with the ad was to get to know Nicole better, to establish a relationship with her, so he declared his interest in running a bigger ad. She advised him against it. "You need to try a different venue. I doubt if many readers of *Sea and Sound* know German."

"I'll try one more time," he said. And he invited her to eat lunch with him again the following week.

He was working hard to engage her interest, to win her trust. She enjoyed talking about books and music. She said she was still reading *Ulysses,* along with a key she had found somewhere that was helping her understand the novel's symbolism and Homeric parallels. She admired the French writers, Colette and Camus, both of whom she called "brilliant." She described Anne Beattie as "a bit too much of a minimalist for me." She believed Norman Mailer was overrated, and she was mystified by his success. On their third lunch date, after her second glass of wine, she opened up a little about Ray Meyers. She referred to him as "the man I'm seeing now" and said she spent most weekends with him on his yacht.

"I believe I met him on the *Eva Marie*," Virgil said.

"That's right."

"Where do you go when you are on the yacht?"

"Sometimes we go down to Charleston to eat at a restaurant he likes down there. Other times we just stay off the coast or go to Ocracoke. We go other places, too. I've been spearfishing a few times in the Keys. I really liked that."

"Do you walk around Ocracoke?"

"Sometimes. Why?"

"Just wondered. I guess I'm just fascinated by how rich people live."

"They have to wipe their asses, too, Virgil."

"Yes," he said. "I know."

On Thursday after the memorial service, he called Nicole and invited her to lunch.

"I don't want to talk to you about an ad," he said. "I just enjoy your company."

Nicole said she was tied up with clients for the next few days and suggested he come to her place for supper on Friday night.

"Fine. Where do you live?"

She gave him directions to her cottage in Kitty Hawk.

"Come on over about seven-thirty."

"Will that be OK with Mr. Meyers?" Virgil was trying to be lighthearted, but Nicole didn't see any humor in his comment.

"It's none of his business," she said.

It was raining when he got to her cottage. She answered the door wearing skintight jeans and a white tank top, with no bra underneath. Virgil could see her nipples under the cotton. As she took his raincoat, he smelled wine on her breath.

She asked him what he would like to drink.

"I'll just take a glass of wine."

"Red or white?"

"Red."

While she went to her kitchen to get him the wine, he looked at the three framed watercolors on the walls—two rural landscapes and a scene of a girl running in the woods during a storm.

When she returned with the wine, he asked her about the paintings.

"My grandma painted them."

"She's really quite good."

"Who's the girl?"

"Me. My grandma said I was always running into the wind."

"Is that true?"

"It was, then. I don't know about now."

"These paintings have a rural feel."

"She lives on a farm in the Shenandoah Valley."

"That where you're from?"

"No. My mom escaped to the suburbs. Her family still lives back there, though."

"Why'd she leave?"

"She wanted to be an actress. She moved to Washington D.C., an intended stop on her eventual way to New York. But she ended up marrying a Marine and following him around. She always claimed she gave up on her career to be a wife and mother."

"Sounds like talent runs in your family."

"It ended with me."

"Really?"

"I used to paint a little. And write poetry. That was before..."

He looked at her, waiting. But she didn't complete her sentence.

"Before what?"

"Before I wised up. Hey, you ready to eat?"

"Sure."

They ate in the dining room adjoining her kitchen. Nicole served seafood pasta with shrimp, scallops, garlic butter, scallions, and sundried tomatoes. Virgil had two servings, but he noticed Nicole didn't each much. She mostly drank wine.

Up until then, he had been careful to avoid asking her many personal questions, but their discussion about the paintings had opened a door, presenting him with an opportunity to learn more about her.

"If your dad was a Marine, you must have moved around a lot."

"That's right. Had to learn how to leave people behind."

"Did you have any brothers?"

"No, just one older sister. My father was hoping for a boy, but he got me instead."

"Doesn't sound like such a bad deal."

"Thanks, but I don't think he felt that way. He even had a boy's name all picked out—Nicholas. I got the feminine form, Nicole."

A career officer in the United States Marine Corps, Nicole's father had served in Korea and Vietnam and retired as a general in 1975. She described him as a distant, reserved man who believed in keeping his feelings under control. "My dad was Scandinavian, all the way back. My mother said my father was a cool customer, but only on the surface. He had a volcanic temperament underneath."

"Does that describe you, too?"

Nicole smiled. "You know the Vikings were farmers during part of the year, but they had to go to sea every so often to rape and plunder. It's that Viking blood."

"Is that why your father became a Marine?"

"Who knows? But the Marines were his whole life, even

after he retired. You know, the first song I ever learned was the "Marines' Hymn." He taught it to me, word for word. I could sing it all the way through when I was five years old."

She said that when her father invited his fellow officers and their wives over, he would often summon her to sing this song. "Andrisson," he would bark out, "front and center!" And sporting a tiny replica of a Marine dress hat, she would march to the center of the room to sing it.

Nicole said she still had a tape of her singing the hymn. Virgil told her he would like to hear it.

"Really?"

"Yes."

She left the kitchen and returned a couple of minutes later, setting a small cassette recorder on the table. "Here's a real stroll down memory lane." Virgil thought he detected an undercurrent of pain in her voice.

Nicole pushed the play button. After some background voices, he heard an authoritative male voice say, "It's time to get Private Andrisson out here to sing. All right, where's Private Andrisson? Andrisson, front and center!" This was followed by laughter and a child's tinny, off-key voice singing.

Nicole kept her eyes closed while the tape played. When it was over, she told him more about her father. He worked out with weights and jogged to maintain his two-hundred-and-ten-pound body. But he was diagnosed with liver cancer at fifty-eight, and nine months later he had wasted away to one hundred and forty. The night her mother called her in to watch him die, Nicole was nineteen years old and pregnant by a third-year medical student at the University of Virginia. Her father had tubes in his nose, another tube in his penis. "I want you to sing for me, Nicole," he'd said.

So she had stood there and sung that dumb song for him. Afterward, she bent over him and said, "Daddy, I love you."

He slipped into a coma that night and died the next day.

Three days after her father's funeral, she had an abortion in Norfolk. She had always wondered if the baby would have been a boy.

After they cleaned off the table, Nicole asked if he wanted to watch the Olympic preview on television.

They sat on the couch in the living room and watched a group of skydivers, holding hands to form the Olympic symbol, falling toward the Olympic Stadium in Seoul. Their chutes burst into colors like blossoms. A group of Korean children began dancing a welcome dance for the athletes, who had come from all over the world to compete.

In the middle of their dance, the screen went blank.

"It's the cable," Nicole said. "It went off last night, too."

She turned the TV off and they just sat there, sipping wine, listening to the rain on the roof of the cottage. Nicole stretched out on her stomach in front of the TV, her wineglass on the floor. Virgil's eyes lingered on the curve of her buttocks in the tight jeans. He had tried to make love to his wife, Allison, from behind once, but she had refused. "That's the way animals do it," she said. "Do you want to make me feel like a dog?"

He stood up and began looking through Nicole's albums.

"If you find one you like, you can put it on."

He picked out a Merle Haggard album, *That's The Way Love Goes*, and put it on her turntable. He had just settled back on the couch when she got up and took the needle off the album.

"I'm sorry. I can't listen to that tonight."

"You can pick something."

"No, you're my guest. Pick anything but that."

He put on an album by Joan Armatrading. Nicole pulled her feet up under her on the couch and rested her head on her knees. They sat there listening to the singer's husky voice. Virgil was curious about Nicole's reluctance to listen to the Merle Haggard album. What was *that* about?

"Are you going out on the *Victory* tomorrow?" he asked.

"Huh?" She gazed at him, her mind somewhere else. Her mood had definitely changed. She seemed possessed by a deep sense of sorrow.

Virgil repeated his question, and she nodded.

"How do you get out there?"

"Raymond's man picks me up in a boat."

When the album ended, she stood up to put the other side on. He couldn't take his eyes off her body while she changed the record.

She walked back to the couch and sat down close beside him. He could smell her tangy, feminine scent—a mixture of sunscreen, sweat, and lime—and feel her thigh touching his. He felt a sudden rush of desire for her.

Remember why you're here, he thought. An image of Jack's body flashed in his mind, and the desire was replaced by a dull familiar ache. Finding the killers is what this is all about, he told himself, not flirting with Raymond Meyers's girlfriend.

After the record finished playing, he stood up. "It's getting late. Guess I'll be heading on home."

"You don't have to go, Virgil."

"I know. But I'd better, anyway. Thanks for the excellent dinner."

He drove home in the rain. Did she want to sleep with him or was she just being friendly?

He lay in bed for a long time, trying to sleep, unable to stop his mind from working, unable to stop thinking about Jack.

Early the next morning he drove to the Kitty Hawk Pier and walked south along the beach, his binoculars around his neck. He saw a white yacht anchored about a mile out from the old Coast Guard station, near the four-mile post. It was the *Victory*. He watched it from behind a dune. Soon he saw some activity on the yacht, a skiff being lowered into the water. Through the binoculars he watched the skiff pull away from the yacht and head toward the beach. He swung the binoculars south and saw

Nicole, waiting on the beach near the station. She had on jeans and a black leather jacket. When the skiff neared the shore, she waded into the surf and the man operating the skiff helped her aboard.

He wanted to get aboard the yacht, but how?

In the afternoon, he checked his mailbox and found the catalogue he had ordered from International Military Supply. It was addressed to "Sam Waterford," the name he had used when he had written to request it. The catalogue contained ads for truncheons, handcuffs, boots, uniforms, thermal underwear, knives, blackjacks, radios, chains, body armor, and many other items. Some of them seemed chilling. On page thirty-seven there was an "electric cattle prod," and on page fifty-six, a blindfold and gagging device.

At the front of the catalogue there was a "note from the president."

International Military Supply is the world's premier provider of supplies for police and military units. In an era of increasingly shoddy merchandise, we strive to provide high quality items at a reasonable cost to our clients. For that reason, we have thousands of satisfied customers throughout the free world. In order to be included in our catalogue all products must pass rigorous field tests, and many items do not meet our high standards. Nevertheless, every product we sell is backed by our guarantee that it can be returned for a full refund if the buyer is not completely satisfied

Cordially,
Raymond Meyers

Virgil studied his signature, noting the exaggerated capital letters, the loops and flourishes. He could picture Meyers holding the pen in his beefy hand, writing in bold strokes. He thought about him in bed with Nicole and felt an immediate repulsion.

What does she see in him besides his money? he wondered.

Maybe that was the only answer.

Still, there was something about Nicole—an aloof and cynical inwardness—that suggested her motives might be more complex than mere gold digging. He thought that after he knew her awhile longer, more of the mystery of Nicole might be revealed.

He drove up to Chapel Hill and found Rilke's untranslated poems in the graduate library of the university. Since he had received no encouraging responses from his ad in *Sea and Sand*, he put up a notice on the bulletin board in the language department advertising for someone fluent in German to work on "a research topic." He included his number at the cottage. At another time, Virgil would have been excited about his research project and the opportunity to work on it in his cottage by the sea, but now he was preoccupied with thoughts of Raymond Meyers. His interest in finding out more about him was complicated by a potential new problem: his growing desire for Nicole. He couldn't stop thinking about her. It wasn't just her beauty; something else about Nicole focused his thoughts on her. Her coolness, perhaps. The Zen-like way she had of seeming to detach herself from a situation to become an ironic observer. But Virgil's attraction to her was accompanied by fear and distrust: he couldn't help from wondering how much she knew about the murders aboard the *Dixie Arrow*.

He spent the night at his mother's apartment in Raleigh. When they had lived in Hatteras, their home had been full of his father's presence: his books, paintings, fishing gear, the aroma of his pipe tobacco. But his mother's sense of order dominated her surroundings now. The only sign of his father was his image in a photograph on the dresser in her bedroom.

As usual, she was delighted to see him, and she insisted on taking him down to the complex's recreational center to talk to her friends, all widows he had met on earlier visits.

Later in the evening, her friend Newton Groves came over to the apartment to watch the Olympic swimming competition on TV. Bald and wrinkled, Newton looked to be at least ten years older than his mother, who was sixty-eight. He fell asleep soon after the swimming competition.

"Newton is just a friend," his mother said at breakfast the next morning. "So don't be getting any ideas. You know your father spoiled me for any other man in this lifetime."

"He wouldn't want you to be lonely, Mama." Virgil said this to ease any embarrassment she might have felt about Newton, but his comment didn't seem to help. His mother was quiet and withdrawn the rest of the morning.

That evening, on his way back to the Outer Banks, he took the Indian Creek exit and drove to Laurel College. He let himself into the building with his key and went to his office. There he located copies of his syllabi for the dean's niece, who would be teaching two of his classes. On impulse, he called up Allison. He told her he was just passing through town and wanted to give her a call to see how she was doing.

He heard a man's voice in the background. Allison covered the mouthpiece and said something unintelligible. "Virgil, could you call back another time? I've got company."

"Of course."

She thanked him for calling before they hung up.

Curious about who was with her, he considered driving by her house just to see if he could recognize a car parked outside. He immediately decided not to do this, however. He didn't want her to nurture a grievance against him. As he thought about this, he suddenly realized he wanted her forgiveness, too, for he had a lingering sense of guilt for ending their marriage.

The fault lay with him, not her. They had gotten married

under a certain contract, but his needs had changed, and the old contract didn't work for him anymore. Although their marriage had failed, he didn't see why there couldn't be mutual respect between them and perhaps one day, a kind of friendship.

As he left Indian Creek, he recalled a conversation he'd had with Sam and Billy one afternoon on the *Dixie Arrow*. Billy had asked him if he thought he would ever get back with his wife, and he said, "No."

"When that fire has died," Sam said, "can't nothing bring it back."

"I don't know about that," Billy said. "I've heard of people who get divorced and then remarried again. Nick Gunderson over in Wanchese divorced his wife and then married her again."

"But the fire hadn't ever gone out. What I'm saying is, when the fire is gone, that's it."

Rocked by the pitch and roll of the sea, he had lain on the bunk, listening to them argue. Both then and now, Allison seemed like someone he had known in another life.

The last ten days in September were cool and rainy. Most tourists had left after Labor Day, and when he went for his daily walks on the beach, he saw only a few surf fishermen. He didn't call Nicole. Although he thought about her often, every time he considered calling her, his will seemed frozen. He had slipped into a mental limbo, a retreat from desire. He spent hours reading and walking on the beach. His reading of Rilke's poetry, with its hypnotic intimate voice, its emphasis on hidden yearnings, drew him deeper and deeper into himself. The poet's lines reverberated in his mind while he walked by the sea:

Exposed on the cliffs of the heart. Stoneground
Under your hands. Even here, though,

something can bloom; on a silent cliff-edge
an unknowing plant blooms, singing, into the air.

A dream shook him out of his lethargy. In the dream, he was back on the *Dixie Arrow*, looking down at the carnage from above. He saw Sam and Billy both get shot, saw the flashes of gunfire from the trawler. The dream landscape shifted to an island, with palm trees and a beautiful, dark-skinned woman lying in the sand. A yacht, shining white in the sun, was anchored about a half mile away. In the tree above the woman there was a parrot and a monkey. The parrot and monkey were communicating to each other, exchanging information about the murders. Virgil kept trying to hear what they were saying, but he couldn't make out the words. He began running toward them, along a sunlit beach. He ran a long time, but no matter how fast he ran he could get no closer to them, and at last, they faded from his sight.

He woke up with his heart pounding, imagining there was someone in his cottage. He grabbed Jack's revolver from the nightstand and walked around the cottage, making sure no one was there.

It was almost daylight. He got up and sat at the kitchen table, drinking coffee. It occurred to him that if he could get aboard Meyers's yacht, he might be able to find some key piece of evidence that would implicate him in the murders. If he didn't find anything, perhaps he could move on somehow, by convincing himself that he had done everything he could to bring the killers to justice.

Even if I fail, I've got to try, he thought. I've got to do it for Jack and the crew.

He wished he could turn the problem over to someone else, but *there's no one else to do this but me.*

On the last two Fridays in September, he set up a morning vigil behind the dunes in Kitty Hawk and recorded the times the yacht arrived: twelve-thirty and one-thirty, respectively. And he ordered more items from International Military Supply: a tube of camouflage paint, black cotton gloves, a set of lock-picking tools, and an inflatable raft which, according to the catalogue, could be used "for night assaults." The raft came with two oars.

He received four phone inquiries about his ad on the bulletin board: two from graduate students, one from an assistant professor, and one from a West German woman working on a master's in public health at UNC. Although she had never read Rilke, she had at least heard of him, and she said she enjoyed reading. He liked her best of the four applicants, all of whom he interviewed over the phone. He told her she had the job and offered to pay her ten dollars an hour.

"How do you plan to keep up with my time," she asked. Her name was Gretchen Bauer.

"I'll just trust you."

"You're the second trusting American I've met."

"Who's the first?"

"My dog."

He laughed. "Thanks, I think."

He got her address so he could mail her copies of the poems. They agreed to talk on the telephone in two weeks.

In early October, he received the items he had ordered from IMS. The lock-pick set had a series of picks and tensioning wrenches. Using the instruction booklet that came with the set, he practiced on the front and back doors of his cottage until he could open them without the key. He wanted to be able to get into desks and cabinets, too, so one night he made another trip to Laurel College, let himself into the locked building with his key and, using the tools and the tensioning wrenches, practiced on the locks on both his desk and his file cabinet, until he could get into them without much trouble. He had to keep the tensioning wrench in the lock at the same time he was inserting the picks and pushing up the series of pins within the lock. This required time and patience, but after a couple of hours he was able to get into all three locked areas without a key.

The first cloudy night, he took the raft down to a deserted section of the beach. Inflating the raft with a bicycle pump, he launched it into the surf. The raft wasn't designed for the sea, but after he got out over the big swells, he could row it fairly well. As long as the sea wasn't too rough, the raft should get him out to Meyers's yacht.

Now what he needed was to get on the *Victory* and learn where everything was—and figure out how to get on it without waking anyone up or setting off any alarms. He was going to have to drop a hint with Nicole and see if she would take the bait.

But he put off calling her. Each morning for three days straight he resolved to call her, and each time he delayed, telling himself he would do it the next day.

When he finally called her, the woman who answered the phone said Nicole wasn't in and asked if he wanted to leave a message. "Tell her Virgil called," he said.

He went for a walk on the beach. The sky was overcast, and there was a strong northeast wind. The heavy surf had churned up a mass of iridescent bubbles on the beach. As he crushed them under his feet, they reminded him how fragile and ephemeral all life was. One day he would be dead, too, like Jack and Sam and Billy. Why couldn't he just accept the killings as fate and leave them up to God to judge?

Maybe there is no God, he thought. Maybe we are all there is.

If that was the case, who else but he, himself, could avenge Jack's death? The killers would have escaped punishment, not only in this life but for all of eternity.

When he got back to the cottage, his phone was ringing.

It was Nicole.

"It's been one of those days when life makes about as much sense as staring down a rathole," she said.

"That's a vivid description of your misery," he said. "Can I buy you lunch tomorrow?"

"I'm tied up with clients at lunch. How about dinner?"

"Sounds great. My treat, your choice."

"That's an offer I can't refuse."

"What time do you want me to pick you up?"

"I'll be ready at six-thirty."

They went to a seafood restaurant in Kill Devil Hills. Nicole seemed melancholy, out of sorts.

"I've backslid again in the smoking department," she said, lighting a cigarette. "Seems to happen every time I get depressed."

"What's the problem?"

"Part of it's my job. We're having trouble selling ads now that the tourists are gone. But the Norfolk office doesn't understand this is a seasonal economy. They keep hounding us to sell more ads. When our regional vice president visits, he keeps dropping these not-so-subtle hints about layoffs if we don't perform. All the ad reps are feeling the pressure."

"At least you have the *Victory* to get away to on the weekend."

"Oh, right," she said, without enthusiasm.

"I'd love to spend some time on a yacht, just to see what it's like."

"That can be arranged."

"It could? That would be great—only I wouldn't want to intrude on your relationship with Raymond."

"I wouldn't worry about that."

He was trying to think of a way to suggest a particular day to visit when she asked him how his research was going.

"Good," he said. "This morning I was reading some poems Rilke wrote about Christ. Rilke saw Christ as a negative figure with no real answers for human suffering. In one poem, 'The Night,' Christ spends the night with a prostitute who tells him, 'Come, don't be a fool. I know something better than gloomily dreaming your life away.'"

"Does he sleep with her?"

"Yes, and in the morning he admits *'Ich Bin Kein Gott,'* which means 'I am not God.'"

"That reminds me of the Scorcese film everyone's been talking been about—*The Last Temptation of Christ.* Have you seen it?"

"No, but I'd like to. Did you know some theaters have pulled it?"

"I read about that. The director has even received death threats."

"People sure can get their noses out of joint about religion. They don't want their cherished beliefs challenged."

"It's all a big fairy tale."

"What—religion?"

"All of it."

"Do you really think so?"

"Look around you. Have you seen any signs of God lately?"

"I don't know," he said, remembering his sense of angst while walking on the beach.

"What's really sacred?"

"What do you think?"

"It's up to the individual to decide," Nicole said. "Don't you think?"

He shook his head, thinking of Jack and Mae. "No. I don't."

Nicole shrugged and ground her cigarette out in the ashtray. "So when do you want to visit the yacht?"

"Anytime."

"Come over to my place this Saturday morning at eight-thirty. We can watch *The Last Temptation of Christ* on the yacht."

"Raymond has it on video already?"

"He has the film."

"I'm impressed."

"Ray can get anything he wants," Nicole said.

Virgil was surprised by the bitter edge in her voice.

Saturday morning he drove to Nicole's cottage.

He arrived a few minutes early, so they had time for a cup of coffee. She sat across from him at her table in the kitchen, her hair pulled back from her face and held in back with a pink band. She had on a black V-neck knit shirt, jeans, and tennis shoes. She wore a pale gold gloss on her lips.

"Does he know I'm coming?"

"I told him last night when he called."

"How'd he react?"

"What can he say? You should see some of the creepy friends he's got. On the other hand, I'm proud to have a friend like you."

"Why's that?"

"Fishing for a compliment?"

"Sure."

"Here's three: you're intelligent, funny, and decent."

Virgil was a little piqued by the word "decent." It sounded like a term a woman would use to describe a man she considered boring and ordinary. He wondered what she would think if she knew he was trying to ferret out information to convince a jury that her lover was a killer.

She drove them to a restaurant parking lot in Kitty Hawk. Virgil asked if it was all right to leave her car parked there.

"Sure."

"Couldn't you get towed?"

"Ray pays the owner a monthly fee so I can park there."

He arranges everything to the last detail, Virgil thought.

They crossed the road and walked down to the beach to

wait for Meyers's man. The yacht looked to be anchored about a mile out.

"How do they get the boat down into the water?"

"They raise and lower it on an electronic winch." Nicole looked at her watch. "He should be leaving right now."

A moment later, he saw the boat pulling away from the yacht.

"Gary is just like a clock," Nicole said.

While they waited, they played a game of tic-tac-toe in the sand, drawing the letters with their feet. Virgil had fun doing this, until it occurred to him that Meyers might be watching them through binoculars from the yacht.

Mcyers's man brought the boat in close to the shore, and they only had to wade a few feet in the icy water to reach it. Nicole and Virgil sat at the bow while Thompson guided the skiff over the swells toward the yacht, white and shining in the sun.

He steered the skiff to the stern, and Nicole climbed out onto the swim platform. Virgil followed her up the ladder and through the transom gate onto the cockpit. A boom with two chains attached swung out from the top deck. Thompson hooked the chains to metal rings at either end of the skiff. Virgil and Nicole watched from the aft deck as the winch lifted the skiff up over their heads and set it down on the top deck.

"Come on, Virgil," Nicole said. "I'll give you the fifty-cent tour."

They went through sliding glass doors into the main salon. She hung their jackets in a narrow closet to the starboard side of the glass doors. They went through a door at the end of the salon into a combination galley and dining area. The galley gleamed with appliances and wood grain surfaces, all in teak and red and black.

"As you can see, there are all the modern conveniences." She took him through another door and up a flight of steps to the wheelhouse. The levers, gauges, and dials were all set in a teak console, and the wheel itself was teak. He ran his hand over the console, thinking how sophisticated and luxurious Meyers's wheelhouse was compared to the one aboard the *Dixie Arrow*. Down on the side of the console, he saw a ring of keys hanging on a hook.

"What are the keys to?"

"Spare keys for the rooms."

Someone was coming up the steps—a man wearing a navy blazer and white pants.

"Welcome to the *Victory*," he said, holding out his hand. "I'm Captain Clay Douglas."

"Virgil Gibson."

"Clay, we're going to watch a film. Can you ask Gary to set everything up?"

"Sure. What film would you like to see?"

"*The Last Temptation of Christ*."

They returned to the galley. A second door, to starboard, opened onto a flight of stairs that led to the lower deck. On the way down, Virgil checked the walls for surveillance cameras or electronic eyes but didn't see any. The stairs ended in a hallway with doors at either end.

"That's the crew's quarters," Nicole said, nodding toward the forward door. "There are two bedrooms, a galley, and a head in there."

"They have their own kitchen?"

"Yes. Class lines are rigidly maintained at sea."

The aft door opened onto a hallway with two guest staterooms on either side. Each room had a queen-sized bed, sofas, chairs, bookshelves, television, and a private head.

The door at the end of the hall opened onto the master bedroom. The carpet, sofas, and bedspread were fire-engine red. Nicole sat on the king-sized bed while he looked around the stateroom. Sliding panel doors opened onto the closets on the starboard side. A door immediately to the portside of the closets opened onto the head. It had a Jacuzzi, marble counters, and gold-plated faucets.

There was a third door near the portside.

"What's beyond that door?" he asked.

"Ray's office. He's in there working."

"Isn't he coming out to watch the movie with us?"

"He doesn't like religious movies."

Nicole unfastened her hair at the back, letting it tumble onto her shoulders. "You look a little spooked, Virgil."

"Guess I'm not used to so much luxury."

"Relax, it's all about personal pleasure."

They went back up the stairs, through the galley and into the salon, where Thompson was winding film onto a projector. Nicole asked if he wanted something to drink.

"No, thanks."

Crossing to the bar, she poured herself a glass of wine and then returned to sit on the sofa.

"Where does that door lead to?" He nodded at a door on the port side of the sliding glass doors.

"Down to Ray's office."

She sipped the wine, watching him thoughtfully. It suddenly occurred to him that his questions were too obvious. Nicole was very quick and observant, and he would need to be more careful in his quest to learn more about Raymond Meyers.

"I can't imagine having enough money to own something like this," he said. "It's a little unreal."

"This is what having money is all about. Creating a safe little world around you—to insulate yourself from the big ugly one outside."

"How are the rich different from you and me?" He wanted to move her past whatever she had been thinking when she had been studying him so carefully a moment before.

She frowned, brushing strands of gold hair out of her eyes.

"They have more freedom."

And more *power,* he thought, but he didn't say it.

"My favorite character was Judas," Nicole announced at lunch.

"Why Judas?" Meyers asked. He was sitting at the head of the table in the galley; Nicole sat to his left and Virgil was across from her, to Meyers's right. Lunch, served by Thompson, was poached salmon, rice pilaf, a cheese quiche, and buttered asparagus.

"I liked his animal magnetism."

"He was actually the strongest of the apostles," Virgil said, looking at Meyers. "And in this version, he never actually betrays Christ. Jesus knew what his fate was, and he asked Judas to tell the Roman soldiers where to find him—in the garden at Gethsemane."

"Judas weeps when Christ asks him to turn him in," Nicole said.

"Is that why people are so pissed off about the film, because of Judas?"

"It's the sex that's got them upset," Nicole said. "In the dream sequence, when Jesus is on the cross, Satan tempts him by showing him what his life would be like if he didn't die. He pictures himself having sex with Mary Magdalene, fathering children."

Meyers waved his hand, as if to dismiss this as a trivial concern. The diamond on his little finger sparkled in the light from the window.

"Let's play a little game," he said. "Professor Gibson, I want you to think of the animal that you most admire, and then let us see if we can guess what it is."

Virgil was immediately on guard, but not wanting to offend his host, he shrugged and said, "OK."

"Ready?"

"Sure." The only creature he could think of was the sperm whale he had seen dying on the beach.

"Nicole?"

She looked at Virgil. "A horse?"

Virgil smiled, wanting to play along, to appear transparent. After all, horses seemed harmless enough. "Yes! How'd you know?"

"Just a lucky guess."

"I wouldn't say that," Meyers said. "Horses have certain characteristics, don't they? Your turn, Nikki."

She had that cool, guarded look now.

"Want to guess her animal, Virgil?"

Virgil sensed Meyers was trying to trap him somehow or else use him to make a point. But what was it? He would have to play along with the game, being careful not to make a wrong move. Nicole reminded him of a cat, but he didn't want to reveal that to their host. He decided to just pick an animal at random to prevent him from gaining any insight into how he perceived her.

"An antelope?"

Nicole shook her head.

"An eagle?"

"No. Not even close."

"A wolf?"

"No."

"I give up," he said. "Raymond?"

"Nikki would most like to be a fox."

"Oh, is that right?"

Sensing the tension between them, he moved to defuse it.

"Let's guess you, Raymond."

"Nikki hasn't told us her secret animal yet."

"Otter," she said.

"Otters are playful, happy creatures aren't they?" Virgil said.

"Fox is your animal, Nikki."

"Let's guess Raymond now," Virgil said. "I'd say bear."

"No," Nicole said. "Python is more like it."

"My animal is the panther," Meyers said. He looked at Virgil. "Ever seen a panther?"

"Only in zoos."

"It's quite an experience to stare into a panther's eyes. The eyes of a dog, even a cat, can look surprisingly human at times. But a panther—never. Look into a panther's eyes—it's like looking into the eyes of nature itself. A panther's eyes are hard and cold and stripped of mercy."

"Sounds like you're very familiar with panthers," Virgil said.

"I owned one once. Had the idea I could tame the animal. I hand-fed it, talked to it through its cage, stared into its eyes. I made the mistake of turning my head once while I was at his cage, looking away at someone who had spoken to me, and he raked his claws across my scalp. It was just a little love tap, but it took twelve stitches to close the wound."

"I didn't know you owned a panther, Ray," Nicole said.

"There are a lot of things you don't know, Nikki."

"What happened to the panther?" Virgil asked.

"I killed it."

"That was stupid," Nicole said. "A waste."

"You killed it for scratching you? Couldn't you have donated it to a zoo or something?"

"I didn't kill it because it scratched me. I killed it because it reminded me of my error in judgment."

They finished lunch in an awkward silence. Afterward, Meyers said he had work to do, and he went back down to his office. Nicole invited Virgil up to the top deck, to sunbathe and look at the sea.

"I'll be up after I visit the head."

"You can use one of guest rooms if you want."

As he went through the galley, he passed by Thompson

cleaning up. "Great lunch. My compliments to the chef."

"Thank you, sir."

He went down the stairs to the lower deck, checking the walls for electronic eyes or signs of surveillance cameras. After using the head, he studied the locks on the doors to the staterooms. They looked like conventional locks. Nothing special there. All three doors were locked by bolts from the inside.

He went back upstairs, through the galley. Thompson was putting dishes into the dishwasher. Virgil could hear Aretha Franklin's voice, singing from the top deck. Somehow Aretha's gospel-inspired singing seemed out of place on the yacht, with its teak and stainless steel surfaces, its emphasis on luxury and comfort. Moving through the main salon, he walked toward the door to Meyers's office, intending to go down the stairs and look for security devices. He had his hand on the knob when he heard footsteps beyond the door—someone coming up the steps. He whirled and headed toward the bar.

The door opened. He turned around and saw Meyers.

"I was going to get a drink from the bar," he said.

"Where's Thompson?"

"Cleaning up."

"What would you like?"

"Brandy."

Meyers walked to the bar. "Looks like we're out of brandy up here."

"I'll just take a beer then."

"I've got some brandy in my office. Come on down."

He followed Meyers through the door, down a flight of stairs and through another door to his office. The door had a conventional lock, no deadbolt. The office, full-width and about eighteen feet long, was furnished with two sofas, several chairs, a coffee table, a bookshelf, two cabinets, and a large desk, forward. There was a computer on the desk. The door to

Meyers's bedroom was to the portside of his desk.

He took a bottle and glass from a cabinet attached to the portside of the room and poured Virgil a glass.

"Thank you."

"So you like Nikki, huh?"

"She's an interesting person."

"An interesting person with a fine mind—is that right?"

"Yes."

Meyers sat down at his desk, folded his hands together and smiled. "You know your animal isn't the horse."

"No?"

"Weasel is more like it."

"I've never actually seen a weasel."

"Then I suggest you look in the mirror," Meyers said.

Virgil drank the brandy down fast and set the glass on his desk.

"I'd better let you get back to your work. Thanks for the drink."

Stepping outside of the office, Virgil closed the door and stood still a moment as he struggled to control his rising anger. He studied the lock on the door and then scanned the walls for hidden cameras or electronic eyes, but if there was anything there, it was too well-concealed for him to notice it.

He climbed the stairs to the salon. Aretha was singing, "Freeway of Love" from the top deck. The yacht looked too easily accessible. He must have a security system aboard, Virgil thought.

He went back through the salon to the galley. Thompson had gone, and the dishwasher was running. He opened the door and went up the steps to the wheelhouse. Picking up the keys from the peg beside the console, he put them into his pocket and went out to the aft deck. He began trying the keys in the exterior lock of the sliding glass door. When he found the right key, he took it off the ring and put it in his pocket.

He was returning the other keys to the peg when he heard someone on the steps.

"Something I can help you with?" Clay Douglas asked.

"No, thanks," Virgil said, running his hand over the console. "I was just admiring the navigation equipment."

"It's state-of-the-art. We've got satellite communications with telex and telfax, a teleprinter telex, and Interface FIU Weather facsimile. Also the newest radar units and Loran receivers."

"Sounds very high-tech."

"Be glad to give you a demonstration."

"Thanks, but I probably wouldn't understand it."

Virgil went up the spiral staircase to the fly bridge, then out to the top deck. Nicole was lying on an air mattress in front of the skiff, listening to her tape player—Aretha singing "Pink Cadillac." She was on her stomach, moving her body to the music.

He sat down beside her. The skiff, secured to the deck with chains, shielded them from the wind. He saw twin images of his face mirrored in her sunglasses. Suddenly, he saw her beauty as a dark and dangerous thing. *If Jack hadn't have been so damned attracted to you, maybe he'd still be alive.*

"I'm sorry Raymond was such an ass at lunch," she said. "I don't know what got into him."

"I ran into him in the bar, and he took me down to his office for a drink of brandy."

She turned down the music. "What'd you talk about?"

"Not much. He told me my secret animal was the weasel."

"He can be a jerk."

"I hope I haven't caused you any trouble."

"Don't worry about it."

Virgil looked up at the flags—one American, the other Virginian—rippling on the mast. The quickest and simplest route to Meyers's office was down the stairs in the salon.

Although he hadn't seen any signs of an alarm system, he was still concerned about that possibility.

"Does Ray ever worry about pirates?"

"Pirates?" Nicole quivered with silent laughter.

"Why are you laughing?"

"I just had a funny image—of Raymond being made to walk the plank."

"Seriously, what kind of protection does he have?"

"I don't think he worries about it around here. When he goes on longer trips, he usually has Sid and a couple of his security guys with him."

Virgil looked at the shore. It had taken Thompson less than ten minutes to get to the yacht. It would take him much longer on the raft. Perhaps an hour or more, depending on how the seas were running.

"What made you think of pirates?"

"I don't know. I guess it's just something I'd worry about if I owned a yacht like this."

"He pays somebody else to worry about things like that."

Friday night, he paced the cottage, rehearsing his plan. Nicole had told him she was working late so Meyers wasn't due to pick her up until Saturday morning. He was still coming down on Friday evening, however, which would allow Virgil the opportunity to get on board the *Victory*. As he paced, he planned what he was going to do. After he got out to the yacht, he would climb up the ladder on the transom, unlatch the transom gate, step into the cockpit, and go up the steps to the aft deck. He would unlock the sliding glass doors to the salon, get the keys in the wheelhouse, and then go down to his office. He would search it carefully—for evidence of Ray Meyers's complicity in the murder of Jack and his crew. He realized his plan was fraught with danger—that he could be discovered and that at the very least he would be guilty of breaking and entering, which would certainly cost him his job and probably his career, too. Maybe his life.

But he had to get on that yacht and look around. He owed Jack that much.

He left the cottage at midnight and drove down the beach road. The moon was nearly full above the sea. Visibility is too clear, he thought. When he got to Kitty Hawk, he didn't see the yacht, so he drove north to Corolla, all the way to the lighthouse. On the way back, he caught a glimpse of what looked like moving shadows out the window: a herd of Corolla's wild ponies, running in the sand by the sea. He stopped the Cherokee and got out to watch them. According to legend, Corolla's wild ponies were descended from Spanish mustangs that had swum ashore from shipwrecks. They had run wild once, but as the Outer Banks's population swelled, motorists had killed many of the ponies, and local residents were trying to find a way to save the ones that remained. There were about a dozen ponies in this herd. They would run a quarter of a mile or so north, turn around, and then come south. Virgil stood there watching them until they disappeared on up the beach.

He got back to Kitty Hawk at one-fifteen. When he neared the old Coast Guard station on the beach road, he slowed down and saw the *Victory*.

He drove three blocks, then backed his Cherokee into the parking lot of a vacant rental cottage. Jack's revolver was in the side pocket of his Army fatigues, along with two speed loaders—small cylinders containing spare ammunition. That gave him fifteen rounds, assuming he would have time to reload. If he found evidence to implicate Meyers and was caught before he could leave, he wanted to be able to defend himself.

He recalled Raymond's smug, cold-eyed expression when he had called him a weasel.

At least I will go down fighting, he thought. *Like Jack.*

Smearing the camouflage paint on his face, he picked up the inflatable raft and slung it over his shoulder. Carrying the oars and the bicycle pump in his hands, he crossed the dunes and began walking north along the beach.

The yacht looked to be less than a mile from shore. There was a light on in the wheelhouse and more lights on deck.

Virgil knelt in the sand and inflated the raft with the pump. The sea shone like ice in the moonlight. I need more darkness than this, he thought.

He stood on the beach, staring at the yacht, trying to get up his nerve to put the raft into the surf. He was worried about how bright everything was.

Then ... voices in the distance.

Two figures came toward him, a man and woman holding hands. Virgil looked out to sea so they couldn't see his face, but the man spoke to him anyway.

He had already been seen. No way could he do it now.

After they went on, he pulled the plug out of the raft, letting the air out. It rushed out with a loud hissing that gradually diminished until all he could hear was the surf.

On Wednesday night, he and Nicole went out to eat again.

The restaurant was crowded, and they had to wait for a seat in the bar. While they waited, Virgil drank two whiskey sours, and he ordered a shot of whiskey and a beer during their dinner.

"How did you meet Raymond?" he asked after they had finished eating. He was drinking his fourth whiskey.

"I worked for his company a couple of summers I was in college."

"He got interested in you then?"

"No, he didn't know me. After I graduated from college I dated one of his vice presidents, a guy named Todd. I met Ray at a party at Todd's house. We had a long conversation. Ray was very polite, charming even, at least for him. He actually took some time to ask me about me instead of bragging about himself, the way a lot of men do. But he was married then, and I didn't think much about our conversation.

"A few years later, after his wife died, I ran into him in a restaurant in Ocracoke. We talked briefly, and he got my number. Asked if he could call me."

"How long ago was that?"

"Last year. Why?"

"I just wondered."

Nicole was studying him thoughtfully. "Why are you so interested in Ray?"

Be careful, he thought. You've had a little too much to drink.

"I don't know, really. Maybe it's because he's so ... successful."

"He is that," Nicole said, lighting a cigarette. "But ..."

Virgil waited for her to complete her sentence.

"But what?"

"But I'm tired of talking about him. Let's talk about you. Why did you become a teacher?"

"Didn't want to have to work hard."

"Come on. I dated a professor once. He worked all the time."

"What did your professor teach?"

"Biology." Nicole smiled and blew a smoke ring at him. "Now that's a subject I know something about."

Virgil laughed, and Nicole began laughing, too.

When the waitress brought the check, Nicole insisted on paying it, over Virgil's protests.

"You have to learn how to receive gracefully," she said. "And that's another subject I know something about. In fact, I'm trying to elevate it to an art form."

Virgil wasn't sure if he liked this comment. The more he thought about it, the more he decided he didn't like it; however, he didn't reveal that fact to Nicole. He only smiled at her and thanked her for buying him dinner.

On the way back to her cottage, he noticed he was weaving a little in the Jeep. At one point, Nicole reached out and steadied the wheel.

When he pulled into her driveway, he said, "Good night. I had a great time. And thank you for dinner."

"Why don't you come in?"

"I'd better go."

"I'm afraid you'll end up in a ditch, Virgil." She took his hand. "Come on. You don't have to be afraid. You can sleep on the couch."

"I'm not afraid," he said, angry now. "Why should I be afraid?"

Going into the cottage, he stumbled a little, and Nicole put her arm around him. Suddenly, he was kissing her, her breasts against his arm. His heart felt like a cannon going off in his chest, but he couldn't tell whether it was from excitement or fear.

When they finally broke apart, Nicole whispered, "I'll get the couch ready for you."

"I don't want to sleep on the couch," he said.

Nicole sat astride him, moving with the easy, graceful motion of a rider on a carousel. As he thrust up into her silky, enveloping warmth, Virgil felt as if he were suspended in that twilight world between dream and wakefulness, and a kaleidoscopic stream of images from the summer flowed through his memory: the woman with a cobra tattoo on her stomach, dancing at Jack's island party; Bobbie walking naked into the surf and kneeling in the sand while Jack entered her from behind; Dave Swain raising the black and silver yellowfin tuna out of the Gulf Stream that day on the *Eva Marie*; the little boy, Evan, in Jack's arms, his hands on the wheel of the *Dixie Arrow* during his party at Oden's Dock; the loggerhead turtles bobbing on the sea, locked in their primal embrace, oblivious to the guitar floating nearby; the herd of wild ponies running on the moonlit beach at Corolla; the sperm whale's luminous eye glowing among the stars over Hatteras. Nicole, moaning softly, rocked back and forth. She leaned forward, grinding herself against him, his hands on her rotating hips. She pressed her lips against his ear and her cries became so intermingled with his own that he could not tell where her voice ended and his began.

When he awoke the next morning, Nicole had already left for work. There was a note pinned to her pillow: *I'm glad you didn't sleep on the couch.*

Instead of feeling touched by her note, Virgil had a sudden sense of panic. He realized he had crossed a perilous new boundary in sleeping with Nicole. What in the hell had he been thinking? The combination of alcohol, loneliness, and his strong attraction for her had confounded his mind, diverted him from his central mission. He looked out the window by her bed, his attention focused on the oleander growing outside. They had made love with the blinds raised. The oleander would have probably prevented someone from seeing in, he thought, but it was still a risk. Nicole is dangerous, he thought, a siren who lures sailors onto the rocks. She was like the toxic oleander growing outside the window—beautiful but deadly.

He couldn't resist the temptation to search her room. To relieve his guilt for this, he told himself he was doing it to find something that would exonerate her of the murders aboard the *Dixie Arrow*. But he also wanted to know more about her, for Nicole was a mystery to him. He didn't understand why someone with her intelligence and apparent independence would be willing to cater to Raymond Meyers's ego and play such an apparently submissive role around him.

Her bedroom contained mostly ordinary items: jewelry, underwear, clothes, a makeup case, brushes, and combs. On her dresser was a photograph of Nicole at about eighteen or nineteen and a woman who resembled her, both of them smiling, their arms around each other's shoulders. There was also a more recent photo of Nicole in a wetsuit, holding a sea bass in one hand, a spear gun in the other. Except for the photographs, her room had a Spartan quality, as if she were only staying there temporarily or as if she didn't want to leave something around that might reveal anything personal. He told himself that her austere room was another manifestation of Nicole's secretiveness, her need to manipulate men. But hadn't she been willing to reveal details of her personal life to him—like playing the cassette of her singing for her father?

The more he learned about Nicole, it seemed the more enigmatic she became.

In the bottom door of her nightstand, tucked into the paperback version of *Ulysses*, he found a letter in an unsealed envelope with no stamp. It was addressed to Ellen Andrisson, at a P.O. Box in Fairfax, Virginia.

Dear Ellen,

I'm busted, sis. Ray has been acting strange lately, and when I asked him if something was wrong, he said, "Do you think I am goddamned stupid?" I asked him what he was talking about and he accused me of spending the night with Jack—he even knew a time and place—July 23, at Jack's house in Avon. Of course I didn't deny it. He wanted to know how many times I'd seen him, wanted to know what I saw in a "two-bit smuggler like Jack Delaney." We were in the master bedroom of the Victory. *He was pacing the floor, furious. Of course I couldn't tell him what I really felt, that I love the way Jack moves, the way he thinks, even the way he smells. Like wood smoke. And those eyes—so full of life and humor. But all I said was, "He was good enough to work for you." That really set him off. He raised hell, wanted to know how I had gotten that idea, and I said I assumed it, because I had seen Jack* leave the office in his yacht with a briefcase one day. Ray got up in my face, told me curiosity was dangerous and added, "Remember what happened to the cat." I knew he wouldn't hurt me—at least I didn't think he would—but I was afraid of what he might do to Jack. I told him it was my fault, not his. "Tell me about it," he said. "I want to hear all about it."

"I don't ask you who you're with when you're not with me," I said. "You've never made any commitment to me. Everything's just been for the moment. Isn't that right?"

He sat beside me on the bed, cracking his knuckles, his rage temporarily derailed by my comment. "You're right," he said. "Maybe we should talk about that. Is that what this was all about?"

"I don't know right now, Ray. I think I need a little time to sort things out."

He sat still awhile, clenching and unclenching his hands, a vein standing out in his temple. Finally, he called Clay on the intercom and told him to get up to the bridge, that I was to be taken back to my car.

I didn't call him, and he didn't call me.

About a week later, Jack called me to ask if he could stop by. I told him to come on.

I was still hot and sweaty from work. I took a shower and put on a cotton dress, with no underpants. I put a Merle Haggard album on the stereo. Jack loves Merle Haggard.

When he came over, he had whiskey on his breath. I poured us both bourbon on ice, and we sat on my couch. Jack was all excited about a trawler he was buying. I asked him if it was like the one that sank. He said she wasn't as big but was in great shape, said she had "a practically new twelve cylinder Detroit engine." He said he was re-naming her the Dixie Arrow.

Then he asked about Ray—he couldn't leave that alone. I told him we weren't seeing each other at the moment. He wanted to know why and I told him Ray had found out I'd spent the night *with him. This information seemed to hit him hard. He asked if Ray had somebody watching his house, and I told him I had no idea. I honestly don't know how he found out.*

"I hope you won't do any more work for him," I said.

"I'm not working for anybody anymore," he said. "I gave notice on the Eva Marie. I'm going back to what my daddy did, trawler boat fishing."

"That's good honest work." I put down my glass, leaned over and kissed him.

I was intending a long slow kiss that suggested better things to come, but he pulled away. "I'm getting married, Nicole," he said.

I felt a chill go through my heart.

"Who's the lucky lady?"

"Bobbie."

"Oh yes. The woman in red."

I looked down at his hands. Lean, brown, scarred—so unlike Ray's. I wanted to cry.

"Is it too late to ask you to reconsider?"

"Nicole—"

"Take it easy," I said, regaining my balance. "I was only kidding."

He looked really hurt, but I could tell our little ride was over. I smiled, raised my glass and offered a toast to the bride and groom.

That was where Nicole's letter ended; evidently, she hadn't finished it.

XIII

To Virgil, the most significant revelation in Nicole's letter to her sister was that Meyers had learned about Nicole and Jack's relationship. Was that motive enough to have him killed? If so, why the others, too? Why such an elaborate scheme involving multiple assassins at night on the sea? Perhaps it was to guarantee their silence, Virgil thought. If Meyers had orchestrated the murders of the crew of the *Dixie Arrow*, along with Mike Jennette, everyone who had participated in the theft of the cocaine shipment would be dead. No witnesses. Although Dave Swain hadn't been involved in the heist, he would have been killed, too, simply for being in the wrong place at the wrong time. They would have killed me for the same reason, Virgil thought.

He had mixed feelings about Nicole's letter. On the one hand, it revealed that she hadn't betrayed Jack, that she had no knowledge of the murders aboard the *Dixie Arrow*. On the other hand, given his attraction for her, he couldn't help from feeling envy for her obvious desire for Jack. *I love the way Jack moves, the way he thinks, even the way he smells.* Virgil's jealousy brought shame and guilt. He loved Jack like a brother, loved him so much he knew he would never be able to rest until he had avenged his death—and yet he was envious of Nicole's desire for him. Nicole's letter reminded him that if Meyers had been behind the plot, Virgil would need strong, convincing evidence to have him arrested and convicted for his crimes.

Leaving Nicole's door unlocked, he took her letter and drove to a copy center in Kill Devil Hills. After making a copy, he returned it to the book in her cottage. Later that day, he put the copy in the safety deposit box at this bank, along with Jack's journal.

He wondered when she had written the letter, since it was obvious that she had made the decision to go back to Raymond Meyers. At dinner Wednesday, she had mentioned that he was coming down late Friday night. He had asked if she was going out to the *Victory* that night, and she shook her head. "I'm working late," she said. "I won't see him until Saturday."

That will give me time to get aboard his yacht and search his office, Virgil thought.

But what would he do if he found any clear, incriminating evidence of Meyers's complicity in the murders?

I'll kill Raymond Meyers, he thought. *I don't care what happens to me afterward. I will kill him, so help me God.*

Friday night, the moon was a red ember smoldering in a blanket of clouds above the sea. As he drove north along the beach road, the stars were hidden. When he reached the old Coast Guard station, he saw the lights of Meyers's yacht.

It was a little after midnight. Meyers had gotten there early.

The sea was choppy, and it took him nearly an hour to row the raft out to the *Victory*. By the time he arrived, he was sweating and winded, and his back and shoulders ached from struggling against the tide with the small paddles.

He rowed to the stern and climbed up onto the swim platform, tying the line around the lowest rung of the ladder.

The cockpit and aft deck were dark. Unlatching the transom gate, he crossed the cockpit to the steps and then walked along the cushioned seating units to the glass doors. The interior curtain had been drawn and he couldn't see inside, but he didn't think anyone would be up this late. Using the key he had stolen on his earlier visit, he unlocked the door, slid it open, and stepped into the dimly lighted salon. He stood still, listening. All he heard was the wind and the yacht creaking on the swells. He went through the salon and the galley and up the steps to the wheelhouse. Lifting the ring of keys from the peg on the side of the console, he went back through the salon and down the stairs to Meyers's office.

The third key he tried on the ring unlocked the door.

He stepped into the dark office and stood still a moment, listening. The room had a faint scent of brandy. He crossed the room to the cabinet on the portside and slid the door open, shining the light inside. Nothing there but liquor bottles.

Ray Meyers is sleeping just beyond that door, he thought. He shined the light at the door to his room. He could feel his heart pounding.

He tried the desk's drawers and was surprised to find they were not locked. Kneeling on the floor, he began examining the contents of Meyers's desk. He found invoices, canceled checks, a planner, and a calendar. On the calendar he noticed that the night of the murders, August 11, had an "X" on the date, nothing else. He looked through the calendar to see if any other dates had been marked with an "X," but it was the only one. When the other dates had writing on them, there were only brief notations or numbers. He examined the canceled checks, but they had all been made out to businesses. Remembering that Meyers had paid Jack in cash, he was sure there would be no record of any money spent on the murders. Most of the other papers he found in various folders seemed business related.

He wanted to get into the cabinet behind the desk, but it was locked. From his rucksack, he took out the lock pick. Picking the lock on the cabinet was somewhat more complex than the one in his office, and it took him awhile to raise the pins with the pick and turn the lock with the tensioning wrench.

He took out the items he found one by one and examined them—plastic bottles of pills, folders with papers in them, a conch shell, a photographic album. The album contained mostly photographs of Raymond Meyers, Sid, and other people Virgil didn't recognize. He thought they might be Raymond's employees. A few of the photos were of Nicole and Raymond. In one photo, Nicole held a spear gun in one hand and a fish in the other. The fish had been impaled just behind the head with the barbed shaft. He could see the wound.

He put the album back and gave the cabinet one last look in the light of the flashlight: He saw something at the back. He couldn't reach it with his hand, so he had to pull it out with the end of the flashlight. When Virgil saw what it was, he felt a chill run along his spine: It was a section of the foreleg and paw of a panther.

As he held the paw, he recalled Meyers's statement at the table: *I didn't kill it because it scratched me; I killed it because it reminded me of my error in judgment.* Virgil had a deep sense of revulsion and disgust. No wonder he kept the thing under lock and key. He was sure Nicole would be equally disgusted if she knew.

He gave the cabinet one last look. The shelf was empty beyond the panther's paw. He bumped the back wall with the flashlight and was surprised to feel it give a little. He applied more steady pressure and it rose up, revealing a hidden compartment at the back. He slid out of the cabinet and, picking up the letter opener from the desk, he inserted his head and arm into the cabinet, this time using the letter opener to raise the hinged section and his left hand to shine the flashlight into the hidden compartment. He felt as if someone had hit him a hard blow just above the heart when he saw the jar and its contents: a severed human hand, floating in a clear liquid.

Virgil let the hinged section of the cabinet fall back and rested his head on the cabinet. "Oh my God," he whispered.

He recalled Meyers's arrogant expression when he had boasted about killing the panther. *Look into a panther's eyes— it's like looking into the eyes of nature itself. A panther's eyes are hard and cold and stripped of mercy.*

And Hurricane Jack had become the victim of that cold, implacable force. Why? Because he had slept with Nicole? Because Meyers wanted to get rid of all the witnesses who could implicate him in the hijacking of the cocaine?

There was no need to kill them, Virgil thought. He wondered if Meyers had been aboard the trawler operated by men who had used Jack's kindness—his willingness to help a fellow mariner in distress—as an elaborate ruse to murder him, or if he had simply pulled the strings from a distance. *That cold-blooded murdering bastard.*

Images of his friend flashed in his mind: Jack in his football uniform when he was a quarterback for the Hatteras Hurricanes; standing on the railing of the Herbert C. Bonner Bridge the night he had jumped in, silhouetted against the starry sky; dancing barefoot at Virgil's wedding; piloting the charter boat toward the Gulf Stream; and, finally, lying dead on the deck of the *Dixie Arrow*, his left hand a bloody stump.

Virgil's reverie was broken by a voice: "*What the hell?*"

Turning, he saw Raymond Meyers standing in the light from his bedroom. He was wearing red pajamas.

Virgil stood up, the gun in his hand. "Don't move!" His hand holding the revolver was illuminated by light from the room behind the office, but his face was still in shadow.

"Who are you? What the fuck is going on?"

"I'll ask the questions," Virgil said. "I want you to tell me why you think you have the right to kill people like they were bugs under your feet."

"What are you talking about?"

"I'm talking about the Coultrane Brothers, Dave Swain, and Leon McRae. I'm talking about Jack Delaney."

"Jack Delaney? His boat was lost at sea."

"Jack was murdered and you know it."

"What makes you say that?"

"Because I was there, you murdering son of a bitch!"

"Where?"

"The *Dixie Arrow*."

Raymond Meyers seemed to shrink before his eyes, like a balloon figure of a man suddenly deflating.

"And I know all about the robbery and murders in the swamp off Gull Rock Bay—how you hired Jack and his crew to steal for you."

Meyers was breathing hard through his nose. His guilt was transparent on his face.

"Mr. Big Shot," Virgil said, relishing the fear he saw in his eyes, "you were used to jerking people around like marionettes, jumping when you said jump. But Jack wasn't a good boy, was he, Raymond? He sampled your own private stock, didn't he? So you not only had to have him killed, you also had your goons do a little something extra, didn't you? I found your goddamned trophy in the cabinet."

Virgil's finger was tightening on the trigger when someone tackled him from behind. Thrown off balance, he fired the gun once before he fell to the floor. The man on his back twisted the revolver from his hand before he could fire it again.

An arm encircled his neck. He struggled to free himself but his attacker had him in a vice-like grip. The pressure increased on his throat until the room became solarized, then everything went black.

Virgil heard someone speaking, as if from a distance. He opened his eyes, trying to get his bearings.

He was on his back, in front of Meyers's desk, his hands secured behind him.

"I still can't believe it," Meyers was saying. "This weasel slinks in here with my woman, eats at my table, drinks my brandy, and all the time he's a walking time bomb. A fucking time bomb. I can tell you one thing, I sure underestimated this little fuck."

"How'd he get the key?" It was Sid's voice.

"He got the key when he was here—from the wheelhouse," Raymond said. "Isn't this a crock of shit? Not only does he use Nikki to try to get to me, know how he got this? The same place he got the raft out there—ordered them from my own fucking warehouse."

Virgil's eyes focused on Meyers. He was standing at his feet, and he looked as big as a giant.

"I spend half a million bucks to get a job done, and look what I get for my time, trouble and money—a piece-of-shit surviving witness."

"He must have been hiding in the fish hole, down in the ice and shrimp," Sid said. He kicked Virgil in the thigh. "That's where you were, wasn't it?"

Virgil suddenly realized where he had heard that nasal monotone before: Sid had been the one in the fish hole.

"That entire operation was sloppy. The colonel lost two of his men, and you let this punk get away."

"We searched the boat and only turned up five IDs." Sid's voice had a faint whining tone.

"I want all the goddamned details. I want to know everything." Raymond kicked Virgil in the side. "Who else knows about this?"

When Virgil didn't answer, Raymond kicked him in the jaw. Virgil, who hadn't seen the blow coming, felt a sharp jolt of pain along the side of his face, radiating up to his skull.

Sid sat on his stomach. Grabbing his face, he jammed a

finger into his left eye. It felt like he was trying to dig his eye out of the socket.

Raymond said something, and Sid rolled off him. He lay there wheezing. His left eye was burning, full of tears.

"I can make him talk!"

"I know, but this isn't the place for that. I don't want my carpet messed up, for one thing. We'll work on him Sunday night in Norfolk. That will give him a little time to anticipate what he's going to experience. C.C. can't get down until late tonight in his boat to pick him up. We'll lock Mr. Weasel in the engine room until then. You and C.C. can take him out of here early Sunday morning. Do it before daylight when Nikki and I are still asleep. I still want you to pick her up in the morning, too." Raymond handed something to Sid. "Put this on him."

Seizing his face, Sid forced a hard object into his mouth. It was connected to leather straps, which he drew tightly around his head.

"Now get that raft, too, and put it in the engine room."

Sid put more cuffs on his ankles, and then he dragged Virgil by his legs into the engine room. Raymond followed him in with a chain. Sid padlocked one end of the chain to the handcuffs and the other end to a steel bar around the engine.

"Sleep tight, professor." He went out and shut the door.

There was a faint red light in the room. All Virgil could hear was the steady humming sound of the generator. He struggled against the chain awhile, but it was no use. His left eye throbbed and burned. The left side of his face had begun to swell from where Raymond had kicked him.

Meyers's strategy of making him sweat first was working. He remembered seeing a torture device on a television documentary about the Sandinistas: a metal clamp that slowly castrated a man by cutting off the circulation in his testicles. A female officer had displayed it for the camera, claiming it had been used by the Somoza regime against political prisoners. He wondered how long he would be able to hold out under torture before he revealed that his knowledge of the hijacking in the swamp had come from Jack's journal and that it was in his safety deposit vault.

I should have told someone else about the journal, he thought. I should have made arrangements for it to go to the cops if I disappeared.

What the hell was he thinking?

He wished to God he had gone to the police. Now he had lost his chance to avenge the murders aboard the *Dixie Arrow*.

In a panic, he began struggling against the chain. He had to get out of there.

But the chain and cuffs held. All he accomplished was to bring Sid into the engine room. "Looks like it's time for a bedtime story."

Closing the door behind him, he switched on an overhead light. He had a paper cup in his hand. "You need a little nightcap first." Bending over Virgil, he undid his gag and poured a briny, sour liquid into his mouth.

"Ahhhh," his said, spitting it out.

"How'd my piss taste, professor?"

Virgil moved his head, trying to wipe his mouth on his shirt, but it was drenched with urine.

Sid sat down on a chair and took a flask from his pocket. He tilted it back and took a drink.

"Part of the problem was that fool of a colonel," he said. "I could tell he wasn't a real soldier when Raymond introduced him to me. 'This is Colonel Juan Comencia,' he says. Another one of his buddies from banana republic land. Only he wasn't a real soldier, like I said. I could tell that when I shook his hand. He had a hand like a girl—soft and limp. Even looked like somebody did his nails for him. They weren't the hands of a soldier. They were the hands of a faggot."

The engine room seemed to be spinning around and around. "Why'd you have to kill them?"

"Ryan didn't want to do it. He thought it was too messy, involved too much risk. But Raymond said Delaney was too unpredictable, couldn't be trusted. 'He's too dangerous,' he said. 'They all have to go.' Ryan said his people didn't want any part of it, because they were American citizens.

"'No problem,'" Raymond says. "'Big ocean out there. Lot of things can happen.'"

Sid took another drink of whiskey from the flask.

"Raymond used his contacts on the docks to get us an old trawler, a floating piece of shit. Barely seaworthy. Colonel Garcia and his cousin, Captain Pablo Bonilla, flew some men in from Guatemala or Nicaragua or whatever country they were from. I get those people Raymond deals with mixed up, to tell you the truth.

"The colonel and me were in charge of the operation. We planned it all out right there in Raymond's office. Contact the trawler by radio, pretend to need help in order to get close to them. Then fire a concussion grenade into the wheelhouse to knock out the communications equipment. Kill them all, then burn the boat.

"The colonel was strutting around, telling Raymond how easy it would be. They hadn't even talked price yet. Big foolish dumb-ass. Raymond warned him to be careful. 'These fishermen may be armed, and the captain of the trawler is especially dangerous.'

"'I have killed many dangerous men,' the colonel said.

"'You have *cojones grandes*,'" Raymond said. "He plays these fools like a harp.

"I was supposed to check all the IDs on board, to make sure we got who we were after. A simple enough job. Only problem was," Sid kicked Virgil in the chest, "one sneaky rat was unaccounted for."

"Who killed Mike Jennette?"

"You want to know who smoked Mike? C.C. took care of that little operation. Drilled Jennette between the eyes while he was counting up his day's receipts."

Sid took another drink from the flask, wiped his mouth with the back of his hand, then continued talking.

"Anyway, the colonel thought it was a fine plan. 'We'll take care of these men for you. No problem,' he said. But there were problems. The first one was that he was a sloppy man with the hands of a faggot and the brain of a woman. His plan to get the fishermen aboard first didn't work out the way he wanted, because he didn't take the time to make it look like a real trawler. Delaney brought his trawler on the starboard side, his bow even with our stern, the outriggers raised so the three men on deck could come aboard. The fisherman asked Ramirez, one of the men who spoke English, where the rest of the crew was, and he told them everyone was below, working on the engine. But this fisherman was nobody's fool. He got suspicious. I heard him say, 'Something's wrong here. They got nets on deck, but there's no cables on the winches.'

"I was standing on top of the stairs leading down to the engine room. I saw the fisherman draw a pistol from a holster on his belt. I turned back to Pablo, who was waiting behind me on the stairs. And I said, 'When I start firing, shoot the grenade into the wheelhouse, through the lighted window.'

"I slipped the safety off the machine gun, stepped out onto the deck, and shot the fisherman with the gun. Then I took down the other two. A moment later, I heard the grenade go off in the wheelhouse.

"One of the fishermen crawled toward the wheelhouse. I watched him stand up and try to walk. I put the laser on his lower back and fired four rounds, knocking him forward over the winch.

"Ramirez was firing a pistol at the blond man, who was

crawling on his belly along the deck. The others came up the stairs and fanned out on deck, taking cover behind the drums and winch. I heard howling from somewhere in the trawler. I knew it had to be Delaney's three-legged mutt.

"I heard a shot, then the howling stopped. I stepped back into the doorway and told the man firing at the one on the winch to get down. What sense did that make—shooting a dead man?"

"His name was Sam," Virgil said. "He had a wife and kids."

"You trying to make me feel bad? Here's what makes me feel bad. I missed you in that fish bin. Now that makes me feel bad."

Virgil was silent, remembering hiding in the fish bin, hearing the shots, and later, the voices above him as he shivered in the ice. He cursed his luck for escaping that death only to face another, more brutal, one.

"Over on Delaney's trawler, someone on the other side of the winch fired two fast shots at Ramirez. He went down on his back, kicking like a baby. Dumb bastard. Can't say he hadn't been warned.

"The others opened fire but they were too late to help Ramirez. His ballistic vest hadn't done him any good. The fisherman shot him in the head.

"The colonel's men were peppering the trawler, shooting wild. I saw the lights on the mast popping out, one by one. Someone on the shrimper was shooting them out. Must have been Hurricane Jack. That was a smart move.

"The Central American guys kept firing at the trawler, bullets whining and ricocheting off the winch and drum. I kept out of sight. I was more worried about being hit by a ricocheting bullet than getting shot by one of the fishermen. Even after the last light has been shot out, the others kept firing, wasting their bullets. After a while, Pablo lobbed the other concussion grenade into the wheelhouse.

"These guys weren't real soldiers. A real soldier is a perfect killing machine. He only fires when he has something to shoot at. Raymond's Third World mercenaries were just mindless blasters, good only for massacres.

"I slipped on my night vision goggles and crawled on my belly along the deck around the starboard side of the shrimper, keeping close to the boat's steel waist so I couldn't be seen from the wheelhouse. I was heading toward the bow, where there was a small hole in the waist of the trawler. I flipped the selector switch on the machine gun, putting it on semi-automatic fire. Activating the laser sight, I poked the barrel through the hole in the bow and waited.

"The gunfire had slowed to an occasional shot. The colonel's men were just shooting at random.

"Then I saw a hand with a gun. I put the sight just to the right of the gun and waited.

"When the man stuck his face around to fire, I shifted the sight to his upper chest and squeezed the trigger.

"One shot. A nice clean kill—unlike these sloppy Central American blasters. Put them in a war against true soldiers and all they do is waste bullets and get their sorry asses killed. That's what happened in the Falklands. Armchair generals and trigger-happy Latino cowboys going up against trained soldiers with discipline and the will to fight.

"I moved the sight along the winch, waiting. I had heard two different weapons, one lighter than the other—a nine-millimeter. The other weapon sounded like a forty-five. I knew there were two men left. It would be easy to flush them out. All we'd have to do is set the ship on fire. But I didn't want to do that because of the other, special request Raymond had made."

Virgil had a flashback of Jack's bloody stump—his glazed eyes, his hair sticking to his forehead.

"What in God's name was he going to do with Jack's hand."

"Dip it in bronze," Sid said, shrugging. "I don't know. I

think he had the idea he was going to make it into a sculpture of some kind." Sid leered. "Maybe as a gift for the slut."

Virgil shut his eyes. He didn't want to hear any more of this. If only he could free himself from the handcuffs and chain—and get his hands on a weapon.

The sea was calm that night, with only a light breeze and a half-moon overhead. There was plenty of light for the goggles, which could amplify light up to seventy-five thousand times. Sid was concentrating very carefully, moving the red dot from the laser around, trying to anticipate where he would appear next.

A muzzle flashed from the wheelhouse window. He fired at it; the others did, too, but he knew they were too late.

This man with the .45 is a true soldier, he thought. He figures we are wearing body armor so he only shoots for the head.

Sid could feel his skin tingling.

There, a glimmer of metal, very low, below the winch.

He waited patiently and finally saw a section of hand.

Putting the red dot from his laser sight on the hand, he squeezed the trigger. The gun's stock slammed against his shoulder.

Got him, he thought. He's lying there in shock, wondering how it happened.

He called Pablo on the radio.

"I think I hit him," he said.

"Did you kill him?"

"No, I think I got his gun hand."

While he was talking to Pablo, a bullet slammed into the deck by his face. He rolled along the deck as more slugs penetrated the steel waist of the trawler.

"He's figured out where I am," he said into the radio. "I'm coming around the portside."

He crawled back around the leeward side of the trawler, then around through the door to the galley where Pablo was waiting with the other three men.

They were talking in Spanish. He heard "*El Diablo.*"

"He's not the devil," Sid said. "But he's a good shot with either hand."

"Let's torch the ship," Pablo said.

"No," Sid said. "I'm going in after him. Our stern is close enough to his bow that I can jump over the railing."

Pablo said something in Spanish to the others, and Sid heard one of them use the word *loco.*

"When I give the signal, I want everyone to lay down a barrage of fire on the trawler," Sid told them. "Cover it up. The wheelhouse, the winch, the doors. Keep it up while I get over there. And remember to shoot high. Once you see I'm on board, stop firing."

"You're taking a big chance, *señor,*" Pablo said. "It would be wiser to set fire to the vessel and shoot him when he tries to run."

"This is a personal matter," Sid said. "It will be done this way."

At Sid's command they began firing. He ran to the boom at the stern of the trawler. He slid along the back of it around to the edge. Taking three quick steps to the waist of the boat, he vaulted over onto the deck of the *Dixie Arrow.* Inching along the deck, he waited by the winch. He could see blood dripping from the man draped over the wench. A dumb-ass fisherman who had the misfortune to run afoul of Raymond and the secret power of the United States government.

He slid on his belly along the edge of the winch, listening carefully. Soon he would have the doorway in view, and he could make the kill.

He could hear him breathing now—the heavy, labored breathing of a man in pain. He's just inside the doorway, he thought. Sid's heart pounded. He was so excited that it didn't occur to him that he might die, too.

He yanked the door open and stuck the submachine gun around inside, firing blindly. Jack got off one shot before Sid's bullets knocked him backward. Sid was holding the gun so close to his face that the ejected casings struck the goggles. He made sure Jack had dropped the gun before he went in. Jack was on his back on the steps at the end of the hall. His right hand was bloody. Sid's bullet had only nicked the fleshy part of the palm. Sid checked the other fisherman to make sure he was dead. A big one, with only one shoe on. Shot through the heart, Sid noted proudly. He called Pablo to tell him he had made the kill.

Quickly, he inspected the galley, the captain's cabin, and the wheelhouse, which had been damaged by the two grenades. Then he slung the machine gun over his shoulder and bent over the captain. Jack was trying to get his breath, but he was finding it hard to breathe with perforated lungs.

"Hello," Sid said. He was taking the knife out of his pocket, opening the sawblade. Sid leaned forward toward Virgil, lowering his voice to a sibilant hiss: "Know what I told your friend Jack? 'I am the angel of death.'"

Jack was already slipping away when Sid finished cutting off his hand. He dragged him outside and propped him up against the wall so the colonel's men could see what a true soldier looked like.

Finishing his story, Sid replaced the gag, pulling the straps tightly around Virgil's head. "Sleep tight, professor. Soon we'll have another bedtime story. Only next time you'll be the star. I'm going to work on you with a power drill first. That's just to get you loosened up. I'm saving the real tricks for afterward."

As he lay in the darkness, Virgil felt an overwhelming sense of defeat. What was left, really, for him except for a quick and merciful death? He spent a long while praying for this very thing, begging God to end his suffering without too much pain. He thought of his mother, of how he would be leaving her alone in the world. He thought of Jack and Sam and Billy and Leon, how he had failed so miserably in his quest to bring their killers to justice. He wished he had told someone of his suspicions, wished he could have somehow had a backup plan for a worst-case scenario, the possibility of getting caught and killed on Meyers's yacht, but he had foolishly rushed into a dangerous situation against a powerful adversary without anticipating the risks. Slowly, with a growing sense of horror, he realized that sooner or later they would be able to force him to reveal his possession of Jack's journal and its location in the safety deposit box. And after his death, sooner or later, the journal would come into his mother's possession, since she was executor of his estate. Wouldn't that place her in danger? Would his folly lead to her death, too? Virgil rued the day he had gone aboard Jack's trawler.

He thought of his students, of his desire to one day have a family of his own, of his Rilke research—all of his dreams that would no longer have a chance of being realized. Why did his life have to end this way?

He dozed, and in a kind of dream he imagined he was on a desolate stretch of beach, with the dying whale, staring into its milky eye. Not wanting to watch it die, he began running along the beach. There was a figure running along ahead of him, a shadow. After a while, he knew the shadow he was chasing was Jack. He drew nearer to the shadow, calling Jack's name again and again. The dream landscape shifted, and Virgil was walking down a long, narrow hallway with concrete block walls. It was deep underground, and as he walked he noticed the floor began to slope down at an increasingly sharp angle. It seemed that he was walking in darkness and that the hallway would never end.

He woke up in a panic, and when he realized where he was,

he began jerking against the chains with all of his might. But it was no use.

A moment later, the door opened again.

Virgil turned his head, squinting in the light.

This is it, he thought.

He saw blue jeans. Tennis shoes.

They were too small to be Sid's.

He caught a familiar scent—of limes and sunscreen.

"Virgil?"

Nicole.

"What in the hell?"

She knelt beside him, unhooking the leather straps of the gag. He spat it out.

"How'd you get here?"

"On a raft. How'd you know I was in here?"

"I heard you, for Christ's sake, rattling this chain. I woke up early, and I was going through Raymond's office so I wouldn't have to go upstairs and walk by Sid or C.C. Virgil. What the hell is going on?" Quickly, he told her about how Meyers had hired Jack and his crew to hijack the cocaine shipment and about the murders aboard the *Dixie Arrow*—how he had hidden in the fish bin and escaped on the hatch cover. He told her about Jack's journal and how he had heard Sid's voice in the fish hole.

"Raymond had them all killed. Mike Jennette, too. He was murdered in his restaurant in Avon."

Nicole's eyes were wide, her lips parted. The color had drained from her face.

"I was afraid something like that might have happened, but I kept pushing it out of my mind. I didn't want to believe it."

"Believe it, Nicole."

"Shit! And you came here to do what?"

"I was looking for evidence. And I found it, too, a whole lot more than I ever expected. I found *Jack's hand*."

"Jack's hand? What are you talking about?"

"Remember when Raymond told us about the panther he killed? He had a dirty little secret he didn't tell us—he had its claw in the cabinet. And there's a secret compartment in back of the cabinet. That's where I found Jack's hand. Sid cut it off before he left the *Dixie Arrow*. Seems Ray Meyers likes souvenirs from the creatures he kills."

"Jesus," Nicole said. Her lower lip was trembling. "This is really hard to believe. You found a hand in Ray's *cabinet*?"

"Yes. In some kind of liquid. Raymond came into the office and saw me, but he didn't know who I was. I was going to kill him, but someone—I guess it was Sid—heard us talking and grabbed me from behind."

"Sid was sleeping in the guest room."

"What was he doing here?"

"Helping Raymond with the yacht. Captain Douglas's wife just had a baby, and Thompson is down with the flu."

"Just my luck. I really wanted to kill him."

"What happened to your face?"

"They roughed me up a little. They're taking me to Norfolk so they can torture me. They want to find out how I got my information about their crimes and who else knows."

"I'll bet they do." Nicole wiped tears from her face. "So that's why you asked all those questions about Raymond's security."

"Yes."

"I guess I was just part of your plan, too. Very clever."

"Nicole, they murdered six good men. And Jack was like a brother to me—"

"Stop, I don't want to hear any more, Virgil. This is all my fault. All my goddamned fault."

"Don't worry about that now. Just help me get out of here."

"I'm going to try to find the keys to these handcuffs."

"Get me a gun if you can."

Nicole went out, closing the door silently. Her scent of lime and sunscreen lingered in the engine room. Virgil's gloved hands were damp and hot. He put them together and began praying.

When Nicole returned, she was wearing her black leather jacket over the white blouse. She was carrying a spear gun and a bottle of water.

"We've got to hurry!" She knelt beside him, unlocking the handcuffs. "C.C. and Sid are in the galley now, drinking coffee."

"Where's Raymond?"

"Still asleep. I found the keys in his desk drawer."

While she unlocked the cuffs on his ankles, he rinsed out his mouth, spitting the water onto the floor. He stood up, steadying himself on the steel bar he had been chained to.

"You all right?"

"Just a little dizzy. My legs are stiff."

Supporting him with her arm, Nicole helped him walk around the room.

"No gun, huh?"

"I've got this spear gun. It won't make any noise."

"How does it work?"

"With compressed air."

Nicole knelt and put the base of the spear gun against the floor. She took the attached arrow off the side, and, using a loading handle tied to a string around her wrist, she pushed the barbed shaft down into the gun. Then she pumped another handle at the base. "Can you carry the raft?"

"Yes." He picked up the raft and put it on his shoulders. Nicole put the paddles under her arm and went ahead, holding the spear gun.

He followed her through Meyers's office, up the stairs. Nicole opened the door a little, looked in, then motioned for him to follow. He stepped quickly into the salon, his chest tight, his temples throbbing. He had an odd, dreaming sensation, as if he were walking in his sleep.

With Nicole in the lead, they went through the sliding

glass doors onto the aft deck. It was just getting light, but fog blanketed the ship and he couldn't see land. Off to the portside of the ship, he could see the outline of a cabin cruiser.

He opened the transom gate and lowered the raft to the swim platform, holding the line in his hand.

"You go first," he said to Nicole.

But before she could go down the steps, he heard the glass doors slide open behind them. "Freeze, assholes!"

Sid stood on the aft deck, aiming a pistol at them.

Nicole said, "Oh, shit!"

"Throw it down, Nicole, and put your hands up."

Virgil briefly considered diving into the water, but he didn't want to leave Nicole, and he knew he'd be an easy target for Sid. Looping the line around the top rung of the ladder, he turned around reluctantly and raised his hands. He was too far away from Sid to make an attempt to grab the gun. I'll wait until he gets closer, he thought.

Nicole dropped the spear gun and paddles, but she did not raise her hands.

Sid flipped a switch on the wall. "Raymond, you awake? I've got two birds up here on the aft deck. Just about to fly."

"What the hell you talking about?"

"Nicole and the professor. She let him go."

Sid clicked the intercom off, leering at Nicole.

"Judgment day, Nikki."

C.C. came out from the salon. He had on a blue windbreaker. "What have we got here?"

"I stepped out to get a breath of fresh air," said Sid. "And look what I found."

"I heard on the intercom. Now we got two witnesses to get rid of."

"Tell him that." Sid pointed the pistol at Virgil. "Both of you—lie down on the deck and put your hands on top of your head."

Virgil did as he asked, but Nicole just stood there.

"Get down, you bitch!"

"Why don't you drop dead, Sid?"

Raymond came out from the salon, his gray hair mussed. He had on a white robe over red pajamas.

"Why couldn't you mind your own business, Nikki?"

"Could I speak to you in private, Ray?"

Sid spat out the word: "Shit."

"If you'll give me a chance, I can explain everything."

"Don't listen to her!"

"Nikki, get down to my office and stay there!" Meyers jerked his thumb at Virgil. "Get this goddamn weasel out of here."

Virgil could see Sid's shoes coming toward him. Beyond Sid, he could see the bottom of Raymond's robe and his feet, encased in bedroom slippers.

How could he get guns away from both of them? There was no way. He exhaled, once again praying for a quick and merciful death.

"Drop the gun, Sid!"

Nicole stood on the aft deck, holding a snub-nosed revolver in both hands. *Jack's gun.* She was aiming it at Sid.

Sid held his pistol at his side, the barrel pointed at the deck. He was looking at Raymond Meyers.

Nicole cocked the revolver with her thumb. "Drop it or I'll shoot."

"Do what she says," Raymond said.

"I hate to waste a good weapon like this," Sid said. "But I'll be damned if I'm going to let you have it."

He tossed the gun over the gunwale, into the sea.

Nicole said, "All three of you—face down on the deck."

As Virgil was standing, he saw Sid and C.C. getting down on the deck, but Raymond just stood there, looking at Nicole, his hand in the pocket of his robe.

"You too, Raymond. I mean it."

C.C. was on his knees, his right side turned away from her. He was trying to get something out of his jacket pocket.

"Nicole, watch C.C.!" Virgil shouted.

The gun in her hand boomed. C.C. grunted and stood up, still trying to get his hand out of his pocket. She shot him again. He took a couple of steps and then fell to the deck. As he was falling, Virgil heard two shots in rapid succession.

Nicole staggered backward, firing the gun in Meyers's general direction. He shot her again, and she fell back against the glass doors.

Meyers walked up the steps, still aiming the smoking pistol at her. A slim black semi-automatic. He must have had it in the pocket of his robe.

Swiftly, Virgil picked up the spear gun by the transom gate. As he raised it, he heard Sid shout. Everything seemed to be taking place in slow motion. Meyers turned around on the steps, his mouth open.

He was raising his pistol when Virgil pulled the trigger.

The metal spear seemed to sprout from the center of Meyers's throat, as if it had grown there. Still holding the gun, he put both hands on the shaft. A thin stream of blood spurted out from around it.

Sid had scrambled up from the deck and was staring at Raymond. He was still clutching the shaft in his throat, as if he were trying to pull it out. The pistol fell from his hand.

Sid went for the pistol, but Virgil tackled him as he was picking it up. They struck the gunwale. Sid lost his hold on the pistol, and it flew over the side. He rolled away from Virgil, got to his feet, and aimed a kick at Virgil's face, the blow barely missing Virgil's chin. Virgil scrambled up the steps to the elevated section of the deck and swung at Sid as he came up the steps. Sid ducked and, moving quickly up the aft deck, he began leaping into the air and kicking Virgil's body—the blows knocking him back into the seating unit.

Sid took something out of his pocket, shook his hand once, and a shiny blade appeared.

Above his head, Virgil saw a fire extinguisher inside an enclosed section of the wall. As Sid came toward him with the knife, Virgil grabbed the fire extinguisher and shot a stream of foamy liquid at his face. Sid backed away, coughing, his head down. He wiped his eyes with his sleeve. Holding the knife low, he feinted to the right, then lunged. Virgil used the fire extinguisher to block his thrust. Then he sprayed him with another blast.

Sid backed off, covering his eyes with his arm.

They squared off on the deck, Sid bobbing around and lunging at him with the knife, Virgil blocking the attacks with the fire extinguisher. He fired another stream into his face, and when Sid put his arm over his eyes, Virgil stepped forward and slammed the fire extinguisher against his head. Sid slipped on the deck and fell down the steps. Virgil followed him down and swung the fire extinguisher against his head, arms, and chest until he stopped struggling and lay still.

Nearby, Raymond lay on his side in a pool of blood, his hands caressing the metal arrow, the point of which protruded about eight inches out the back of his neck. His eyes looked as if he were in deep meditation.

Virgil went up the steps and crossed the deck to Nicole. She lay on her back, her face turned toward the glass doors. He sat beside her, cradling her head in his lap. "Nicole."

She tried to lift her head, but she couldn't make it. There were three red stains about the size of a quarter in her blouse, one on her sternum, one over her left breast, one on her lower side.

He took her hand in his.

"Hold on, Nicole. I'm going to get help."

She closed her eyes, her grip on his hand weakening.

"It hurts," she said.

"I'm so sorry."

"Ray ..."

"He can't hurt anyone else now."

She tried to smile, but couldn't quite make it.

"I've been so blind, Virgil. I wish ..."

She never finished her sentence. Her eyes closed, her hand went limp, her head rolled to the side, and a moment later, she stopped breathing.

Virgil watched the color ebb from her face until she looked like an alabaster statue. The stains on her blouse dried to the color of rust. Her lips were slightly parted, her eyes half-open, as if she were already looking into some other world. He pressed her hand against his lips, trying to think of some words of prayer to go with her spirit to the country of the dead, but nothing came to mind.

Some sixth sense caused him to look up. He saw Sid staggering up the steps, the knife in his hand, blood streaming from a gash in his forehead.

Picking up the revolver that Nicole had dropped, he shot Sid once at point blank range. Sid staggered but didn't fall. Virgil pulled the trigger again but the hammer clicked on an empty shell.

"Your gun is empty," Sid said, grinning. His lips were bloody.

Sid was between Virgil and the fire extinguisher. No way to reach it without being stabbed.

He dashed through the sliding glass doors and ran through the salon to the galley. He was looking around for something to use as a weapon when Sid came through the galley door.

He tried to pick up a chair, but it was bolted to the floor.

Sid laughed and opened one of the drawers. Virgil turned and ran up to the wheelhouse. Hearing Sid coming up the steps, he ran up the staircase to the flying bridge. He stepped out to the top deck, looking frantically around for something he could use as a weapon. But there was just the skiff, secured with chains, the mast, and the flags fluttering in the wind.

He ran to the skiff as Sid stepped down from the flying bridge, flashing a demonic smile. He had one hand behind his back.

"I've got a surprise for you."

Sid raised his arm to show Virgil what he had been hiding: a meat cleaver. Then he came around the skiff toward Virgil. There was a bloody foam on his lips.

Around and around they went. Virgil thought his only chance was to run around the boat until his attacker collapsed from blood loss. But Sid seemed to be moving faster and faster. When he coughed, red specks splattered on the skiff's hull.

Suddenly, he leaped up into the skiff and ran over to the side nearest Virgil. He backed away as Sid jumped off the skiff and ran at him, holding the meat cleaver above his head.

Virgil tried to jump to the aft deck, but he slipped and fell. He rolled toward the starboard side.

Sid ran along the edge of the deck, howling, but in his frenzy he lost his balance. He tottered on the edge, his hands moving in frantic little circles before he fell backward into the sea.

Virgil opened the hatch and climbed down the ladder to the aft deck. He picked up the fire extinguisher and headed toward the transom. If Sid tried to climb up out of the water, he would stop him before he could get back into the yacht.

Virgil was waiting for him by the transom gate when he heard Sid scream.

He ran to the starboard gunwale and saw Sid thrashing around in the sea. He went down and came up again, one hand reaching for the sky in what looked like a last-second bid for salvation. He rolled over and Virgil saw that his other arm was just a stump.

He turned away, sick to his stomach.

It didn't take the sharks long to devour what was left of Sid.

When Virgil looked again, he saw only a few fragments of flesh floating on the metallic-gray water.

He lay down on the deck, panting. The fog was lifting, and he could see patches of blue in the morning sky.

When he sat up, his eyes focused on Raymond Meyers. The man responsible for the murders of Jack and his crew lay on his back, his eyes open, one hand still resting on the shaft in his throat. His cashmere robe was soaked with blood. Death had imbued his face with a rapt, meditative quality that softened its fleshy arrogance. C.C. lay on his stomach nearby. Virgil turned him over, feeling for a pulse. He wanted to make sure he was dead. Remembering that he had been reaching for a gun when Nicole shot him, he took a pistol from the pocket of C.C.'s windbreaker.

In the bar, he drank down three glasses of water. Pouring himself a glass of brandy, he sat on the sofa and tried to decide what to do. If he contacted the Coast Guard, he would have to tell them everything, and he would be arrested for murder, conspiracy to commit murder, and breaking and entering. He decided he should leave on the raft. He was anxious about putting it in the sea, in view of what had happened to Sid. To reassure himself, he thought he could use C.C.'s pistol to shoot any sharks that might still be hanging around.

All he wanted was to lie down and sleep in his own bed. He washed the glass, dried it, and returned it in the cabinet.

Revived by the brandy, he went down to the Raymond's office. He used one of the oars from the raft as a tool to slide the jar containing Jack's hand out to where he could reach it. He took the container up onto the deck, unscrewed the lid, and dumped the contents into the sea. "So long, Jack," he said. He threw the container in, too. He went back down the stairs to the engine room, where he found the parka he had left in Raymond's office. He picked it up, along with his rucksack, the lock pick set, the oar, and the spare cartridges they had taken from his pocket; then he returned to the aft deck and sat down beside Nicole. He didn't touch the gun beside her. It was Jack's Smith & Wesson. He guessed she had found it in Meyers's desk. He wondered why she hadn't given it to him.

She had been trying to protect him, he thought. Perhaps she thought he would get killed trying to use it.

Virgil kissed her forehead and prayed for her soul. Then he picked up the paddles, untied the line, and climbed down the ladder to the swim platform. He got the raft into the sea and began rowing into the fog.

Above the yacht, the seagulls circled on invisible currents, yammering over the dead.

XIV

Virgil didn't leave his cottage for two days. He kept up with media accounts of the deaths aboard Raymond Meyers's yacht by watching TV. Several stations from North Carolina and Virginia sent news teams to the Outer Banks to report on the deaths and subsequent investigation. In one broadcast, the reporter mentioned Raymond Meyers's ties to "right wing groups in Central America," and said a "police source" had suggested that C. C. and Nicole might have been killed by mercenaries working for leftist guerillas in El Salvador or Nicaragua. When questioned by the same reporter in front of the courthouse, the Sheriff of Dare County said, "There's a lot of people working on this case, and we're investigating a number of leads. That's all I have to say right now."

Coast Guard divers recovered the weapons thrown overboard. Virgil assumed that when the police added up the physical evidence, it would be clear that Nicole shot C.C. and Raymond had shot her. He hoped they would also conclude that Sid had killed Raymond. But he thought the police might have trouble determining a motive. Why, for example, would Nicole want to shoot C.C., and why would Raymond shoot his mistress?

Ten days after the deaths, two Coast Guard investigators visited his cottage. Their names were Saunders and Dunlow. The men explained the questions were "routine." They were talking to everyone who had been aboard Meyers's yacht within the past few months. The ship's log had listed him among the visitors.

Saunders asked most of the questions while Dunlow took notes. He wanted to know more about Virgil's relationship with Nicole.

"We were just friends," he said.

"You ever have a physical relationship with her?"

"No, it was just ... platonic."

"She ever talk about any other men she was seeing?"

"She mentioned Mr. Meyers a few times."

"What did she say about him?"

"Said she spent weekends on his yacht."

"She ever mention any other men?"

"No. But we weren't that intimate, as I said before. We mostly talked about books and films, things like that."

"You visited the yacht on October fourteenth. Is that correct?"

"Yes."

"Could you tell us the purpose of your visit?"

"Nicole invited me to watch a film, *The Last Temptation of Christ*."

"Who else was on the yacht?"

"Raymond Meyers, his captain and the first mate. I think his name was Thompson."

"Is that the only time you were on the yacht?"

"Yes."

"Did you know Sid Hinton?"

"Raymond's nephew? I met him once."

"When?"

"Fishing trip I took with Jack Delaney early in the summer."

"You remember the exact date?"

"It was sometime in May. Around the second week, I think."

The fishing trip seemed to pique their interest, and they asked several questions about it. When Agent Dunlow asked him why he was aboard the *Eva Marie,* he said Jack had invited him. Saunders seemed interested in this and inquired about his relationship with Jack. Virgil explained they had known each other since high school and had continued their friendship over the years.

They wanted to know the last time he had heard from Jack. After thinking a moment, Virgil said he wasn't exactly sure. "Sometime in August." Then he mentioned the party on Oden's Dock.

Near the end of the interview, Agent Saunders casually asked Virgil where he had been on the morning of the murders.

"Here. In my cottage."

"Can anyone verify that?"

"My mother. She was visiting me." Virgil had already spoken to his mother about an alibi. He had kept things simple, explaining that some people he had known were killed and that the police might try to involve him. Although his mother had been horrified at the possibility of his being involved in a murder case, she had promised to provide him with an alibi, if necessary.

Virgil was relieved that the investigators didn't ask for his mother's name and address or any other details about the visit.

The men thanked him for his cooperation and said they would be in touch if they needed anything else.

Three days later, Agent Saunders called and asked to talk to him again, this time at the Sheriff's office in the Dare County courthouse in Manteo. Virgil agreed to meet them the following afternoon at one.

He was highly anxious about talking to the investigators

again. He wasn't a very good liar, and he was afraid they might consider him to be a suspect. Although he had worn gloves the entire time he had been on the yacht, and he had carefully cleaned Jack's gun of his fingerprints before he had taken it aboard the *Victory,* he worried that they had found some other evidence placing him at, or near, the crime scene. He had come ashore on the raft before the fog had lifted, but had someone seen him?

After a nearly sleepless night, he arrived at the Sheriff's office ten minutes early. Saunders shook his hand and said "a government man" wanted to talk to him. The FBI agent left the room then and another man entered. He was bald, heavy-set, and dressed in a dark suit. What Virgil would remember most about him, however, were his shoes. They were so highly polished that he could see his image mirrored in their surface. He introduced himself as "T.J. Jones," but did not produce any identification or state the agency that employed him.

T.J. Jones recorded the interview. Like the other investigators, his first few questions dealt with Nicole. He wanted to know if she had ever mentioned Raymond's contacts in Central or South America.

"She said he knew a lot of people down there."

"She ever mention any specific individuals or countries?"

"No."

"She ever express any anger against Mr. Meyers?"

"Not directly. But I got the feeling she had some sort of resentment against him."

"Can you give me an example of what you're talking about?"

"I once heard her say, 'Raymond can get anything he wants.' It was just the way she said it. There was a bitter edge to her voice."

"I see." The man looked a little bored by this. He asked Virgil how he had first met Raymond and Nicole. He repeated what he had told the other investigators.

"What do you think happened out there?" Virgil asked, after the session was over.

"Three people got killed," the man said, a note of irritation in his voice. "Maybe more."

After Virgil left the sheriff's office, he ate a late lunch at the Duchess of Dare Restaurant in Manteo. Nicknamed "The Diner" by local residents, it was the place to go in Dare County to find out what was going on.

A group of men in an adjoining booth were discussing the case. One of the men, a deputy sheriff, sounded more authoritative than the others. The deputy said that although "the federal boys" had their own ideas about the deaths, he believed the killings had resulted from a fight over Nicole, whom police suspected of having an affair with Sid at the same time she was seeing Raymond. The deputy said he figured Raymond and C.C. had confronted Sid and Nicole on the yacht about the affair, and in the culminating fight she shot C.C., Raymond shot her ,and Sid killed Raymond with the spear gun. The deputy wasn't sure about what happened to Sid after that. "He might have tried to escape by swimming to shore, but if he tried to swim with blood on him, it's possible he ended up in a shark's belly."

The deputy admitted this theory had some loose ends, but he hoped they would be tied up when the investigation was completed.

"Way I figure it, it was just a case of a woman two-timing a jealous man," he said. "Tempers got hot, and the guns came out."

"Looks like she'd have had sense enough to leave the nephew alone and just stick with the older man, rich as he was," someone said.

"You can't tell what a woman's liable to do," the deputy replied.

The other men at the table agreed that this was true.

That fall, aside from his Rilke research, Virgil began trying to put his life back into order. Like Ahab, whose rage at the loss of his leg was directed at the universe, he had been holding all of creation accountable for the murders of Jack and his crew, and he could see he needed to put things in perspective. After all, the murders aboard the *Dixie Arrow* seemed insignificant when measured against the Holocaust, and they were no worse than mass murders he read about in the newspaper. But coming to terms with his personal ordeal wasn't easy. He suffered from nightmares, cold sweats, anxiety attacks, and flashbacks of the deaths: the limp bodies, the glazed eyes—as if they were already looking into the next world.

And he couldn't stop thinking about Nicole. The haunting image of her on the deck of Meyers's yacht—dead and lovely.

He not only missed her, he also couldn't seem to release himself from his guilt for her death. He kept thinking that she might still be alive if he had turned Jack's journal over to the police instead of trying to dig deeper into the case on his own. He had once heard someone say that the pain of hell comes from regret, not fire. At the time, he had dismissed this theory, but now he could see the truth in it.

In early November, he ran into Bobbie in Food Lion. Her skin had the glow that pregnant women often get, but her sorrow was evident in the tightness of her mouth and the abstracted expression in her eyes.

Virgil avoided mentioning Jack, but Bobbie brought him up. She said she knew Jack was never coming back. "I used to pray he'd turn up, that he'd somehow been cast ashore on an island, and that someone would find him. But I know now he's gone."

"It has been a long time," Virgil said, choking a little on the words. It was all he could think to say.

"Jack never knew about this," Bobbie said, touching her swollen belly. "I found out after he went to sea."

Virgil turned away from her, faking a cough.

Bobbie wanted to know if he was all right.

"Allergies," he said. "They kick up every once in a while."

He invited her to his cottage for dinner. She was lonely and depressed about Jack. Like many Hatteras residents, she believed his ship had gone down in a storm, and he saw no need to tell her anything different. They had dinner several more times after that. Virgil liked Bobbie and enjoyed her company. She was fine and decent, the kind of woman who holds up the whole world. For a while, he considered pursuing a more serious relationship with her. But he eventually decided against it. The problem was Hurricane Jack: He would have always been between them in a way that Virgil could never overcome or forget.

Virgil wished Jack could have known that Bobbie was pregnant, but there was no way to tell him now. *She won't ever find another man like Jack,* he recalled Mae saying. *But someone else will come along in time, and she'll start all over again with him. And Jack, he'll fade in her memory. He'll become someone she'll think of every once in a while. Some little thing—a song, a smell, a word—will bring him back.*

Jack won't fade from Bobbie's memory in the way that Mae predicted, Virgil thought. She'll see Jack every time she looks at their child.

In January, Bobbie asked him to be her baby's godfather, and he gladly accepted. He wasn't quite sure what a godfather was supposed to do, but he liked the sound of it. And he wanted to do it for Jack's sake.

He finished the Rilke research and began work on his essay. His central focus was on how Rilke's last fifty poems, including the previously untranslated ones, reflected his awareness of a unifying force flowing throughout nature. *"Rilke felt a mystical synchronicity with trees, insects, stars, tides, and wind,"* he wrote. *"To Rilke, everything in the universe was interrelated.*

This awareness imbued the poet with a stoic acceptance of life
as it is, a willingness to see beauty and suffering as different
sides of the same coin—or, more accurately, different facets
of an infinitely complex, multi-dimensional puzzle."

Virgil would later see that his interpretation of Rilke's work seemed relevant to a change he had sensed in himself. Although he continued to grieve the deaths of his friends, he felt blessed simply to be among the living. And he had begun to look forward to each day as an opportunity to participate more fully in the unfolding mystery of his own life.

He returned to Laurel College for the spring term with some of his old enthusiasm for teaching. He was no longer quite so frustrated by his students' indifference to learning. He even now saw them as victims of America's emphasis on instant gratification and the glittering surface of things. The insidious ways it tells us to define ourselves in terms of possessions and power rather than our capacity for love and work. How could they know anything different if someone wasn't willing to help them learn? He wanted to challenge them to think, not just about literature but about themselves and all of life, too. Its beauty, its cruelty, and its ineffable mystery.

Monica Simpson had signed up for his composition class again, having failed it again with another instructor. She visited him early in the semester, claiming she wanted to discuss her problems communicating her ideas on paper. She hadn't been in his office five minutes, however, before she hiked up her skirt to show him what she had to offer him in exchange for a passing grade.

"Please pull down your dress, Ms. Simpson," he said gently. "You don't have anything there that I haven't seen before."

After she stopped crying, she told him she had always lacked confidence in her mental ability. She had grown up in the shadow of an older sister who had recently finished medical school and whom had been heavily favored by their parents.

Monica, on the other hand, had always thought of herself as "the dumb one who got all the looks."

Virgil assured her that she was just as valuable and worthy as her sister, but that she would have to find her true purpose in life, just as her sister had. And he spent the next hour helping her write a descriptive essay. Her topic: "The Most Beautiful Thing I Ever Saw."

The most beautiful thing I ever saw was a picture of the earth taken from up in space, she wrote. *The sea was as blue as a sapphire and sparkling with tiny points of light. The land was big and green and looked alive.*

In early April, Bobbie called from Greenville to tell him she was going into labor. She had gone home to live with her parents during the winter.

"Mama's taking me to the hospital now. I wanted you to know."

"Did you call Mae?"

"Yes. She's coming as soon as she can."

Virgil arrived at the hospital in Greenville three hours and twenty minutes later. He and Bobbie's father spent two more hours in the waiting room before a nurse told them they could see her.

When the nurse took them to her room, Bobbie was sitting up in bed, holding her baby against her chest. The baby was wrapped in a blue blanket. Bobbie's face was pale and drawn, but she smiled when she saw them. Her hair lay against her head like a helmet. "I have a boy, Virgil."

Mrs. Russell, who had been with her during her labor, sat by the bed, fanning herself with a magazine. Bobbie introduced him to her as "Jack's best friend." He wondered if Jack had ever referred to him that way or if that was just Bobbie's effort to confer legitimacy on both him and her baby. He felt sorrow for her—at how lonely she must feel without Jack.

Mr. Russell and Virgil stood there looking at Jack and Bobbie's son. His eyes were tightly shut in his pink, swollen face.

"You want to hold him, Daddy?" Bobbie asked.

Bobbie's father picked up the baby. "Would you look at this little fellow? Good God almighty, he's a beauty, isn't he?"

When her father moved to return Bobbie's baby to her, Bobbie said, "Let Virgil hold him."

Mr. Russell put the baby in Virgil's arms. Holding him against his chest, Virgil touched his open palm, and his tiny hand closed around his finger. "What's his name?"

"Daniel Jack," Bobbie said.

Daniel Jack opened his eyes then, and Virgil saw that they were going to be blue like Jack's.

The baby held on to his finger, and he wouldn't let go.

Grateful thanks to Joe Coccaro,
Julian March, and Diane Patterson
for insightful and vigilant editing.

Read all four
Beach Murder Mysteries.